10/23

THE

BEAUTIFUL

AND THE

WILD

THE
BEAUTIFUL
AND THE
WILD

PEGGY TOWNSEND

Berkley
New York

BERKLEY
An imprint of Penguin Random House LLC
penguinrandomhouse.com

Copyright © 2023 by Peggy Townsend

Library of Congress Cataloging-in-Publication Data

Names: Townsend, Peggy, author.
Title: The beautiful and the wild / Peggy Townsend.
Description: New York : Berkley, [2023]
Identifiers: LCCN 2023000964 (print) | LCCN 2023000965 (ebook) |
ISBN 9780593638088 (hardcover) | ISBN 9780593638095 (ebook)
Subjects: LCSH: Wilderness survival--Fiction. | Alaska--Fiction. |
LCGFT: Survival fiction. | Novels.
Classification: LCC PS3620.O97 B43 2023 (print) |
LCC PS3620.O97 (ebook) | DDC 813/.6--dc23/eng/20230113
LC record available at https://lccn.loc.gov/2023000964
LC ebook record available at https://lccn.loc.gov/2023000965

Printed in the United States of America
1st Printing

Title page art: Mountain landscape © Galyna Andrushko / Shutterstock
Book design by Alison Cnockaert

THE
BEAUTIFUL
AND THE
WILD

1.

The silence was so thick I felt like I was drowning.

It filled my ears and throat with a watery quiet that made it hard to breathe. I leaned my forehead against the cold steel door that imprisoned me, and willed myself to draw in small gulps of air until finally the feeling of suffocation began to lift. It was only then that I turned to look at my surroundings.

I was locked inside a rusted shipping container, its walls pockmarked with tiny holes that let in slivers of light. A mildewed mattress on a low frame sat in one corner, with a ragged upholstered chair and a steamer trunk next to it. There was a shelf with an old-fashioned lantern on it, a small woodstove that vented through the back wall of the space, and a cluster of fifty-five-gallon drums in the corner near where I stood. It looked as if someone had once lived here but had abandoned it the way people did in ghost towns, leaving everything behind as disaster and illness struck. I shivered and pulled my jacket tighter around me.

Gray light filtered through a high rectangular window and I pushed myself away from the door to look.

Outside, the sky was pewter with dark clouds that scudded in the wind. Dense stands of spruce pressed around the container. In the distance, a muscular line of serrated mountains poked the sky. Everything here in Alaska seemed oversized and unrestrained. Even the summer daylight had no boundaries. I didn't have my phone or a watch but I guessed it was after midnight.

In front of me was a clearing that had been hacked out of the wilderness. A small greenhouse, a couple of graying outbuildings and a scattering of broken equipment edged the compound. A good-sized vegetable garden had been planted in the center of the opening, although the plants looked tired and anemic. On the far side of the garden was a sagging, low-roofed cabin with a set of weathered antlers nailed above the door.

Yellow light spilled through the front window of the hut, illuminating a male figure bent over a table as if performing some intricate work. He wore a plaid flannel shirt and his golden hair was long.

He was my husband, the father of my child. A man everyone said was dead, and yet here he was, very much alive.

He was also the one holding me prisoner.

I couldn't help but wonder how everything had gone so wrong.

2.

—— THEN ——

I met my husband, Mark, nine years ago when I was still struggling to find my way. I was living in Sacramento with three roommates and waitressing at a cheap diner where the mediocre food was matched only by the sullenness of its customers. I sometimes wondered if the meals were what made people grumpy or whether the sourness of the customers caused the cook to do only a halfhearted job because he knew he would never please anybody. Either way, I felt like I needed to blow off a little steam and decided to go to this country-and-western bar called the Holdup with another waitress from work. Mark was the first person I saw when I walked in.

I was wearing a short denim dress and a pair of cowboy boots I'd borrowed from my housemate Maggie, and he was sitting at the bar in faded Wranglers and a white T-shirt. He had shaggy golden hair and boyish blue eyes; when he smiled, a dimple appeared in his left cheek. I tried not to stare but I couldn't help myself. I was like a moth with a beautiful yellow flame in front of it.

When Mark caught me looking, he came over with a bottle of Coors and sat at my table. My friend got up and went to the dance floor. My whole body vibrated with his nearness.

First, he asked me questions about myself and then told me he was a freelance filmmaker who'd studied at UCLA and just finished a documentary about a Marine amputee who'd run the length of Africa as a penance, basically, for being alive when the rest of his squad was dead. He told me about watching a sunset in Morocco, hiding from bandits in Uganda, and surfing at J-Bay in South Africa. He seemed confident and adventurous. One of those people who went off to climb mountains or motorcycle across Siberia just because the unknown was out there waiting to be experienced. He was so different from me and yet, from that moment on, he was the only thing I wanted.

I could say it was the beer I drank followed by three whiskeys on the rocks but I would be lying. We closed down the bar with talk and I went home with him, where we made frantic and then slow love on a mattress on his bedroom floor. I would have gone with him sober. I never left after that night.

When his Africa documentary won the grand jury prize at a prestigious New York film festival four months later, the combination of excitement and optimism caused him to propose marriage and we drove up to South Lake Tahoe, where we tied the knot in a wedding chapel off the main drag. The truth was, as we lay in our hotel bed that night—the new Mr. and Mrs. Russo, as the officiant had loudly announced—I felt like, even though I didn't deserve it, I'd won some kind of prize too.

After that, we rubbed shoulders with celebrities at Sundance and spent a weekend at a fancy house in Tahoe with some hedge fund guy who introduced Mark to a couple of big-time producers. We went to elaborate parties in San Francisco and LA and spent all day in bed just because we could.

Life seemed shiny and bright then, especially after the two producers Mark had met hired him to replace the cinematographer on their most recent film, a guy who'd had an unfortunate accident involving a BMW, a power pole and a bottle of Don Julio tequila. Mark was flown to Utah in a private jet. Three weeks in, everything fell apart.

First, the producers told Mark that they had to make cuts to the budget and then that they wanted to take the film in a different direction: more commercial, more explosions, and with a love story. Mark told them they would ruin the film and made the mistake of sending an email to a fellow shooter telling him what a clown show the production had become and how the married director had been having sex with an eighteen-year-old girl on set. The story somehow made its way into the trades, including the detail that almost everyone on set called the two producers the Brothers Dim. Mark was fired and told he would never work in Hollywood again. He took a Greyhound bus back to Sacramento.

The next day, I found him passed out on the couch, an empty bottle of vodka on the carpet next to him. It was three in the afternoon. I helped him into bed and went to work, thinking he would sleep it off. He didn't. For the next five days, he huddled under the blankets, refusing to speak, refusing to eat, refusing suggestions to get up and take a shower. His stillness felt scary and dangerous, like a hand grenade had been deposited in our bedroom.

On day six, just as I was getting ready to call Mark's brother to ask if this had happened before and what I should do, Mark stumbled out of the bedroom. His hair was wild and his smell zoolike, and he went into the kitchen and fried himself three eggs.

"Don't," he said, and held up a hand when I started to ask how he was.

He spent the next two weeks on the phone. No one would take his calls.

After that, he got a job at one of those big-box hardware stores and started a portrait business on the side. Then, one day, he burst into our apartment and said a guy he knew from film school worked as a fire lookout in Washington State and needed someone to fill in for him while he went off to take care of his ailing father.

"Think of it, Liv. We'll be on top of the world and no one will bother us. We'll be part of nature, free from the money-grubbers, the phonies, the idiots. Just us."

It scared me a little but he folded me into his arms and said: "Trust me, you'll never feel more alive than when you don't know what's coming next."

And he was right.

By the time fire season was over, I was weightless from the freedom of being unchained from rude customers, routines and responsibilities, and so we kept traveling. We crisscrossed the West, sleeping under the stars, drinking beer in dimly lit bars and getting temporary jobs when we were low on money. Once, we worked clearing out hoarder houses for a rehab outfit in Los Angeles. Another time, we spent three weeks in a commune outside of Portland, Oregon, where we canned vegetables, milked goats and fixed fences.

Then I got pregnant and Mark shifted from the restless wanderer to the superhero of fathers. He'd come into a little money after his mother died—his cardiac surgeon father had passed three years before—and he made a down payment on a house on the outskirts of Sacramento. It was beige stucco, 1,120 square feet, and had been built in 1939 when the Depression was still fresh on everyone's minds.

There was a tiny front porch, two small bedrooms, noisy plumbing and a galley kitchen that looked out onto a sprawling elm tree in the backyard. And yet it was ours.

He carried me over the threshold with my seven-months-pregnant belly. Later, we laughed about how he had grunted with effort when he hefted me up.

When Xander was born, Mark dove into fatherhood as if he had been destined to do just that. He changed diapers, read child-development books and paced the floor for hours when Xander had colic. When Xander began missing some of his milestones, Mark was the one who insisted we take our boy to Stanford.

I remember sitting under a buzzing fluorescent light in the tiny exam room and listening as the doctor spoke about genes being deleted from a certain chromosome that would make our son's health as fragile as an old man's and leave him with developmental delays. He said, however, that surgery could repair part of what was wrong with our son's heart and that if we did a lot of occupational and physical therapy, we could get him fairly close to "normal."

He smiled when he said it, as if we should have thanked him for such wonderful news.

Instead, Mark's eyes lasered in on the doctor. "Who the hell wants normal?" he said. "Normal is just a prescription for unhappiness. You should know. Look at you." The doctor reared back on his wheeled stool. "My kid is perfect," Mark said, "an old soul who was placed here for a reason, and he's going to change the world."

It turned out both he and the doctor were right.

Xander was an old soul, a beautiful boy who changed our lives. But he also needed surgery to enlarge his narrowed aorta and therapy to help him learn to walk. Our hearts filled while our bank account drained.

I started cleaning houses because of the flexibility the work offered and Mark took on different jobs: shelf stocking, house painting, hardware clerking. We tried to keep alive some vestiges of our
former life with overnight camping trips to the mountains and
watching old movies on the couch with a bottle of wine between us.
Eventually, however, our lives dissolved into routine and I couldn't
help but think we were traveling the same stretch of road day after
day, never getting anywhere except the state of exhaustion.

We worked and ate and fell into bed, sometimes without even a
good night kiss. We still had sex but it tended to be more hurried
and less intense than in the old days. A few times, I faked an orgasm
but most of the time I didn't have to. Mark was always careful to
make sure we were both satisfied.

Still, I was never quite sure what Mark saw in me. I wasn't thin
or tall or beautiful like the women in LA, who all appeared to have
stepped out of the pages of a magazine. I was shorter and more com-
pact but my hair was thick and the color of roasted coffee beans and
my cheekbones were high and sculpted. Mark always said my looks
reminded him of a warrior princess.

"How could I look at another woman when I have you?" he
would say.

Despite that, there was a part of me that suspected he wanted
more than me and our little house, our low-paying jobs and our
suburban lives, so when he got a job at a custom-motorcycle shop
delivering bikes to customers all over the West and discovered a
subject for a new documentary, I was thrilled.

But maybe our quiet life was what I should have wanted. Maybe
that should have been enough.

3.

—— N O W ——

I awoke on the bare mattress under a striped wool blanket I'd found
in the steamer chest. My eyes were full of grit and my mouth dry as
dust. It took me a few seconds to remember where I was, and when
I did, panic fluttered inside me.

I sat up and told myself to calm down, that Mark couldn't keep
me locked up forever, although I could no longer be sure of that fact.
Not since so many things I thought I knew about him had turned
out to be wrong.

I pushed myself out of bed, my back muscles protesting against
the lumpy mattress on which I'd slept. The plywood floor was rough
under my bare feet. I went to the window, which was set high enough
so that my chin just came to its bottom sill. I wiped away the desic-
cated corpses of a half dozen flies and tapped the barrier with my
finger. Plexiglass. No way to escape there.

Outside, the sky had turned cornflower blue and a hard breeze
sent cloud shadows racing across the garden. The dirt was dark with
moisture. It must have rained during the few hours I'd slept.

I thought of my drive here: the pouring rain through Seattle, the graveled highway with its frost heaves and the dark forest pressing in on either side, the fast food Xander and I had eaten so I could surreptitiously charge my phone because my twelve-year-old Subaru was too ancient to have a charging port. Somewhere in the Yukon, however, the fast-food places disappeared and I had to be even more creative. Once, I tried to charge my phone at an outlet I found behind a gas station/mini-mart and was chased off by the attendant, who threatened to have me arrested for theft of electricity. Pretty soon, though, finding outlets didn't matter. Cell service became so spotty it was basically nonexistent. It made me feel cut off from the world but free in a way too.

It had taken Xander and me ten days to get to the compound where I was now, each road getting progressively worse until we were driving on a dirt track with potholes so big they threatened to swallow our car. I had to stop once when Xander declared his "axle was dragging," which was what my client old Mr. Martin said when he was tired. Mr. Martin was a widower and a Vietnam vet who adored Xander and insisted I bring him along on my cleaning job whenever Xander wasn't in school.

I gave Xander a juice box and we played a quick game of tag before we started off again. Forest gave way to brilliant green meadow and then returned to swallow the road. A river, its water wide and smooth, flowed parallel to the track for a while. Narrow driveways branched off the road here and there, but if there were other houses nearby, I didn't see them. The only evidence of a neighbor was a half-burned and apparently abandoned single-wide trailer I saw about eight miles in.

Finally, I located the small wooden sign with an arrow painted on it and turned the Subaru onto an even narrower track. The opening was so overgrown, I almost missed it. Branches squealed against the side of the car, and at one point I had to steer the Subaru through a shallow stream that crossed the road. My heart jackhammered in my chest. I'd risked so much to come here.

"Is this I'll-ask-ya?" Xander said from the back seat.

Before we'd left, I told him we were going to a place called Alaska, where there were lots of trees and new people we would meet.

"This is Alaska all right," I told him.

"Then where's all the people?" he wondered.

"That's a good question, Xan. Maybe we'll find some at the end of the road."

But we didn't.

The track climbed and twisted before curving so sharply downhill that I had to shift the Subaru into first gear to keep the brakes from overheating. Finally, we came to a small clearing. Instead of the road continuing, however, it stopped. I told Xander to wait, and got out of the car. There were faint tire tracks in the dirt but no sign of a vehicle, and I wondered if I'd driven all this way only to find the place abandoned.

The air had a chill to it. Goose bumps rose on my bare arms. I could hear the thunder of rushing water ahead and walked to the edge of the forest opening. There, twenty feet below me, was what I guessed was the same river that I'd glimpsed from the road. Only instead of being wide and calm like before, it had narrowed through a rocky cut to become a noisy scrum of white water. A concrete support column stood empty in the river, the bridge it once held lost to time or storms or both. Next to it was a rickety walkway made of graying wood planks. It was suspended from a pair of rusting cables that had been laced with rope to serve as a feeble barrier against the maelstrom below. It looked as if a slight gust of wind or a scampering squirrel could have sent everything crashing into the water.

Looking out the window of the container now, I thought of the nerves I had felt when I saw the shaky walkway and how I'd zipped my cell phone, wallet and keys in the pockets of my jacket, left the rest of our things behind and taken Xander's hand.

I had never even considered what would happen next.

Now I watched the cabin for signs of life. Pale smoke rose from a stovepipe in the hut's patched metal roof and went horizontal in the breeze. A small gray-and-white bird landed on a branch in front of the container. It bobbed up and down on the thin bough, cocked its head in my direction and flew off. Its sudden absence made me feel even worse for some reason.

A few minutes later, the front door of the cabin opened and Mark came out. He wore jeans and a long-sleeved red T-shirt with a ball cap pulled low over his eyes. He looked rangier than he'd been in Sacramento: thinner, weather roughed, his cheekbones carved more sharply. If anything, the change made him more handsome.

Once, when we were at Sundance for the screening of his first documentary—the one that had given him his bright future, which was later yanked away—I'd overheard a woman stage-whisper to a friend, "He should be in front of the camera instead of behind it," and it was true. He had the kind of looks that made people stop and stare, although he never seemed to notice.

I saw him purse his lips and heard a faint whistle through the window. A second later, the black-and-white Australian shepherd I'd seen when I first arrived barreled out of his plywood shelter and ran over to Mark. I thought the dog's name was Shadow.

Mark bent over and ruffled the dog's ears. The canine barked once, turned in a quick circle and sat at attention. Mark grinned. Then he turned and called into the cabin and Xander came out into the sunlight. He wore his green sweats and a too-big sweatshirt I didn't recognize. The wind lifted his corn silk hair. My heart squeezed at the sight of him.

Mark said something, hoisted Xander into the air and spun him in a sweeping arc in a game of airplane, which Xander loved. Xander's mouth opened in a laugh while the dog barked around them. After a few turns, Mark set Xander down and took his hand.

I pounded on the plexiglass. "Let me out," I shouted.

Xander stopped and frowned toward the container where I was being held.

I banged on the window again.

Mark looked over his shoulder. His face was hard and his lips set. He shook his head at me, took Xander's hand and disappeared around the far edge of the cabin, and I thought that no matter what you want to believe, the truth is that none of us really know our spouses. We may think we do, but really, we see only what our partners allow us to perceive. All the dark things—the secret desires, the obsessions, the uncontrolled needs—tend to stay shoved deep inside, and even if we glimpse our partners' shortcomings and depravities, our tendency is to look away because their sins are now ours too. Think of the spouses of alcoholics and abusers and corrupt politicians. Aren't there always those questions? Why didn't the spouse do something to stop the drinking? Why didn't the partner grab the children and run? Aren't you complicit if you stay with someone who uses power to destroy anyone who stands in their way?

I think that's probably why I didn't ask the questions I should have asked back in Sacramento or look below the surface to see what was really there.

4.

―――― THEN ――――

There are animals that move in packs and pods, needing companion-
ship and protection as they travel. But there are others, like wolver-
ines or mountain lions, that prefer to travel alone. I read about that
somewhere and I think people are the same way. If I had to catego-
rize Mark, I would put him on the wolverine list. Even as a little kid,
he liked to go off by himself.

When we first met, he told me the story of how he had gotten
bored with first grade one day, slipped out a back gate and headed
to the beach before he was caught by a sharp-eyed cop. Later, he told
me that he'd been kicked out of summer camp because he kept wandering into the nearby woods and that he'd run away from home at
ages ten, eleven and thirteen. He never got very far, he said, because
either someone would spot a young kid trying to hitchhike and call
the authorities or he'd run out of money, get caught shoplifting and
be returned home defeated and covered in grime.

His mother was a homemaker and his cardiac surgeon father
spent more time at the hospital than with his family. He had one

brother and they lived in a large Colonial-style house in Charleston, South Carolina, where his parents hosted cocktail parties and dinners for other doctors and their wives. Mark's father wanted him to go to his alma mater, Yale, and although Mark was accepted to the university, he decided to get as far away as he could from his parents and attend UCLA instead. His father said Mark could stay in California as far as he was concerned.

Maybe I should have paid more attention to Mark's stories. That way, I might have understood why the need to be free was such a part of him. But I kept thinking that I didn't deserve a husband like him and that my hold on him was tenuous at best. As if the slightest attempt to restrain him would send him running away from me.

Sometimes, in the earliest months of our marriage, for instance, I would come home after a lunch shift and find our apartment empty. I would tell myself Mark was out for a long run or had gone to buy groceries, since my cooking skills were limited to toasted cheese sandwiches and spaghetti. I'd pull off my shoes, grab a cold beer and drink it while I lay in the tub, trying to soak away the smells of grease and burned coffee that lingered long after I'd left the restaurant.

We couldn't afford a cell phone in those days, so after I dressed, I'd clean the kitchen or fold laundry while listening for the click of the front door opening and Mark coming in to say that he was home and hoped I'd like linguine and clams, or that his run had felt so damn good he'd just kept going. Instead, on some occasions, night would arrive and drag into the zero hours and Mark would still be gone.

I'd perch on the couch in the darkness, reminding myself that in our marriage vows we had pledged to be together until death did us part but not that we had to be glued to each other twenty-four hours a day. As time wore on, however, my mind would conjure up images of him lying injured in a ditch or zipped in a body bag at the morgue, and I would get up and pace the apartment and start to call the police but remember I didn't trust them and instead search one more time for a note or a clue to where Mark had gone and when he might be back.

Each time, he'd come home as the sun rose and say that he'd heard that the spring bloom in the Sierra was spectacular, so he'd hitchhiked to Tahoe, where he photographed fields of lupines and mule-ears and the red stalks of snow plants rising through the forest duff. Or that a friend had called and said a swell was running and they'd driven to Santa Cruz to surf and found a fine band playing at the little Mexican restaurant where they'd gone to eat and decided to stay until closing. He'd smell of dust and pine or his feet would be spackled with sand and I'd tell myself not to hold too tight or I would lose him forever.

When I'd mention later how worried I'd been, he would tell me that worry never helped anyone or anything and to trust him to come back to me. When Xander was born, his disappearances mostly stopped. Still, sometimes he'd go off to buy milk and see something he wanted to photograph and wait for the light to be just right in order to capture the shot. He was one of those restless creatives—people whose minds seemed to be constantly seeking—and yet, when he was interested in something or someone, he would focus every bit of his energy and attention on that one thing. It was why his art was so wonderful.

He'd study a single seedling rising from the ashes of a great fire, and when the image emerged in his photo, you could almost sense the willpower of that single living thing, the feeling of hope against a background of despair. It was also why every single boss at every one of his crappy jobs wanted to hire Mark full-time. People would wait patiently for him at the giant hardware store because he would listen intently to them describe their houses and their lives, and he would tell them exactly what shade of blue to paint their bedrooms. Or they would hunt him down at the grocery store where he stocked shelves to tell him how their spouses had loved the canned Italian tomatoes he'd recommended, and what did he think about this brand of strawberry jam? Everyone seemed to crave his attention, his light. He was that kind of person. The truth was I craved it too.

One time, when Xander was five, however, Mark didn't come home for three days.

I'd taken Xander to Goodwill to get school clothes, and when I got back, our house was empty. There was a pot of water on the stove and some chopped onions and garlic were on the cutting board, and I thought Mark must have ridden his bike to the grocery store to get some ingredient he'd forgotten. When he was still gone an hour later, I went to his studio in the garage and found his bike leaning against the wall. I called his cell but it went straight to voice mail. The only clue to his whereabouts was that his running shoes, which were usually by the front door, were gone.

I made scrambled eggs for dinner, put Xander to bed and reminded myself of what Mark had said about worry. At one a.m., I called his cell, but again it went to voice mail without ringing. By six p.m. the next day, I'd sent Mark ten texts and phoned his boss at the motorcycle shop; he said Mark had had no deliveries scheduled, and he seemed almost as upset as I was that Mark had disappeared. He said he would make a few calls and insisted I phone him the minute Mark returned.

I also called Mark's two best friends along with every hospital within a hundred-mile range. His friends said Mark was a capable guy who'd maybe just needed a break from his routine—not very comforting—and every hospital I called had no record of an unidentified, comatose man being brought through its doors.

I imagined Mark being trapped in the wreckage of a car under the waters of a still lake or lying dead at the base of a steep peak in the Sierra that he'd gone off to photograph. Or maybe he'd suddenly gotten tired of our life and simply left.

I took Xander to school and went to work and spent most of the night worrying and watching reruns on TV.

Finally, seventy-four hours after I discovered Mark gone and fifteen minutes after I'd put Xander to bed, the kitchen door opened and Mark stumbled in, sunburned and tangle haired. Before I could even ask him where he'd been, he said I should sit down because he had the wildest story to tell, and he went over and got two bottles of beer from the fridge.

He drained one of the beers in a long gulp and started in on the second. According to him, he had been prepping dinner when he'd gotten a phone call from an old film school classmate named Hopper, who said he was headed to Nevada and asked if Mark would like to grab a drink. The friend picked him up and told him about this spirit ceremony he was going to film in the desert. The ceremony was going to be overseen by some South American shaman and, before the guy could even ask, Mark said he wanted to go.

"It was trippy and wild and completely unexplainable," Mark said of the ceremony, which apparently including drinking some kind of foul concoction, dancing and drumming under the moon. He leaned toward me as he talked about the nature of reality and whether we believed what other people perceived us to be instead of what we truly were. He finished his second beer. "I think my whole worldview just shifted, so everything is clear now."

Later, he apologized for not letting me know where he was and said he would never again leave without writing a note or calling me first. I was so relieved he was home that I didn't press for details. At the time, I did wonder briefly why his clothes weren't dustier than they were if he'd been in the desert and why he smelled slightly of oregano, but I let it go. I understood that sometimes you had to take the not so good in a person in order to have the wonderful, and that trying to tie him down would only break the connection we had. However, he was never quite the same after that trip. Sometimes I'd catch him staring off into space and he began to bring home books with strange titles he wanted me to read. I said I would, but who had time between work and parenting and laundry and grocery shopping?

So, when everything happened and he disappeared that night in November, I told myself he'd gone off on another one of his wanderings, and tried to keep myself busy. Two days later, however, a detective from the San Francisco PD, Inspector Louise Hardy, showed up on our front porch in a navy blue pantsuit and asked if she could come inside. My heart stuttered and I showed her into the kitchen, where we sat at our small table. Her eyes were brown and there was a dark mole on her right cheek.

She told me she was sorry to have to bring me the news, but apparently, two nights earlier, Mark had jumped off the Golden Gate Bridge.

5.

———— N O W ————

It was cold and damp inside the container, the air scented with mildew and dust, which had probably been accumulating for years. I went back and sat on the bare mattress, brushed the dirt from my feet, pulled on my socks and shoes and wrapped the wool blanket around my shoulders. I was hungry and thirsty and needed to pee. I wondered how long Mark planned to keep me here.

Something scraped against the outside of the container and I returned to the window to see what it was. A breeze made the tree branches lift and fall. The raspy sound came again and I guessed it was the wind. Nothing else moved.

The compound where I was being held was cupped in a small wooded valley with the clearing and the sagging cabin in the center; the shipping container from where I watched was set a few yards up an incline on the north side of the property. To the south was another rise. To the east, rugged gray peaks rose like watchful giants. Above them, the sky burned bright blue.

A small greenhouse was situated at the western edge of the

garden. Next to it was a rototiller without any wheels, a dented aluminum rowboat, a rusted set of box springs and a snowmobile with a broken track. Nearer the cabin were two small structures made out of graying plywood. One might have been an outhouse. I didn't know what the other one was for. The place looked sad and used up, as if it had grown too tired to go on and was just waiting to be reclaimed by the forest. And yet I knew Mark would have loved this place for the wildness of the land, for the self-sufficiency it demanded, for the isolation and for the challenge. A place like this would be a giant middle finger to rich white jerks like those two LA producers—men who, Mark always said, bought huge houses as a way to display their manhood and drove overgrown SUVs that would take them nowhere more adventurous than Palm Springs.

The forest cast shadows over the container and I yearned for fresh air, for the ability to walk more than a dozen feet and for a drink of water. I willed Mark to return from wherever he'd gone and head toward the container so we could talk. I didn't know how long I stood there, but finally I saw the dog Shadow emerge from the aspens on one side of the cabin, sniff the air and flop down in the sun. He'd been the first to greet us after Xander and I had crossed the footbridge.

We had been following a narrow trail through the forest when the dog raced up, gave a single bark and rushed away again. Xander started to run after him and I grabbed the back of his sweatshirt.

"You have to stay with Mama," I said, although what had that gotten him over the past nine months? Sad dinners of canned soup and ramen noodles. A mother who was about to lose the only house he'd ever known. A mom who'd dragged him into the woods because she thought she could fix something she'd broken beyond repair.

"But the doggy wanted to play with me," Xander protested.

His blue eyes under pale lashes began to fill with tears.

"I know, baby," I said, and dropped to one knee, pulling him into me.

Xander had just turned seven but was small for his age, with a forehead that was just a little too high and a mouth that was a little too wide for his face. They were the only outward signs of the genetic glitch in him—the subtraction of just three genes from the thousands that each of us is supposed to carry—that changed everything for him. And yet I always thought the subtraction had added things too. Xander was a happy kid with such an enthusiasm for people that it would take only a few seconds for him to become your best friend. He also had keen hearing and a love for music that was infectious. I'd watch his face light up when his favorite country songs came on the radio, and all you had to do was hum a few bars from a tune on his playlist and chances were he could name the title and artist before you got to the chorus.

"We just need to go slow so we don't get lost, all right?" I told him, and wiped the tear from his cheek with my thumb. "Remember how we always stay together?"

He nodded. "Eyes on me. Eyes on you," he mumbled.

It was a trick his occupational therapist had taught me as a way to focus his attention.

"Exactly," I said, and kissed him on the forehead.

He rubbed his nose and I stood and took his hand.

"Come on, let's find that dog."

The trail wove through thick stands of brush and around skeletal gray logs. Trees rose high around us. We walked for about ten more minutes before we emerged into the clearing where the dog stood in front of that run-down cabin, trembling with barks. A hardy-looking young woman wearing a long paisley skirt and a flannel shirt stood in front of the hut with a rifle cradled in her arms. She had long chestnut hair with colorful beads twined into a braid near her face, but all I could focus on was the weapon. My pulse ratcheted upward.

"What do you want?" she hollered.

I pulled Xander behind me. "I'm looking for Mark Russo." I tried to make my voice sound confident and powerful, although I felt neither.

She lifted her chin. "There's nobody here by that name."

There was something about the way she glanced away and then looked back at me that made me think she was lying. "How about you let me check?" I called.

"Are you a cop or something?"

"How many cops show up with a kid?"

I could feel Xander poke his head around from behind my legs. The muzzle of the rifle in the woman's hands lowered and she frowned at me.

"Who are you?" she asked.

"I'm his wife and this is his son and I think you should go get Mark."

The woman's mouth opened but nothing came out.

I was just starting to tell her that I was pretty sure Mark was there, when a figure slipped from a stand of aspens next to the cabin.

The man was tall and slender, with long golden hair and an ax in his hand.

"Daddy," Xander cried.

I swallowed at the memory of that moment. How naive I'd been to come here.

I turned and looked around the container. The urge to pee was stronger now. Whoever had lived in this awful box must have used the forest for a bathroom and hauled water to drink because there was no toilet or faucet or sink. I wondered what Mark expected me to do.

I thought, *I will not give him the satisfaction of my humiliation by wetting my pants or peeing in the corner like an animal.* My bladder pulsed and I knew I couldn't wait much longer. I tossed the blanket from my shoulders and began my search. I dug through the steamer chest and looked behind the woodstove. Nothing. My discomfort grew. I hurried over to the fifty-five-gallon drums and spotted a small aluminum pot wedged between one of the drums and the wall. I didn't have time to look further. Quickly, I unzipped my jeans and squatted over the container.

I felt exposed, vulnerable, animal-like. I finished, zipped up and looked again at the container's corroded walls, the high window, the horrible mattress, and thought that there wasn't a single person in the outside world who knew or cared where I was.

6.

—— T H E N ——

I became a house cleaner after Xander was born, mostly because I could make my own schedule. Nearly all my clients' houses were big, with high windows that let in waterfalls of light, and furniture with price tags that exceeded what I earned in a month. I would find expensive clothes crumpled on bedroom floors, fancy pots and pans grimed with food on kitchen counters and kids' crayon marks streaking white walls and I would think, *How can you abuse a beautiful house like this?*

And yet there was something about bringing order to chaos that I liked: replacing stale and wrinkled sheets with ones that were clean and freshly ironed, turning full trash cans into empty ones and making fingerprints disappear from mirrors and stainless steel appliances.

I scrubbed farmhouse sinks, polished marble countertops, swept miles of hardwood floors and washed pyramids of towels and bedding. My clients gave me keys; they let me in and most of them hardly knew anything about me. Only my name (Liv), rank (house cleaner) and phone number. Like a prisoner of class war.

But I knew a lot about them.

I knew, for instance, that Juliette Monroe was a lawyer who traveled a lot, loved handbags and had a closet full of Prada and Chanel in size zero. She also had boxes of laxatives and a bottle of ipecac syrup hidden behind the toilet bowl cleaner under her bathroom sink.

I knew that Andy and Clare Iverson ate takeout nearly every night and liked gin martinis (a lot) and that their ten-year-old son still wet the bed. I knew when the Chens were fighting—his pajamas would be on the floor next to a rumpled bed in the guest room—and that Mr. Chen kept a pair of size eleven, red high heels behind an old set of golf clubs in his walk-in closet.

I might have known more intimate things about them than their friends did, and yet it was lonely work. Only white-haired Mr. Martin, who survived on a pension and the insurance money after his wife died, would be around to talk with me. Otherwise, the only personal interactions I'd have with my clients were scrawled notes asking me to also sweep their massive decks, or checks with my name scribbled on them. I was the ghost that floated into their homes and left gleaming floors and tautly made beds behind. If I didn't show up, they might wonder why the laundry was still on the floor and the beds unmade but they wouldn't worry about me. They'd just get angry that I hadn't been there to do my job and didn't answer my phone when they called to complain.

Sometimes I would sit on the couch in a client's living room after I'd cleaned it, stare at all the beautiful things and pretend the house was mine.

It only made me feel worse.

7.

—— N O W ——

I was lying on the mattress, the wool blanket pulled up to my chin, when I heard the squeal of the metal bar that held the container's doors closed. I sat up quickly, a sudden flash of dizziness forcing me to close my eyes for a moment. When I opened them, the young woman I had met yesterday was coming into the container. Her name was Angela.

She wore the same paisley skirt and flannel shirt but her hair looked freshly washed and she carried a tray containing a plate covered with a pot lid, a large Mason jar of water and a mug of what smelled like coffee. She wasn't pretty in any conventional sense. She had a nose that turned up a little too much and a chin that was a bit too strong. Her green-gold eyes, however, were stunning and there was something attractive about her, a *Mona Lisa*–like calmness.

"Good morning," she said.

"Where's Mark?" I demanded.

She set the tray on the steamer chest near the bed and straightened.

"He and Xander took your car and went to town," she said. "We needed some supplies. Plus he wanted to check things out."

She smiled and gestured at the tray as if bringing food to a prisoner were an everyday thing. "You hardly ate anything at dinner, so I knew you had to be hungry. I made you toast and a nice herb omelet. The eggs are from our hens," she said.

I wanted to shove her to the ground, to sprint for the door, to lock her inside the container and escape. But how could I leave if Mark had taken Xander? If my car was gone? The Subaru had been the only vehicle at the road's end and the nearest house I'd seen had been that scorched and empty single-wide. There was nowhere to run, which was probably why she had left the container door partially open.

"I don't care where the eggs came from," I told her. "What I want to know is why I'm locked up."

The smile faded from her face. "We need to stay safe, Liv, and, well, after yesterday, we can't be sure, can we?"

Yesterday had been one gut punch after another.

The first was seeing Mark stride out of the aspens. It felt like a miracle, like Lazarus rising from the tomb, like those people at Lourdes who suddenly got up from their wheelchairs and walked. Unlike with those people at Lourdes, however, the sight of my living, breathing husband rooted my feet to the ground.

Mark dropped the ax and Xander ran and jumped into his arms. Mark buried his face in Xander's neck, his hands pressing hard against his son's back. His shoulders convulsed in a kind of rhythmic shudder.

When Mark looked up, tears streaked his face.

While we were on the road, I'd rehearsed what I was going to say when—and if—I saw Mark again. In my practice sessions, I'd been like a lawyer: calmly asking questions, keeping my mind open, allowing for forgiveness if needed. And yet all of it had flown out of my head the minute I saw him. All I could think was that my husband, the man I loved, was alive and not dead. It's what people who've lost someone wish for more than anything: the chance to hold their person, to talk to them again. And yet I couldn't move or speak.

Xander turned in Mark's arms. "It's Daddy," he shouted.

There was a humming in my ears.

Mark moved toward me. He had a necklace of brown beads at his throat.

"You cut your hair," he said quietly.

"I did." It was all I could manage to get out.

"It looks good."

"Thanks," I said. "You look good too."

A tear zigzagged down Mark's face and my throat tightened. He pulled me against him with one arm, enfolding Xander and me in an embrace. He was warm and solid and alive, and he smelled like cedar. I couldn't help myself. I began to cry. Finally, we pulled apart and Mark wiped his eyes with the inside of his elbow. "I've been waiting so long. I thought you'd never come."

It took a few seconds for his words to sink in.

"Wait," I said. "How would I come? I thought you were dead."

"I left you a note."

"I know," I said. "The horrible one in the car."

Even though Inspector Hardy had warned me, I demanded to see the scrap of notepaper the police had found in the Subaru, which had sat abandoned by the bridge for two days before it was noticed.

To Liv, the note read, *People might say I ended my life but you already did that, didn't you?*

31

The detective had been right. It only made things worse.

"I know. I'm sorry. I had to make it look real," Mark said. "But I'm talking about a different note. The one I left on my desk in the studio. I put it there right before I left."

An image flashed of him coming out of the studio on the night he had disappeared.

"There was no note, Mark."

Xander wrapped his arms around Mark's neck and squeezed.

"Daddy," he said happily.

"It was in the folder marked 'Bills,'" Mark insisted. "I knew you would find it when you went over our budget. It had the latitude and longitude for this place, plus the first line of that poem I wrote for you on our fifth anniversary. You know, 'Surrender me to the woods.' I knew you'd figure it out but nobody else would."

I shook my head.

"The next line: 'for that is where I must go,'" he prompted.

"I never saw a note."

I remembered going to the studio as the bills began to pile up, hoping that I could figure out our finances. I told Xander he could play mini basketball with the hoop Mark had mounted on the wall and I handed him the little plastic orb that went with it. I was on my third cup of coffee and was buzzed and exhausted at the same time.

I sank into Mark's chair, fired up his computer and stared at the confetti of documents on the screen. I was just wondering how I was going to find what I needed in the mess when Xander went after a wayward shot and crashed into the desk. The impact caused a pile of manila folders to avalanche to the floor, creating a spill of old bills, bank statements, photos and scraps of paper with what looked like notes for stock photos Mark could take and sell. I remembered gathering everything up and not really looking at anything beyond a few of the photos: a shot of an old man with wild gray eyebrows and a colorful knit cap; a portrait of a wrinkled woman in what looked to be a small country store; an athletic-looking blond woman holding a bow and arrow in the woods.

But even as I remembered, I thought the message still might have gone over my head. I had no recollection of the poem, let alone the second line. That was the difference between us. Mark believed in poetry and symbols while I trusted what was right in front of me: mortgage payments and accusing notes left inside cars.

Mark's eyes filled again. "Every day, I prayed I'd see you and Xander walk down that path. I was so worried. I thought maybe Xander had gotten sick or something bad had happened to you."

"Why didn't you call? Or send an email? How could you rely on a note?"

Xander grabbed Mark's ears and pulled Mark's face into his own. "We walked across a bouncy bridge, Daddy, and Mama said, 'Hang on tight.'"

Mark grinned. "Such a brave little man." He rubbed his nose against Xander's. "And now you're here and I'm so happy."

Xander giggled.

Mark's presence felt like a miracle and yet somehow wrong. How could he have relied on a few lines of poetry to keep our lives from falling apart? Why had he pretended to jump off the bridge when he could have just said he needed to get away for a while, like before?

Mark looked at me over Xander's shoulder, his brows knitting together for an instant. "So, how did you find me, then?"

I reminded myself to be patient and told him that I'd found a few clues that made me think he might be alive, and that since we were in the process of losing the house anyway, I'd decided to come to Alaska to see if I was right.

"Did you tell anybody you were coming here?" There was the slightest edge to his voice.

"No." The only person I'd told was old Mr. Martin, who had said he'd miss us and given me a hundred dollars for the trip, but I never said exactly why or where I was going in Alaska. I was too embarrassed to admit I was following my gut and a very slim trail of clues despite the fact that Inspector Hardy and all the media said they were almost certain Mark was dead. There'd been a strong outgoing tide when Mark had jumped and sharks outside the bay, plus there were a number of instances when jumpers' bodies had never been recovered. Besides, there'd been a witness: a nurse returning from a late shift in the ER who'd seen a man fitting Mark's description going over the railing around two a.m.

Mark exhaled at my answer. "That's good. Did you use a credit card?"

I shook my head. "No. Cash. I sold your cameras."

"All right. That's OK. How about your phone?"

I frowned. "It ran out of battery somewhere past White-horse. Why?"

"Just checking," he said.

Xander gave Mark's neck another hug.

"I know it's a long drive. You must be exhausted and hungry," Mark said. He pointed to the woman with the beaded hair. "Angela has made some wonderful soup."

"I want soup, Daddy," Xander shouted. His whole body trembled with excitement.

"Come inside, Liv," Mark said. "Let's eat."

But my head, which had been emptied of questions, now filled with them.

"But why did you come here? Why did you pretend you were dead?"

Mark studied the boots on his feet as if the truth might be buried in the dirt beneath their soles. "I had to," he said finally.

"You had to?"

"It's a long story."

"Well, I'd like to hear it."

"You will."

"You could have just asked for a divorce if that's what you wanted."

"I didn't want a divorce."

"Then why did you do what you did?"

"Let's eat something, and after, you and I can talk about things." He held out his hand. "Please, Liv."

I could no more eat than I could fly to the moon. However, I also knew that if I didn't quiet the anger and hurt rising inside me, I would ruin whatever chance I had of making us a family again. And deep down—despite the betrayal I felt—that was what I wanted. Not just for Xander but for me too.

Maybe it was because love doesn't die as easily as people think. That you can wound it ten, fifteen, even dozens of times before it finally succumbs. Or maybe it was because I'd lived so long without love that when I'd finally found it, I didn't want to give it up.

Now Angela was nodding at the omelet in front of me. "You should eat before it gets cold."

"I'm not hungry," I lied.

"At least try the coffee, then. I added some licorice root to restore balance. It will help you feel better. I don't know if Mark told you, but I'm a healer and an herbalist." She spoke as if she expected me to be impressed by the news.

It was the least of the things Mark hadn't told me.

8.

—— N O W ——

I accepted the mug from Angela, mostly to blunt my hunger and the damp cold that had seeped into my bones. The coffee was dark and strong, the way Mark always drank it. I took a few sips and Angela smiled again, then rearranged my breakfast plate on the tray as if that would convince me to eat what she'd cooked. The dusky light of the container made her hair look mousy, and I remembered following Mark into the cabin yesterday and noticing the changes in him: the new hints of copper in his blond hair and the shoulders that had broadened in the months he'd been gone.

Inside, the cabin seemed even smaller than the outside made it look. It was low ceilinged, with dark log walls and bunches of drying plants hanging from a central rafter. The only natural light was provided by a decent-sized window at the front of the house.

Against one side of the main room, a rough kitchen was set up with a tiny four-burner propane stove, a short stretch of plywood countertop and open shelves filled with plates, pots and pans and big glass jars of rice, flour, brown sugar and coffee. A section of pipe came through a hole in the log wall, sending a thin but constant stream of water splashing into a deep sink and down its drain. A half-sized refrigerator was tucked in one corner and an ancient-looking woodstove was in the middle of the room. There was an old plaid couch, along with a tarnished brass lamp and a smoke-streaked stone fireplace that looked like it hadn't been used in years. A short hallway with two doorways led from the kitchen. Bedrooms? Storage? Whatever they were, they couldn't have been very big.

The place smelled like woodsmoke with hints of mouse nests and mildew. The floor was cracked yellow linoleum.

We sat ourselves on wood benches on either side of a worn pine table while Angela ladled soup into bowls and set them in front of us, along with a plate of sliced bread and a round of what Mark said was goat cheese.

"It's lentil and morel soup. Angela foraged the morels herself," he said.

Suddenly, the cabin door flew open and a boy with pale blue eyes and white-blond hair burst into the room. He stopped when he saw us, the door half-open, his stare bordering on rude.

"That's Rudy," Mark said to Xander. "He's ten. Rudy, this is Xander. Say hi."

Rudy's gaze went to Xander but no words came out of his mouth.

"I'm seven 'cause I had a birthday," Xander announced, and held up three fingers. Mark laughed and reached over to ruffle Xander's hair.

Rudy plopped himself onto the bench across from Mark. His fingernails were dark with dirt and I remembered how I wondered who he was and why he was here and watching as he grabbed a slice of bread and shoved half of it into his mouth.

Angela scowled at him. "Dude, slow down," she scolded in a way that made me think he must have been a younger brother or something. She didn't look old enough to have a ten-year-old child.

After we had eaten—I could choke down only a few spoonsful of soup—Mark suggested we head outside. I remembered feeling disoriented, stranded between anger and relief, love and a hundred questions. Mark sent Xander off with Rudy to see the goats, which he said were staked just behind the cabin, and then he gestured toward a splintery board set on two upright logs.

"Sit, please," he said, and I sank onto the makeshift bench.

"Well, that's the garden," Mark said, and swept out his hand. He went on to tell me how they'd planted beets, carrots, onions, potatoes, squash and kale and that they'd even started a few tomato plants in the greenhouse but that their yield had been disappointing so far. A dozen Rhode Island Red hens pecked in the dirt and Mark said that on the east side of the cabin, there was a coop, which they hoped to expand someday, and that Angela made herbed goat cheeses from the plants she gathered and sold the rounds to a shop in Valdez. It felt weird the way he talked. Like Xander and I were friends who'd stopped by for a visit instead of a family he'd abandoned.

Angela wore a pair of work gloves and was walking slowly through the garden with a hand basket, harvesting carrots and picking bugs from what looked like potato plants.

I turned toward Mark. "What I really want is to know why you're here." I hated how my voice trembled.

Mark rubbed his palms against his thighs. It made me think he was nervous too. "That's fair," he said.

The story he proceeded to tell me made complete sense and no sense at all.

Apparently, Rick's motorcycle shop was successful not for the skill with which the company built and rehabbed custom bikes but because it was a front for a larger and more lucrative business: drug distribution. As Mark told it, right after he was hired, Rick's wife left him, causing him to nose-dive back into drug use after years of sobriety. Within the space of six months, Rick had lost his house and his kids and begun to neglect the shop—until a guy, an ex-con who'd once bought a bike from Rick, dropped by. Over a six-pack in the back office, he offered a solution to Rick's problems and it wasn't long before a new stream of customers were leaving with packets of homemade methamphetamine in their pockets. Meth paid more than motorcycle work did, and Rick and his buddy decided to expand. They rented a warehouse outside of the city where they cooked larger batches of the stuff and began shipping their product around the West, hidden in the gas tanks of custom motorcycles and in the panels and tires of the trucks and trailers that delivered them. Mark had discovered what he was hauling only after he came in early one day and caught Rick stuffing product into the door panel of the delivery truck. Mark did the only thing he could. He said he was fine with hauling drugs but thought he should get a small cut of the profits because of the danger involved. There was a tense moment but Rick liked Mark and agreed. He warned, however, that if Mark ever double-crossed him or his partner, he would find himself floating in the Sacramento River with a bullet in his head. Mark didn't doubt the threat—he'd seen a couple of guys with prison tattoos come into the shop—but he figured he could extract himself after he proved his loyalty and made enough money to restart his film career.

"You remember how messed up things were at the time?" Mark asked. "What you'd done?" he prompted.

"It's not something I'd forget, Mark."

"Don't be that way. I'm just trying to tell you what happened."

"All right. Go on."

"So, while I was doing that delivery, my investor called and backed out of my movie. Remember? I told you."

I nodded.

"He said it was because of some legal stuff but I knew the real reason was you. I was shook up, so I stopped for a drink at a casino in Elko. Just a couple of quick ones to take the edge off. When I came out and saw the load had been stolen and the drugs were gone, I knew I was screwed." Mark swallowed hard.

"Rick and his partner are bad people, Liv. The last guy who crossed them ended up dead and he stole only one pound. I lost forty."

I felt like the wind had suddenly been knocked out of me.

"You see why I had to go?"

"Why did you get mixed up with them in the first place?"

"I don't know. I thought I could handle it."

Of course he had. Mark had always thought that no matter what happened, he would land on his feet.

"You should have told me."

"I couldn't. I had to protect you and Xander from them." He took my hand and I yanked it away. "I figured the best way was to make them think I saved them the trouble and killed myself. The less you knew, the better."

"And was leaving me without any money also part of this great plan?"

"It happened so fast. I needed somewhere to hide. This is Alvin's place."

Alvin Jones had been the subject of Mark's first documentary.

"I know," I told him. "It was part of how I found you."

Mark frowned. "How did you . . . ," he started.

"This is about you, not me," I said.

"All right," Mark said, and took a breath. "So, Alvin called back in September before everything happened. He said I should come up, maybe even buy his property. He had met this woman online who lived in Thailand."

A sudden gust of wind made the green willows at the far end of the garden bend and sway.

"When everything happened with Rick and the bikes, I thought this place was the answer. We talked about moving anyway, remember?"

I interrupted. "*You* talked about moving."

"Whatever. I knew you would love it here. The city was strangling us. Xander's health was being compromised by all that pollution and the tule fog. You were always working. Once I saw this place, I knew it was exactly what we needed. Nobody would find me. I made Alvin an offer. Cash. Fifteen thousand dollars. It was all I had. Alvin accepted."

I thought of how he'd let me work my butt off when he'd apparently had that kind of money stashed somewhere.

"Alvin sent some of the money off to his girlfriend, put the rest in the bank and said he'd stick around for a month or so to show me the ropes. Then he flew to Thailand."

"But you left us with nothing. Only that note."

"I know. I'm sorry. There was no time to really think. Besides, I thought you'd come here sooner than you did."

"Don't blame me for your shitty plan."

Muscular slate-colored clouds piled against the mountains in the distance.

"I said I was sorry."

"And who is she?" I lifted my chin at Angela, who now had a basket half full of carrots on her arm.

Mark fell silent for a few moments. Then: "Love is not finite. Love is abundant and all around us if we let it come to us."

I frowned. "What are you talking about?"

"Remember that book I kept asking you to read, *Mind, Self, Love* by Kai Huang?"

I shook my head.

A hint of exasperation crept into Mark's voice. "It's that translation of an ancient manuscript, one that was discovered in a cave near Dunhuang, China. If you'd bothered to read it, you would know what I'm talking about and understand how mind-blowing it is. It's about creating a new society, a new way of living that guarantees happiness and absolute freedom."

I studied the familiar lines of his face: the slightly crooked nose that he'd broken surfing at Ocean Beach, the deep blue eyes with their flecks of green. *Like sunlight on the sea*, I thought.

"Freedom from what, Mark?"

"Freedom from a society controlled by a few. The freedom to throw off the chains of greed and our capitalistic society and stop the fake Christian morality that makes us feel guilty for any pleasure we feel. The freedom to quit bowing down to those who try to stop us from being happy by creating rules about money and sex and relationships. About monogamy. You would have seen the beauty of it."

"Omigod. She's your girlfriend."

"Kai Huang prefers the term 'play partner.'"

I stood. "Are you kidding me?"

"I wouldn't kid about something so important," he said.

Angela had stilled and was watching us.

I pointed at her. "How old is she?"

"Twenty-two."

"Where did you meet her? At prom?"

"Don't be that way, Liv. She worked at the Granary. She managed the herb-and-supplement section."

The Granary was a food co-op near downtown Sacramento where Mark bought the coffee he liked.

"How long?" My insides trembled with rage.

"Two years, about."

I thought of his supposed trip to the desert.

"But we were friends first."

"Well, of course. That makes it OK, then."

"It wasn't like that."

"I can't believe this."

My head pounded and I massaged my temples with my fingertips.

Mark let out a long breath. "I was going to tell you. I needed to tell you. We were dying. Couldn't you see that?"

"No, Mark, I couldn't. We were just doing what we needed to do."

"Which is exactly what I'm saying. We were turning into roommates with a shared calendar. We were becoming one of those couples you see at restaurants who sit there and don't say a word to each other. It was all work and bills and taking care of Xander. There was no joy, no spontaneity in our lives anymore. But this . . . this is rebirth. This is opening ourselves up to the abundance of love and happiness that comes with the freedom to be who we were meant to be. Just think if we had to choose each other every single day? Kai Huang says, 'An open hand guarantees we will never be hungry.'"

"What does that even mean?"

"It means not being tied down by fake rules and being released

44

by pleasure. It means rejecting the views that have corrupted this country. It's so clear but nobody sees it. Capitalism has made us believe we can be happy only when we possess things, which chains us to jobs we hate and bills we can't pay and a system of marriage and family that strangles us. The so-called American Dream." He leaned forward. "And what do we do? We swallow the whole myth and all the rules and work harder without understanding we are building our own prison. It's what religions and governments want. To lock us in with rules and then reap their profits from our ignorance. They control us with false desires for fancy houses and nice cars. But if we turn away from that, if we reject society and capitalism and turn toward pleasure and the freedom to live without constraint, we will have the happiness we were meant to have."

I stared at Angela, who was walking slowly toward us. "And she's the one you chose for your little experiment?" My voice rose.

"It's not an experiment. It's real life, and yes, I had to bring her because I needed someone to pick me up from the bridge and help me sneak across the border. Someone Rick couldn't connect to me. If you had disappeared at the same time they thought I'd killed myself, it would have cast doubt that I was really dead. I figured you'd see the note, settle things and then come north. So we could be together. I love you. I want you to share this life with me."

He took my hand again and I yanked it away.

"Fuck you, Mark," I said. "I want a divorce."

9.

—— THEN ——

My parents weren't exactly the poster children for a happy marriage. They were two people who never should have been together. Like fire and water: my mother hot and destructive, my father quiet and still. And I was the product of that meeting: a kid who was never loved, never wanted and never good enough.

We lived, back then, on two sections of ranchland northeast of Paducah, Texas, with about two hundred head of Hereford cattle, which brought in just enough money to keep my parents from quitting ranching but not enough to live without a lot of belt-tightening during certain years. My mother, Helen, was as loud as she was mean and as thin as an oat stalk from the diet pills she should have stopped taking but refused to quit. My father, Jim, was a sturdy and quiet man—a hard worker with a streak of something hurt and brooding beneath his silence.

I'm not sure why my mother was the way she was. She never talked about her family. All I knew was that she had been born in the hills of Missouri and raised by a single mom who had five kids, took in laundry and cared for her own mother, who, it was once said, could have taken off a squirrel's head with a single rifle shot at fifty feet.

As for my father, his quietness apparently came out of a hundred-twenty-five-acre wheat farm outside Great Falls, Montana.

From what I understood, my paternal grandfather, William, was like my dad, strong as an ox and a hard worker. His wife, Maureen, was dark haired, green eyed and known both as a fastidious house-keeper and an excellent pie baker. Like me, my dad was an only child, but, unlike my parents, my grandparents had longed for a whole brood of kids. The sadness over the offspring that never ma-terialized was said to have hung over their house like a cloud.

By the age of ten, my father was already working the farm. He fed the chickens and mucked out the henhouse. He milked the Hol-stein, Betsy, hoed the vegetable garden and helped his father with the cut. In school he was a so-so student, never attaining a grade higher than a C but never causing problems with his teachers either. By the time he was in high school, he was a strapping kid who'd grown strong from moving irrigation pipe and digging ditches. The football coach kept trying to recruit him but my father apparently couldn't see any sense in the hitting and tackling and fighting that went on just to get a leather ball over an arbitrary line, and he re-fused.

Instead, whenever he had a free day, he would grab his fishing rod and a canvas pack and head for the distant hills. The land undulated low and wide around him, spreading as far as he could see, and there was a nice trout stream about five miles away. He would hike there and catch brookies and then use an old cast-iron skillet he'd hidden under a log to fry the fish over a campfire, with salt and a little oil he carried in a small jar in his pocket. Afterward, he would set his back against the log and roll himself a cigarette as he thought about everything and nothing.

It was a simple life but one that suited my father. One day, however, a neighbor called. He'd broken his arm thanks to a stubborn horse that had kicked him when he wasn't looking. The neighbor asked my dad's father if he could help with the threshing, just until the neighbor could hire someone from town.

Somehow, on that sun-filled day, my father's dad got tangled up with the thresher, and even though the neighbor's wife rushed him to town in her truck, he died of his injuries that night. The funeral was small.

My father, who was nineteen, tried to keep the farm running but eventually lost it to the bank. By then his mother was showing signs of dementia, which would take three long decades to claim her. She went to live with her sister in Billings and my father made his way to Colorado, where he got a job as a hand on a big cattle ranch and sent checks back to his mother. He met my mom on a trip to town. She was already two months pregnant from a boy who, whether from patriotism or fear of marriage, had left to join the Navy.

My father never had a chance.

My mother suggested a picnic by a creek and baked a pie like his mom did. She wore low-cut blouses and curled her hair. She took him to a dance at the Grange. A month later they were married.

When my mother lost the baby a few weeks after their wedding and my father's boss offered him a job in Texas with a pay raise, they went south. Then a settlement check arrived from the threshing company and they put a down payment on their own ranch, which was where I was born.

My mother named me Olivia with the lofty expectations of the talented beauty I would become—Olivia de Havilland, Olivia Hussey, Olivia Newton-John. However, I was a hardheaded and fussy child and I was quickly demoted to Liv. And my father found himself hog-tied to a ranch and to a mean and bitter wife.

At least that was how my paternal grandmother put it when I went to visit her and my great-aunt the summer I was twelve. My mother said it was dementia that made my grandmother tell those lies but it seemed to me like she told the story during one of those moments when she was as lucid and clear as anybody. My great-aunt, who would die two years later, said the story was "about right."

The older I got, the quieter my father seemed to become and the more bitterness filled my mother. I watched him silently shovel his supper into his mouth while my mother sat there with a cigarette between her fingers trailing smoke and asked him about his visit to the feedstore that day or whether he thought they should get a new truck or if he knew the Howells down the road had gone to Galveston for a week at the beach. He would mumble one-word answers until she got so angry she'd accuse him of cheating on her with the clerk at Murphy's Feed and Supply or selling our stock for too low a price or being too much of a "hayseed" to go anywhere besides town.

He absorbed every insult and accusation she threw at him, sometimes saying, "I'm not cheatin', Helen," and other times going off to finish some chore or head into the pasture for a smoke. A few times, he slammed the door behind him or curled his fists into hard balls but he never hit her or yelled. He just retreated into a quiet that seemed to grow darker as the years went by. Once, I saw him kick at a barn cat after my mother called him "dumb as a post" but the cat was too fast and my father's foot missed and I heard him curse under his breath. When I asked him once why he put up with her, he said he'd made a vow and he wasn't a man to go back on his word.

I promised myself right then that my marriage would never be like theirs, and yet look how mine turned out.

10.

———— N O W ————

As we sat there on the rough bench in the middle of the wilderness, our voices rose. Mark said I was too uptight to see the freedom that living with pleasure gave and the only reason he'd smuggled drugs was so we could have a better life. I told him that if "uptight" meant I didn't approve of him screwing another woman behind my back and also that I wanted a house where my son could live, then that was what I was, and that I was going to get a divorce lawyer who'd make him pay for what he'd done. I'd also tell the cops he was alive. Mark stood and bellowed that if I did that, Rick and his partner would know he was alive and then he would really be dead.

I told him I didn't know who he was anymore and he said that was because he was his true self now.

Xander, who'd come back from the goats, started crying at our shouting. Rudy took his hand and led him gently into the cabin.

Mark said, "Look what you've done."

"What I've done?"

"You've made him upset."

"And having him think you were dead was fine?"

We went on like that for a while: me accusing him of being both a liar and a cheat, and him asking if I thought he hadn't suffered too.

A gust of wind pushed through the forest with a sound like a far-off highway, and a shiver ran through me. Suddenly, I was cold and exhausted. The light around us was milky gray. I felt like a fool for chasing after a selfish cheater, for coming to a place so remote and wild. Slowly, I got to my feet.

"I can't stay. It's over."

"Liv," he started.

I held up my hand.

"You look tired," he said. His voice was kinder now. "It's probably better if you leave tomorrow. It's late and the road isn't well marked. I'd worry about you guys getting lost out there."

I thought of the horrible track, the turns Xander and I had navigated, the state of our gas tank, which was barely a quarter full.

"There's a bed in the shipping container on the hill," Mark said. "You can sleep there." His gaze locked onto mine and I remembered how he could draw you in with that look, how it was like being pulled by a magnet you couldn't resist. "I'd like to spend a few hours with Xander. Please," he said. "Then you can leave. We'll figure something out."

"I can't stay."

"Babe," he started, then hung his head.

I turned and he followed me into the cabin. Heat radiated from the woodstove. Angela was on the couch and the lamp next to her threw a yellow circle of illumination that didn't reach the corners of the room. She looked up from her knitting.

"The boys were tired. I made them hot cocoa and put them to bed. Would you like a cup?"

Mark pulled the jacket from my shoulders. I was too tired to object.

"Or Angela could heat up more soup. You should eat," he said.

I shook my head. "I don't want her soup."

Mark hung my jacket on a hook by the door. "She wants to leave," he told Angela.

"But you just got here," she said.

"Where's my son?" I asked.

"He's in the bedroom on the right," Mark said.

I went down the short hallway and stepped into the room, let my eyes adjust to the dimness. A pearly gray light came through a small window above a pair of twin beds. The boys slept in one of them, Xander's back curled against Rudy, the other boy's arm flung protectively over my son. They looked so innocent and peaceful and my heart cracked. My sweet little boy. Abandoned by his father, living with a distracted and overwhelmed mother, watching too much TV, eating cheap food, wearing hand-me-down clothes. How would I tell him his father was disappearing from his life again?

I heard a murmur of voices from the living room and moved to the side of the bed. I touched Xander's warm cheek and thought, *What will it hurt to let him spend one night here? What will it hurt to let him wake up to his father?* It would be so much worse if I loaded him half-asleep into the car and he woke up in another new place with his daddy gone again. This way, I could try to explain what was happening. I leaned over and kissed the top of his head.

"We'll stay here tonight and leave in the morning," I said when I came out of the room.

"OK. That's good," Mark said. "I'll walk you to the container."

"I can do it myself," I said.

"There's been a brown bear hanging around. I'd feel better if you didn't go alone," he said, and took a rifle from a rack above the doorframe. I'd never known Mark to carry a gun before. Angela was still at her knitting.

"Sleep well," she said.

I ignored her, put on my jacket and followed Mark outside and around the edge of the garden. I was drained of everything: thoughts, hope, anger.

Mark stopped at the container and lifted a metal bar that held the doors closed. The squeal of it broke the silence that had fallen between us. I went inside and Mark offered to make a fire. I told him just to go.

I watched him walk across the container's plywood floor and the door slowly close behind him.

It took a few seconds to register the next sound: the screech of the metal bar falling into place.

"Mark!" I yelled, and ran to the door. I pounded a fist on the cold metal. "Unlock the door," I shouted.

"See you in the morning," he called.

I pounded again. "Open it right now."

Silence fell then and I waited, realizing after a few moments that Mark wasn't coming back. I told myself he'd locked the door against the bear he'd talked about, and tried to stay calm. The air inside the container was dank and cold and I blew on my hands and then shoved them into my jacket pockets to get warm.

It took a moment for the absence to register.

My wallet, keys and cell phone were gone.

And here I was now, with the woman he was screwing, because apparently I'd been too busy trying to keep our lives afloat and my son healthy instead of becoming some free spirit who gathered herbs and mushrooms and wove beads into her hair.

Angela was still talking.

"I think you'll really be pleased by the difference in taste in organic, free-range eggs," she said. "They're much healthier for you than the store-bought ones. I also put in some dried chanterelle to add umami."

I stared at her. "What the hell are you talking about? Do you think this is some weird bed-and-breakfast where you lock your guests in a box and screw their husbands?"

Something flashed across her face but it was gone so quickly that I wondered if I'd imagined it.

"There's no reason to be hurtful," she said. "Believe me, we're as unhappy about this as you are."

"I doubt that," I told her.

"This isn't a game," Angela said. "You have to trust us. These are dangerous people who don't forgive or forget. If you did what you said you'd do yesterday and told the cops, Rick would find out Mark is alive and then he'll be dead. Just like he said. You put us in a very bad spot." She gestured around the container. "That's the only reason you're in here. You were threatening us."

I stood. "The reason I'm here is because my husband is a lying, cheating, drug-dealing jerk who apparently likes to screw women who aren't smart enough to see that this whole free-love thing just means he'll cheat on you too." I reached over and dumped the plate with the omelet and toast onto the floor. "And I don't want your stupid free-range umami omelet either."

Angela's eyes flashed. "Don't think you're any better than me. I know what you did."

It wasn't the first time I'd heard someone say that. In the days and weeks after the terrible thing happened, I heard it more than a few times. Sometimes it was hissed in my direction. Sometimes it came filled with accusations. The worst was the psychologist in the shapeless green dress who was assigned to examine me. We sat in a small, windowless room while she poked and prodded and finally said the phrase with such pity that I felt like I didn't even deserve to be alive. Even the detective who had terrible coffee breath and sat across the scratched metal table from me saying I might as well confess because he knew what I'd done hadn't made me feel as bad as that psychologist had. And now here was my husband's lover making the same charge.

I don't know how people fall for the idea that a sin can ever truly be forgiven. Even though I paid my price, the dark stain I carried never went away.

11.

—— THEN ——

It was what I had done—or hadn't done—that brought me to the Goodridge Juvenile Correction Center the year I turned seventeen. It was June and the driver of the transport van had rolled his window down, so the hot wind slapped my hair against my face like a thousand little whips. There were two other girls in the van, both of them tough-looking, with homemade tattoos and hard eyes. I wanted to tell the driver that I wasn't like them and that I didn't belong here. Although there was also the possibility that I did.

None of us said a word as the van pulled up to a pair of towering wire gates and waited for the guard to check the documents the driver had brought. I bent low to look through the grimy van window and see where I was.

Goodridge didn't look like a prison, exactly. It was more like a boarding school that had fallen on hard times. There were rows of concrete-block dormitory buildings surrounded by packed-dirt yards and a high fence topped with razor wire. There was a cracked basketball court with hoops but no nets, a potholed dirt track and a few cement picnic tables under rusting tin shelters that provided the only shade in the place. Outside the fence were ugly fields of cotton that baked under a yellow sun. The wind blew almost constantly. Everything was bleached, like bones in the desert.

When the driver came around and opened the van's sliding door and ordered us out, I didn't move. My legs were trembling so badly, I thought they wouldn't hold me if I stood. After a minute or so, a guard poked his head in and said I could either obey the rules or start off my sentence in the behavioral unit. I wasn't sure what that was but the way he said it made me get myself to my feet and shuffle out of the vehicle. I thought I might fall but I didn't.

I followed the two other girls into a holding room where the handcuffs were removed and we were searched and handed the orange pants and shirt we were to wear, along with two pairs of cotton underwear, two pairs of crew socks, an ugly white bra and canvas shoes that turned out to be a half size too big for me. Everything felt unreal, as if I were watching some other girl take off her clothes and pull on the baggy pants and too-stiff shirt.

After we dressed, a matron came in and explained the rules, and then, one by one, we were escorted to a windowless interview room where, when it was my turn, a woman in a bright red pantsuit opened a thick folder on her desk and looked over my records. "It says here you claim you can't remember what you did."

All I could manage was a nod.

She closed the folder and stared at me. Her lipstick matched her clothes.

"I think you'll find that remorse and rehabilitation work better than denial as far as your time here," she said. "I urge you to participate in session, to confront your actions and to learn."

After a different room and another lecture, this one on personal hygiene, I was handed a stack of folded sheets and a pillow and escorted to C dorm: forty young women crammed together in a space with narrow chicken wire windows set high on one wall and not much ventilation. The musk and constant noise made us feel like cattle. Some of the girls adjusted. Some did not.

Two weeks into my sentence and an hour before wake-up call, one of those nonadjusting girls began to scream. She had brown eyes and short coal black hair and had been brought in, I'd heard, for taking a hatchet to her boyfriend, who would end up living the rest of his life without four fingers on his left hand. She was fifteen but looked about twelve. Her lawyer had claimed self-defense. She screamed for eight hours straight.

We could hear her through the walls of the isolation room when we were herded into the yard for our hour of exercise. We could hear her down the hallway as we walked to the cafeteria for lunch. We could hear her as they loaded her into an ambulance and drove her away. That night, when I lay in the narrow prison bunk, I thought I could still hear her high-pitched howls.

The only way I could cope inside was not to think about my school or my friends or the trial that had put me in that place. Instead, I squeezed my world down to my bunk, the yard and the sewing room, where I worked with twenty-four other girls, hemming and stitching zippers into little girls' dresses, their parents never realizing their precious daughters were wearing clothes made by mutilators and murderers, by assaulters and thieves.

My only friend was a girl who'd accidentally killed her boyfriend by injecting him with a syringe full of heroin that, unbeknownst to her, had been laced with some kind of prescription sedative. She taught me how to avoid the roughest girls and a way of breathing that calmed the panic attacks that kept rising whenever I thought about being where I was. She also taught me how to lie, which I'd never been good at before. It's the thing they don't tell you about prison. You might go in with bad behaviors but you always leave with more than when you arrived.

My Goodridge year went by slowly, each day being stretched by meals you didn't look forward to eating, nights that came with terrible thoughts and days filled with a horrible sameness broken only when girls got into fights or decided to cut themselves after discovering their boyfriends or partners had broken up with them. Now here I was, locked up again, the differences being the quiet and the fact that, at Goodridge, I had known when I would get out. Now I had no idea if or when that might happen.

Angela's visit had made that clear.

12.

──── N O W ────

I spent most of the day either lying on the bed or staring out the window, so I saw Mark come home with Xander and go into the cabin. He carried a bulging pack on his back and a white propane tank in each hand. He didn't even glance at the container. His whole body seemed to droop. Later, Angela came out and shooed the chickens around to the east side of the cabin, where the coop was located, while Rudy brought in the goats. Then nothing. The cabin door remained closed, the stovepipe trailing smoke. I'd finished off the water and my stomach clenched with hunger. I wished I'd been smarter and not thrown my breakfast on the floor. The only person I'd really hurt was myself. Or maybe I wounded Angela more than I thought. Maybe that was why she and Mark were ignoring me.

I stared up at the container's ribbed ceiling and felt a wave of anxiety. What if they planned to starve me? What if I died here and they buried my body in the woods? What if they told Xander I had left and he had only a hazy memory of a mother who hadn't loved him enough to stay?

Light still shined through the container window but that meant nothing during an Alaskan summer. How did anyone get used to it anyway? My throat closed and I felt slightly nauseous. I got up from the bed and went over and rattled the door.

"Hey, I need water," I shouted even though there was no one to hear.

I laid my palms against the metal doors and breathed liked the girl at Goodridge had taught me, until I felt some of my panic recede. I told myself people could survive a long time without food but then thought it took only four or five days to die from thirst. I knew I needed to find a way out of here and escape. That was when I noticed the rectangle of darkness that cut across the narrow slice of light between the container's two doors.

It was the bar that held the container shut and I thought, *What if I can find something narrow and strong enough to slide through the crack and lift the metal arm?* I could wait for the right opportunity to slip out, grab Xander and run to the car. Later, I would realize that the plan also required me to locate my car keys and wallet, but right then I didn't think of that. I was just desperate enough to come up with a plan that didn't go very far.

For a moment, my spirits buoyed and I wished Angela had given me a regular spoon with breakfast or, better yet, a table knife. Instead, all I had was the fragile bamboo fork she had left, which was stamped with the note "100 percent recyclable." The only thing I wanted to recycle it for was something metal and strong.

I began to search methodically, digging carefully through the blankets and sheets in the steamer chest (unlike the hurried search I'd done before) and then through the supplies in the fifty-five-gallon drums. Inside were sacks of feed, tarps, rope and packets of batteries. One held a couple of rotting potatoes. I slammed the lid back on, as I started to gag from the smell. Finally, I got on my belly and slid partway under the bed, then reached around the floor with my fingers. I felt grit and dust and then something light scurrying across my hand. I yanked it back and saw a big fat spider escaping across the floor. I shuddered, gathered myself and tried again, exploring the edge of the wall until I touched something hard and tool-like. I pulled it toward me.

It was a pair of rusting scissors with the tip broken off one blade. The blade might be too short to do the job I needed and yet it offered a ray of hope. I slithered back out from under the mattress but I was too elated and too slow to react when the bar groaned, the door opened and Angela came in. She held a tray with dinner in her hands.

Her glance fell immediately on the dust on my clothes and the shears in my hand.

"Get the scissors, Rudy," she said, and the boy, who was behind her, dropped my duffel, which he was carrying, and scurried over to snatch the scissors from my hand. His pale eyes never met mine. He reminded me of the skittish feral cat that had lived in the alley behind Mr. Martin's house, surviving on mice and garbage scraps—and always biting the hand that tried to feed it. And yet I'd seen how gently he'd taken Xander's hand.

Angela made a small tsking sound, then told Rudy to take the scissors into the house and come back after he'd finished his dinner. The door closed and the bar fell into place.

She stared at me for a moment and said she wanted to apologize for the cruel thing she'd said that morning, as if that were the only thing that had caused me to try to break out of the container.

"I let my ego get in the way of understanding. I let my ears listen instead of my heart and of course you reacted." She glanced at the congealed breakfast on the floor. "I hope once you get to know me, you'll see I have only good intentions for you."

I wondered exactly what kind of good intentions included screwing a woman's husband, but didn't say that.

"I thought nobody was coming," I said.

"Sorry. Yeah. It's just that we had some news that made Mark get one of his headaches. I had to put him to bed with some willow tea. I'm sure he'll feel better in the morning."

She carried the dinner tray to the steamer chest, pointing out venison sausage and rosemary-roasted potatoes on the plate and setting a fresh Mason jar of water along with a mug of tea next to it. I gulped some of the water and she pushed the plate in my direction. I stabbed a piece of potato with the flimsy fork and shoved it into my mouth. Angela began to clean up the omelet remains with a towel. She looked up at me from where she was crouched on the floor.

"The news was pretty scary for us."

According to her, a stranger had arrived in town this morning in a rented Ford Expedition. Mark had heard the news from Evan at the gas pump, who had learned it from Dale at the hardware store. The only reason outsiders came to the town of Cohut, which was the closest town to here at fifty miles away, was to hunt or fish. This guy, however, had rolled in without any gear. No rifle, no fishing pole, not even a decent pair of boots. He was dressed in jeans and expensive-looking loafers. Dale said the guy had bought a topo map and a shovel and asked questions about the town and what kind of people lived in the area and said he was a developer but Mark didn't believe that. Especially since the stranger had showed up right after I did.

"He thinks maybe you weren't telling the truth when you said you never used a credit card and your phone battery died," Angela said as she rose to her feet.

I told Angela that I'd told the truth and that if the guy had been sent by Rick and his pal, it was even more important that Xander and I not be trapped here.

"I'm afraid leaving isn't advisable right now," she said. "Don't worry. Xander is our highest priority. We're going to take every precaution we can."

I could hardly stand to look at her.

She set the messy towel aside, lit the lantern on the shelf and sat in the upholstered chair.

"What are you doing?" I asked.

"I wanted to read to you while you ate." She pulled a slim paperback from her skirt pocket. Its cover was creased and the pages were swollen as if they had once gotten wet. It was the book *Mind, Self, Love*. "I thought if you understood us, if you knew what we were trying to achieve, you might not be so angry, so blame-placing." She leaned forward as if she were imparting a secret. "That way, you could see the beauty of how we live and Mark would let you out. It's what Mark wants more than anything. He wants you and Xander to stay and to be a family again and maybe you would want it too. After you understand." She was so close, I could see a faint half-moon scar on her left cheek. "I want to help you. I want to be your friend."

I started to tell her she would never be my friend but I remembered one of the mean guards in prison, Sheila, a heavyset woman with bottle-brush eyebrows. Defy Sheila in even the slightest way and she would find an excuse to write you up and take away your shampoo or your library privileges or toss your bunk for contraband five days in a row. Suck up to her, however, and life would be smooth.

"So, if I listen and eat, I can get out of here?"

Angela smiled. "It would be a start."

"How about letting me see Xander too?"

Angela cleared her throat. "Maybe later." She opened the book and proceeded to read the first chapter. The book turned out to be the story of a boy, the son of a Chinese papermaker, whose entire family died in a great plague of smallpox. Driven out of his village because the scars on his face were too big a reminder of what the little community had been through, he wandered the country, begging for food and sleeping with pigs for warmth. Eventually he made his way to the Kunlun Mountains, where he met a gnarled old man, a ritual master. The man sent the boy on various quests to learn lessons about finding happiness. The book pledged ten lessons in all.

I choked down the meal and drank the tea while she read. I didn't know when or if I would be fed again.

"What do you think?" Angela asked when she was done.

Right then the door opened and Rudy peeked in. "Dad needs you," he said.

"Dad?" I said, but Angela was already up and grabbing the meal tray with my empty dishes.

"I'll be back," she said, and hurried out the door, and Rudy closed it behind her, the bar falling into place.

I stared after her.

Wasn't it enough that she'd stolen my husband? Did she have to create a fake family for him too?

13.

—— N O W ——

It took me a while to fall asleep that night. All I could think about was men coming with guns and me being trapped, so I couldn't save Xander, and about being locked up for the rest of my life. It was like a movie except everything was real and I couldn't relax with the knowledge that everything would turn out fine in the end and that the main character would walk into the future happy and strong and whole.

I tossed and turned and finally got up. The dampness seemed to have seeped from the mattress into my bones. Before I decided to try to get some sleep, I opened the steamer chest, found some old cotton sheets and made the bed with tight military corners the way I did for all my clients. I thought it would help me sleep but it didn't.

I padded across the floor and looked out the window. The world was bathed in a gauzy light that made everything seem slightly out of focus. I stared at the cabin and thought of Xander curled up in the twin bed with Rudy, of Angela lying next to Mark, her tight young body cupped against his. It filled me with a kind of dark metallic rage and I thought, *Why did I accept Mark's excuses instead of seeing the signs?* Mark getting a call and taking the phone into the backyard (one of Xander's movies had been on and it had been hard for Mark to hear the caller); the sudden interest in herbal supplements (a guy at work had turned him on to them); coming home late (overtime).

I thought of one of my earliest housecleaning clients, Phoebe Walters, who'd grown suspicious of her CEO husband and snuck back to her house one day instead of going to her yoga class and found her fifty-four-year-old spouse in bed with the twenty-one-year-old dog groomer.

"I say, let her have him," Phoebe said when she called to tell me she'd sold the house and was moving to Portland and no longer needed my services. "The little whore can spend her thirties buying diapers for him and for her kids."

When I told Mark the story about Phoebe's husband, he said, "Talk about cliché."

I started to turn away from the window. It did no good to think about Angela and Mark lying together, about how clueless I'd been. Before I turned, however, I saw something move at the far edge of the garden and leaned closer to the window.

It was a fox.

The tip of its tail looked as if it had been dipped in white paint, and there was a matching spot on its snout. It trotted purposefully through the plants, stilling once to sniff the air and then looping in my direction before turning again and disappearing around the edge of the cabin where Mark said the coop was located. I waited to see if Shadow would come barking out of his shelter but there was nothing. I guessed the fox knew enough to stay upwind of the dog and the thought came suddenly: *That is exactly what I will have to do with*

Mark and Angela. Stay upwind of suspicion, act as if I am fine with this strange life of theirs and then make my move.

Which is why I went over and picked up the *Mind, Self, Love* book, lit the lantern with a match from the box next to it and began to read.

The second chapter described how the wandering boy had carried with him a jade necklace that had belonged to his mother. Even as he starved, he refused to sell the piece and slept only in snatches for fear someone would steal it from him. The ritual master said if the boy wanted to stop his suffering and find riches, he needed to cast the bauble into the river.

The boy went to the river, where he paced for three days before, exhausted from worry and tired of his world of hunger and fear, he finally did what the ritual master had said. He waited for his riches to arrive, and when they didn't, he hiked back to the ritual master's house to complain. The master said the riches he had promised was actually the freedom of living without having to carry the burdens of his past, and the boy realized that indeed he felt lighter and happier without the necklace constantly weighing on his thoughts. He slept eight hours for the first time that night.

I thought about my past. I didn't think it was as easy to toss it away as this Kai Huang guy made it seem.

14.

—— THEN ——

If you look back at your life, you'll see the moments when everything changed. It might be the instant when the technician's voice shifted from breezy to matter-of-fact as she did your mammogram. Or maybe it was when your phone rang as you were driving and you looked down for just a second to see who was calling instead of keeping your eyes on the road. They're the tiny shifts that send us careening onto another path or nudge us in a different direction. For me, it happened on an overly hot Tuesday morning last October. The day the baby fell from the sky.

I was on my way to Xander's occupational therapy appointment and I remember the feel of the heat rising off the sidewalk and Xander's sweaty little hand in mine. We were already late.

"Come on, Xan, let's race," I said. "See if you can beat me to the door." I tugged on his hand. "One, two, three, go."

Instead of running, however, Xander dug his heels to a stop and pointed.

"Look, Mama, a pirate," he cried.

I looked up to see, walking our way, a bearded man with an eye patch, and that was when I saw the flash of pink above my head. For the briefest of moments, a nanosecond of time, I thought it was a bag of laundry.

Then some part of me realized it was a child.

I didn't even think before I dropped Xander's hand, leaped forward and curled my arms outward.

The weight of that tiny falling girl drove me to the ground.

My knees skidded across the sidewalk and my left elbow smashed into the concrete. I felt myself start to roll and I hugged that little girl tight against my chest. There was a dull thud as the side of my skull hit the hard pavement and I heard a scream. For a moment, I saw stars.

Then I was flat on my back, the toddler's big brown eyes staring into mine, so close I could see the little flecks of gold in them.

"Oh my God," someone cried.

The girl's mouth opened and she let out a wail.

Above me, a white curtain fluttered out from an open second-story window.

"Call an ambulance," a man shouted.

My ears rang like a fire alarm and faces appeared above me. The world took a single jerky turn. I squeezed my eyes closed.

Then a gentle voice: "You can let go, honey. I've got her. I'm a nurse."

I didn't want to let go. Yet I felt the little girl being pried from my arms. A mumble of voices rushed in and then receded like waves on the shore.

"She saved that baby's life," a woman said.

"She's a hero," a man agreed.

Which was the same thing the cop called me later as I sat in the back of an ambulance after "the Catch," as it would come to be known.

"That was something how you caught that kid," the officer said. His voice was full of admiration.

He had reddish blond hair, a gap between his front teeth and a rash of freckles that covered his face and arms. He looked like a boy in my sixth-grade class, a kid named Wilson, whom everybody had teased.

"If you don't mind me saying, you would have made a helluva wide receiver," the officer said.

I was staring through the ambulance's back windows, watching a clump of television cameras aim their lenses at the second-floor window of the apartment from which the girl had fallen. Officer Freckles, as I thought of him, told me the baby's mother claimed she'd opened a window in their new home to catch a breeze and hadn't noticed the screen was missing. While she was on the phone, her daughter, an active twenty-month-old, had somehow scrambled up onto the back of the couch under the opening and tumbled out. The baby's name was Molly. I hoped she was OK.

"What?" I said.

"You know, like catching a football?" Officer Freckles said.

"Oh," I said, turning back to look at him. "I clean houses."

The officer's forehead crinkled into a frown. "I'm not sure I'm following you there, ma'am."

"I mean I've got strong arms. That's how I caught her."

"Oh, gotcha," he said.

Xander lay on his back on the ambulance floor, listening to his playlist on my phone. "George Strait. 'I Cross My Heart,'" he said, and thumped his heel once on the ground as if to punctuate the point.

"Lucky for her you came along when you did," the officer said. "Otherwise . . ." He let his voice trail off.

An image formed of the little girl Molly lying on the ground with blood pooling beneath her small head, her limbs splayed in unnatural positions, a bit of brain matter leaking out.

"I think I might throw up," I said.

The officer grabbed a tube-shaped plastic bag and handed it to me. I held the bag over my mouth and breathed deeply until the nausea passed. Finally, I lowered it to my lap.

"All good?" Officer Freckles asked.

I wasn't "all good" but I nodded anyway.

"Can I go now?" I asked the officer. "I've got to get home."

"You should go to the hospital. Get checked out."

"I don't have insurance," I said, which was true, but mostly I wanted to get away from the cop, from the commotion outside.

"How about I take you home?" the officer said. "You might black out or something. You hit your head pretty hard."

"I'm OK. I need to get out of here." I handed the tube back to the cop. "Come on, Xander."

"Really, you ought to get checked out." Officer Freckles looked at his notes. "Mrs. Russo," he added.

Outside, another TV truck pulled up. I turned to the cop. "Do you have to put my name in your report?"

"Sorry," he said, although he didn't look like he was. "SOP. Standard operating procedure."

"It's just that I'm a pretty private person." I looked out the ambulance windows again.

Officer Freckles followed my gaze. "I hear you. Those reporters are scum."

"Vultures," I said.

I didn't explain more.

"Listen, I'm not supposed to do this," the cop said, and looked out the window again, "but I know the EMT. I'll get him to drive us around the corner so those clowns don't see you, and I'll walk you to your car, make sure you're OK."

"All right," I said.

The officer winked. "It's the least I can do for a hero like you."

Which is exactly what I wasn't.

I didn't tell the cop that, however. Maybe I should have. Instead, I let him walk me to my Subaru and wait on the sidewalk until I drove off. The scrapes on my knees and elbow burned, and I wished, for a second, I could rewind time so the mother would have noticed the missing window screen and the baby wouldn't have climbed up onto the couch and I wouldn't have been the one walking by at the moment she fell and somebody else had caught her—an ex–baseball player, for instance. But then maybe I should have rewound even further. To what had happened before I went to prison. To that winter's evening when I was seventeen.

Xander was in his booster seat behind me and Carrie Underwood was on the radio. I debated canceling my regular Tuesday afternoon cleaning clients, the Kiplingers, but what would that change other than creating an even bigger hole in our bank account?

The Kiplingers were a pair of fussy real estate agents who lived in a seven-thousand-square-foot house that looked as if it should have been located on a vineyard in the South of France but had accidentally been dropped into a gated community on the outskirts of Sacramento, California, instead. They insisted that their house should resemble a model home rather than a place where people actually lived. The granite countertops had to be shiny enough to see your face in them, the towels were required to be hung just so and the throw pillows needed to be fluffed and then chopped, so the corners stood up like Doberman pinscher ears.

Six months earlier, they'd also installed one of those camera-based alarm systems that not only recorded the comings and goings in the house but allowed them to watch whoever was inside. Once, Mrs. Kiplinger had sent me a text saying she had noticed that I was putting the burgundy-striped sheets on their bed when she'd specifically left me a note to use the sage green set.

Their finicky little hearts would have stopped if they had seen Xander wandering around their house, and yet there hadn't been enough time to drop him off at home so Mark could watch him and also get to their house on time. We had only one car. Besides, what if Mark had asked why I was all skinned up and saw the worry in my eyes when I told him?

"Xan, baby," I said, and looked into the rearview mirror, "Mama has to go to work and I need you to help me."

He wrinkled his nose.

"If you can watch cartoons and be quiet as a mouse, I'll buy you an ice-cream cone when I'm done. How's that?"

"I can do it," he said solemnly. "I like mouses."

At the Kiplinger house, I parked my car in the shade of a giant oak, grabbed my cleaning caddy and step stool and told Xander to wait in the car. I let myself into the house, went into the kitchen–family room area with its expansive hardwood floor, overstuffed furniture and giant TV and got out my feather duster. I tied a bandanna over my hair and began to swipe the duster over the Kiplingers' walnut bookcase, atop which the telltale camera blinked its red light. I tried to act nonchalant as I climbed the step stool to dust. Instead,

I gave the camera a little shake and tossed a white cleaning rag over the lens.

Let the Kiplingers think that their fancy camera system had malfunctioned or that I'd accidentally jostled it and turned it off while I cleaned. I knew I couldn't get away with the stunt twice but I hoped it would work for now.

I hustled back outside, moved the car in front of the garage, where I knew there was a blind spot with no cameras, and snuck Xander into the house. I gave him a Fruit Roll-Up, turned the TV to the Nickelodeon channel and went to work.

I stripped the Kiplingers' bed (they'd had sex this week, which wasn't always the case), started the laundry and cleaned the four bathrooms, the two guest bedrooms, the office and the formal living room before I headed for the kitchen–family room area.

Xander said he had to go to the bathroom, so I took him into the garage and had him pee in one of my cleaning buckets.

"Let's always pee in buckets," he said as his stream drummed against the plastic.

"Let's not," I said.

My head thumped as I scrubbed the kitchen sink and wiped down the granite countertops. Outside the Kiplingers' big French doors, their pool shimmered cool and blue in the heat.

If I could, I would have stripped off my clothes and waded into the water, letting myself sink below the surface and opening my mouth so the water rushed in and I wouldn't have to think about the trouble that might be coming. Instead, I shook off the thoughts, grabbed my mop and went to work on the kitchen floor. The scrapes on my knees and elbow flamed every time I moved.

When the house was done, I snuck Xander back to the car, returned inside and changed the TV channel back to PBS. Then I climbed the step stool and used the handle of my duster to flip the cloth from the camera.

On the way home, I stopped at the drugstore and bought Xander a vanilla ice-cream cone for a dollar fifty-five.

"You're such a good boy," I told him.

15.

—— THEN ——

I saw the TV van the minute I turned onto our street. It was parked in front of our house.

"Shit," I hissed.

"You said a bad word, Mama," Xander announced from the back seat. His face and red T-shirt were streaked with vanilla ice cream, so it looked like he'd been caught under a flock of loose-stooled pigeons.

"I know. I'm sorry, sweetie."

There were two guys—a big one with a TV camera on his shoulder and a smaller one wearing a tie. They were on the front porch talking with Mark.

Xander strained against the seat belt on his booster seat. "Who's that?" he asked.

"Nobody," I said.

"Not nobody," he insisted.

I told myself they couldn't have uncovered my past so quickly. Every six months or so I would Google myself. Luckily, what had happened had occurred before the Internet and social media made every transgression, every bad choice, part of the public record. Also, the weekly paper that had covered my story had gone out of business without archiving its articles, and I'd changed my name when I'd gotten married. Each time, I assured myself my secret was safe although, as I understand now, all it took was a tiny sliver of light to reveal the secret you'd tried to tuck away in the darkness.

The reporter, the cameraman and Mark all looked over as I pulled into the driveway and I knew that the moment I stopped the car Xander would jump out and tell the reporter that his name was Xander, that he was six years old and who knew what else. Which is exactly what he did.

The cameraman was aiming his lens at us when Xander leaped from the car and yelled, "I'm Xander, and guess what. I peed in a bucket." He stopped, grabbed his crotch with two hands and mimed the episode.

"Xan, stop it," Mark said from the porch.

I got out of the car. "Don't you film my son."

The guy in the tie made a cutting motion at his cameraman and came toward me with a car-salesman grin. He had blazingly white teeth.

"Paul Rodriguez, Eye First News. It's an honor to meet you," he said, and held out a hand as if he thought I welcomed his arrival on my front lawn. I didn't. When he saw I wasn't going to return the handshake, he went on like nothing had happened. He must have been used to things like that. "That video of you catching the baby was something else," he said.

"What video?" I asked.

"The one that's blowing up the Internet," he said. "Some guy filmed the whole thing."

Xander gave a little dance on the grass. "And I ate ice cream," he said.

"We'd just like to talk to you for a few minutes," the reporter pressed. He glanced at the Subaru with its magnetic sign that read LIV'S GREEN CLEAN. "You, the hero house cleaner, and Mark here, the man who shot that Africa documentary. Wow."

"I really don't want to talk," I said.

"Why don't we all go inside?" Mark said from the porch. "It's hot out here and I know my wife must be exhausted."

He came down the front steps and wrapped his arm around me.

"Why didn't you call me?" he whispered.

"I don't know. I thought you were busy," I said. "It wasn't a big deal."

And I tried to convince myself it wasn't. Instead, the story of the Catch hit all the major networks and morning shows. The amateur video, which some college kid had posted on YouTube, had ninety million views and counting. Reporters flocked. Four of the moms at kindergarten drop-off who'd never spoken to me before came over and said that we should do lunch sometime and that they'd love to have Xander over for a playdate if that was all right with me. Somebody even started selling T-shirts on Amazon that read LIV BRAVE above a line drawing of a woman with her arms stretched in a V over her head.

At a gas station, when a woman wearing one of those shirts shouted, "Liv!" and waved her hand like she knew me, I started to wave back before I realized I had no idea who she was.

"Let's see those strong arms," the woman yelled, and I shut off the fuel, shoved the nozzle back into the holder and left even though I'd put only four gallons in the tank.

Why would she think I wanted to perform like some trained seal?

She wasn't the only one.

Strangers stopped me in the grocery store to shake my hand or take selfies with me. Some people would raise their hands in a V over their heads and shout, "Liv brave, Liv strong." One man told me he was going to name his daughter Liv because he wanted her to be fearless and quick thinking like me. I said, "Thank you." What I really wanted to say was that the Catch had been nothing more than a reaction, like being at a ball game and snagging a line drive coming at your head, and that because of what had happened, I needed two big glasses of wine before I went to bed at night. The first glass was to stop the worry. The second was to keep away that image of the baby falling through my arms and smashing onto the sidewalk.

Mark, on the other hand, seemed to thrive on the attention.

After the first TV reporter left, he got ice for my knees, fussed over the bruise forming under my right eye and splurged on steaks to barbecue for dinner. He even brought back a bottle of chilled champagne to toast what I'd done. All I wanted was a cold shower and everything not to have happened.

When the phone calls started later that evening, Mark fielded them all. He agreed to interviews with the *LA Times*, the *Washington Post*, *People*, and NPR. When one of those national morning shows called, we took a red-eye to New York and flew back the next day to LA to be interviewed on some drive-time radio show.

"All the important people listen to him" was what Mark said of the radio interviewer, although I wondered if by "important" Mark meant people in nursing homes because the guy looked like he was a hundred years old and he kept calling me "young lady."

After that, two literary agents called, followed by an LA pro-ducer who said he wanted to make a movie about me, although, as we talked, it became clear he saw Xander as the boy version of Helen

Keller and me as a God-fearing woman trying to keep my family afloat. I turned them all down. I just wanted everybody and everything to go away. Mark, however, said what had happened was the best thing for us.

He'd been working on his new documentary, a film about a former monk who lived in a yurt in Big Sur with a coyote he'd raised from a pup. The hermit was said to have cured three people of cancer although he said he'd only taught them to pray with faith.

Mark had shot some early footage and pitched investors, and now, after the Catch, one of them had called to say he had decided to back the documentary and would be sending a contract for Mark to sign once his lawyers cleared up a few things.

Mark said the Catch had changed our luck.

But luck is a fickle thing that can turn off as quickly as it's turned on. Mine shut off seventeen days after the little girl fell.

16.

--- N O W ---

"I'm sorry I didn't get to see you yesterday," Mark said as he came through the container door.

He was dressed in jeans and a Billabong T-shirt I didn't recognize, and carried a tray with a pot of coffee, two mugs, a plate of biscuits and a small pot of honey. Outside, rays of sun slit through the forest. I could smell the scent of loamy earth and decomposing bark through the half-open door.

I thought of my naivete in coming here and how I'd let hope override any critical thinking I might have done. For instance, why would you have faked your death if all you'd wanted to do was leave your wife—unless something else had been going on? And why did I think I could fix his problems when I didn't really know what they were? Instead, I had made up stories to fit what I'd wanted to be true and not what had been right in front of my eyes.

Mark set the tray on the steamer trunk. "I thought we could have coffee and talk." His eyes seemed sunken in his head.

"You look tired," I said.

"I didn't sleep much. I have a lot to think about."

I thought that locking up your wife in a steel box should have been enough reason for insomnia; however, I didn't say that. Instead, I told myself to be the fox.

"Angela told me about the guy showing up in town," I said.

"I don't like it that he came right after you did." Mark slumped into the upholstered chair. A long red scratch ran across the back of his left hand. He still wore his wedding ring.

"Nobody followed me, if that's what you're thinking." I'm not sure why I felt so defensive. It wasn't my fault his boss and his boss's partner were after him.

"We just can't be too careful," he said.

"There were stories on TV and online about you jumping," I said. "The police said it would have been a miracle if you'd survived. Hardly anyone does."

"Which is exactly my point," he said. "They couldn't just say I was dead, could they? No, they all have to cover their asses. There was even a witness, for God's sake." He rubbed his forehead. His voice sounded peevish.

"I still don't know how you did it."

He told me that he'd gotten the idea from a movie and that he'd purposely waited for a car—a Prius, as it turned out—hefted himself up on the railing as the vehicle approached, then dropped to the ground as it passed. Angela had been driving right behind the Prius and he'd scrambled into the back of her pickup, which had almost rear-ended the witness's vehicle when the driver slammed on the brakes.

"If the cops had had enough balls to say I was dead, I wouldn't have to worry about Rick or his goons following you."

"Maybe it's not as bad as it seems."

He blew out a breath. "Remember I told you about Tyler, the guy who stole a pound of product?" He didn't wait for an answer. "So, not long after it happened, Rick asks Tyler to take this motorcycle out for a test drive, and at seventy miles an hour the handlebars detach. Basically, they had to scrape Tyler off the pavement with a shovel. Rick tells the cops it's a terrible accident but handlebars don't come off bikes unless someone loosens them or puts in a bad bolt."

He must have seen my eyes widen because he said, "Now you get what I'm up against."

He leaned forward, filled two mugs with coffee and handed me one as if we hadn't been talking about narco assassinations and drug deals. "That's why I couldn't let you leave. It was just too dangerous."

I took a sip of coffee. An idea formed.

"I've been thinking," I said.

"Oh?"

His eyes met mine and I forced a smile. I needed to make him believe I was sincere.

"I was upset when I said those things about getting a lawyer and calling the cops," I said.

He took a long pull of his coffee. "More than upset. You were pretty much out of control."

I snuffed out a flash of anger. *Be the fox,* I reminded myself.

"Whatever. It just seems like we should be able to work this out."

He cocked his head. "Go on."

"I was thinking if you could manage some cash and a little child support, I think I might be able to hang on to the house. Then, when five years are up, like Inspector Hardy, the one who investigated your case, told me, I can ask for a death declaration and Rick and his pals would have to believe you're dead. I wouldn't file for divorce. You'd be officially dead and you could be with Angela like you want. We could both get on with our lives. I wouldn't tell a soul."

I sat back on the bed, expecting him to say he was glad I'd come to my senses. Instead, his eyes darkened, and for a moment I felt the slightest tingle of fear.

"So you're going to take my son away from me. Is that what you're saying?" he asked.

Too late, I realized my mistake, but I backtracked quickly. "We could make a visitation schedule. Summers with you. The school year with me. How about that?" I asked even though I had no intention of letting Xander live here.

"And I'd have to wait five years for that to happen so you could declare me dead?" Mark set down his coffee mug with a deliberateness that sent a chill up my spine. "I think what you're really saying is that you won't even try to open your mind to this life, to me. That you'd rather go back to scrubbing toilets and living the big capitalist lie because of some outdated view of what a family is." Mark shook his head. "You were always afraid of change. But I didn't realize until now how closed off and repressed you are, how pedestrian your thinking is. And you wonder why I looked for something more."

One of the legacies of growing up in a household where you believe you're not good enough to be loved is that you tend to feel less-than whenever anyone says something bad about you. But not now.

"If being repressed means I don't hang around with drug dealers or think it's fine to screw other people when you're married, then yeah, that's me. And if the big capitalist lie is making sure my son has health care and enough to eat and a roof over his head and doesn't get killed by some meth dealer, then I'm all for it. And in case you've forgotten, you were all for it too when those two producers wanted you to do their movie."

Mark stood. "Why are you making this so hard?"

"Why are you such an asshole?" I stood too.

He looked away and then back at me. I could tell he was trying to stay calm. "Listen. All I want is for you and Xander to have more happiness than you've ever had before. All I want is for you to be free like I am but you won't even try. Christ," he said. He turned and started for the door.

I went after him. "If you want me to be free, why are you locking me up?"

He shoved open the container door. "Maybe because you need to figure out why you're so stuck on a life that doesn't work anymore, why you believe the lies of society instead of the truth your husband is telling you."

He shook his head and stepped outside into the sunlit day.

"Wait. You can't just leave me here."

"I *can* leave you here, and you should have thought of that before you made your threats," he said.

For a moment, I didn't recognize him, this man I'd once loved and worshipped.

"I'm your wife, not your enemy, Mark."

"Then act like it," he said. "I won't let you take Xander. I want both of my sons here with me."

He turned and slammed the metal door shut, closing off the sun like a curtain had fallen.

Both of your sons? I thought. So that's why Rudy had called Mark "Dad."

I ran to the window and watched him stride toward the house. I knew I'd blown my chance of leaving by challenging him and by not thinking things all the way through. My fingers trembled against the windowsill and I wished I could suck back my words. You were never supposed to make your captor angry. I had learned that in prison, where confrontation with a guard or refusing to speak in a session just made things worse. I turned and leaned against the container wall, seeing the dank space and imagining spending months, or maybe even years, here. I sank to the floor, trying to calm my breath, to slow the beating of my heart. I closed my eyes and slowly counted to one hundred. When I opened them, I saw the answer.

While I had been under the bed, I'd noticed that the mattress was set on an old-fashioned web of woven wire and that some of the cables were rusted and snapped. I thought if I slid back beneath the bed, found those broken wires and untangled them, I might be able to use them to get out of here. I heaved a breath, lay on my back and slid beneath the bed frame. The light was dim and I used my hands, running them over the weavings until I felt the sharp spike of a broken wire. I unwound the metal lengths, feeling the tickle of dust on my skin and wondering how many more spiders lived here. Were there black widows in Alaska? I didn't want to know the answer to either question.

I tried to work quickly but it still took me a while, the wire stabbing my fingers with a dozen tiny pricks. Finally, I managed to unwind two pieces of wire, which I planned to wrap around my toothbrush handle. In prison, girls had always been making things out of toothbrushes: shivs, tattoo needles, blades for those who were into cutting. My plan was to use the wire to strengthen the toothbrush, slide it through the crack and, if it was long enough and strong enough, lift the bar so I would be ready to escape. Or if that didn't work, maybe I would sharpen the end and turn it into a weapon. I had to do whatever was necessary. Mark's visit had made that clear.

I came out from under the bed, slapped the dust—and any wayward spiders—from my clothes and hair and started to work. Every now and then, I'd stop and look out the window. Angela was at the far end of the garden. I never saw Mark or the boys.

I took the pieces of wire and wrapped them around the tooth-brush handle to give it strength. When I tried to shove it through the door slot, it was too thick, however, and I had to unwind one of the strands, leaving a piece of wire that snagged and bent when I tried to push it through the crack.

I heaved a sigh of frustration and rewound the whole contrap-tion, wrapping the excess wire around the bristles, and tried again. This time, the bar lifted an inch, then an inch and a quarter. My fingers strained against the toothbrush and the weight of the metal shaft. All I needed was another half inch. I grunted, leaning against the door for leverage.

The action, however, caused the toothbrush to slip and the metal bar crashed back down.

I cursed and hurried to the window to see if anyone had heard. Angela was still working in the garden and Mark was still missing. I rubbed the cramp out of my fingers and tried again: lifting, strain-ing, trying to ignore the way the wire cut into my flesh. The bar moved upward an inch, an inch and a half. I was almost free.

I bent my knees and used my whole body to push upward.

The toothbrush snapped and the bar clanged back into place.

I wanted to scream. Instead, I turned and leaned my back against the door and tried to convince myself I would find another way out. I remembered the time Mark and I had gotten turned around while hiking in Washington State. I'd started to panic at the thought of dying in the woods without water or food and he said, "You're in a room with no windows or doors and all you have is a mirror and a table. What do you do?"

I told him it wasn't a time for riddles and couldn't he see that we were in serious trouble? He smiled instead and said, "You look in the mirror and see what you saw and then you take the saw and cut the table in half and two halves make a hole and you climb out." Then he'd waited as if he thought I would laugh.

"What the hell, Mark?" I'd said.

"What I'm trying to tell you is there's always a way out. You just have to throw out all the old, tired ideas and look at things through new eyes."

So we hiked to the top of a ridge and waited until dark, when Mark somehow used the stars to figure out which way was north. He lined our position up with a distant peak, and the next morning, we trekked two hours in that direction until we came to a narrow road and hitchhiked our way back to our car.

It was one of the things that had first attracted me to Mark: his ability to find a path different from the one most people followed. It was like he always stood on some high place where he could see all the possibilities laid out below him, and he would choose the one that might not be the most apparent but worked best for what he needed. Of course, that was before I had found out he'd taken a path that included a mistress and a drug ring.

I told myself that, like with Mark's riddle, I needed to keep my eyes open to whatever opportunity arose, think differently and, meanwhile, keep my true feelings hidden.

I drank some water, ate the breakfast Mark had brought, read some Kai Huang and watched the coming and goings at the farm: Angela hoeing weeds, the chickens scratching in the dirt and the sun tracking across the little valley. To an outsider it might have looked like the perfect answer to a life of complications and struggle. The isolation, however, felt dangerous to me. Even when I'd lived on the ranch with my parents, town was only a twenty-five-minute drive away. Now it was as if the forest had swallowed me alive.

I vowed to do anything to escape.

17.

—— THEN ——

The weather turned the day my luck gave out. It was the middle of November and a gray drizzle leaked from the sky. I'd spent the morning cleaning a new client's three-story Victorian, which had not only a sitting room, a parlor and an attic library but also front stairs, servants' stairs and a stairway that went inexplicably from the kitchen straight to the owners' bedroom. I felt like I'd cleaned Mount Everest.

After the Catch, seven people had called wanting to hire me as a house cleaner, but with my regular clients, I could manage to accept only three of them. I considered telling this one I needed to raise my rates.

I stopped at the market after I'd picked Xander up from school. I got a whole chicken on sale for fifty-nine cents a pound and had to high-five the bag boy, who said his mom thought I was "rad."

When I got home, I swallowed two ibuprofen and we were halfway through Mark's dinner of roast chicken and mashed potatoes when there was a knock at the door.

Xander jumped up and I told him, "You finish your dinner, Xan."

Mark was answering a text from his prospective investor.

"I'll get it," I said.

The woman at the door had dark, chin-length hair and a tiny diamond in her right nostril.

"I'm from the *Sacramento Tribune*," the woman began.

"We're eating dinner," I said. "I don't have time right now."

"I just need a comment," the reporter said quickly. "It's about your mother."

My legs suddenly felt as if they could no longer hold me up.

"You need to leave." It was all I could get out.

"Don't you want to tell your side of the story?" the reporter persisted.

"No. Go away," I said, and started to close the door.

The reporter blocked its swing with her foot. "It's just that it's always better to get out in front of this, you know," she said.

"Leave," I said, and started to push the door closed again. I wanted to halt what was coming even though, deep inside, I knew it was like trying to stop a tidal wave.

"Hey," the reporter cried, and put up her hand.

"What's going on?" Mark appeared beside me.

Xander was there too, his chin shiny with chicken grease.

"I'm just doing a follow-up on a story from *PRIME News*," the reporter said. She looked at me. "The one about your wife spending a year in prison for accessory after the fact and abuse of a corpse."

"What's a 'buse of course'?" Xander asked.

"Why don't you go watch your movie, bud? It's all set up," Mark told him.

"Yay," Xander cried, and scurried away.

"Let's take this outside," Mark said.

We stepped onto the porch and Mark closed the door behind us.

My head buzzed as if a swarm of bees had taken up residence inside of it.

"Who did you say did this story?" Mark asked.

"*PRIME News*," the reporter said.

"Well, they got it wrong," Mark said. "And I don't appreciate you coming here making wild accusations. And I especially don't appreciate you making them in front of our son."

"You're saying your wife has never been arrested?"

"Yes. That's what I'm saying," Mark said.

"Have you seen the piece?" the reporter asked. She took a step toward us and tapped her phone awake.

"This is ridiculous," I said to Mark. "Let's go inside."

"What happens when a hero turns out to not be so heroic?" a male voice intoned from the small screen. "What if a hero was implicated in the murder of her mother twenty-one years before?"

I could feel Mark go still.

The voice continued: "Liv Russo, or Liv Crocker as she was known then, was arrested for helping her father, Jim Crocker, a rancher, bury her mother's body in a manure pile after he'd killed her with a hayfork on a winter's day in 1997."

The bees now swarmed to every part of my body as the voice of our former ranch hand, Slim Cadwallader, rose out of the phone.

"It was about eleven o'clock when I heard loud voices coming from the barn," Slim said. "Weren't nothing unusual about that. The boss and his wife, they was always fighting. She could holler louder than a hog in heat."

Slim was a narrow-faced man who'd come to us from a ranch in Wyoming. His teeth were stained from the tobacco he chewed. Once, I'd seen him touch my mother's underwear as it hung drying on the clothesline beside our house.

"Then, around midnight," Slim was saying, "I look out the window, and what do I see but the boss with a shovel on top of the manure pile. He weren't usually awake at that hour."

He went on to recount how he had asked my father about it the next morning and my dad had said an old sow had died and he needed to get rid of it. "That's what ranchers started to have to do once the tree huggers took over the government," Slim said. "They made all these rules about composting dead stock or taking the body to a rendering plant instead of just digging a hole or letting the varmints get to it, which is the way my daddy did it." Still, he said, he had thought seeing his boss digging so late at night was strange. Now the prosecutor was on the small screen describing how my father had told everybody that he and my mom had had an argument and she'd gone off to stay with her sister.

"But," said the *PRIME News* reporter, "Slim kept thinking about what he saw and finally dug down into the manure pile and found Helen Crocker's corpse. There were four puncture wounds in her upper abdomen that matched a hayfork found on the property. That's why Slim said he called us here at *PRIME News*. He said nobody should be called a hero when they weren't one."

On the screen, the reporter was walking toward our old red barn, although whoever owned it now had painted it green.

"According to the sheriff at the time, Jim Crocker's fingerprints were found on the hayfork handle and Helen's blood was discovered on his jeans," the reporter said. "However, investigators found something else: a hair clip belonging to Liv Crocker, their seventeen-year-old daughter. It was uncovered under Helen Crocker's body in the pile of dung."

I could feel the *Tribune* reporter's eyes on me.

Then it was back to the prosecutor, who said they'd also found my mother's blood and manure on my sneakers, which pointed to my guilt as an accomplice, although, he said, I'd claimed I had no memory of that night.

"She hears her dad telling people her mom went to visit her sister and yet she knows the truth and doesn't say a word. She just goes to school like nothing happened," the prosecutor said on the video. "The only reason to stay quiet is because she was part of it and we had the forensic evidence to prove that. We charged her with what we thought we could get to stick. If I had my way, though, we'd have arrested her for criminally negligent homicide."

I backed up and sat heavily on the wooden chair on our front porch.

The prosecutor was followed by a sound bite from my court-appointed attorney, who said that I'd been traumatized by what I'd seen and that the only reason I'd been charged with any crime was that the district attorney was running for reelection and wanted to show he was tough on crime.

"My God, she was just a kid," my attorney said. "She was a victim as much as her mom was."

The video ended noting that I'd been found guilty by a judge and spent a year in a prison for juvenile offenders.

Across the road, our neighbor started up his SUV and backed out of the driveway. The drizzle had turned to rain now.

Mark turned to me. "You told me your mother died of cancer."

I opened my mouth. Nothing came out.

The reporter scribbled something in her notebook.

"And you said your dad died," Mark said.

"He did," said the *Tribune* reporter. "He died in prison six months after he was convicted."

"Christ, Liv," Mark said.

"I'm so sorry." My voice shook. "I would have told you but . . . ," I started.

"But what?" Mark said. His voice was a mixture of anger and hurt. He turned to the reporter. "We have no comment. You need to go."

18.

—— THEN ——

Everything happened fast after that reporter's visit. By eight the next morning, the Kiplingers had already fired me.

We won't be needing your services any longer, they texted.

Then it was almost all the rest of my clients, my phone pinging with short messages of outrage and dismissal. Only Beth Andrews had the decency to call and fire me over the phone.

"We just don't think it's good to have you around our children," Beth said, although the only contact I'd had with her kids was cleaning their Sharpie scribbles off the walls, putting away the hurricane of their toys and seeing the slashes in the couch where one of them had taken a steak knife to the fabric.

I wanted to tell Beth Andrews that her kids would probably grow up to be juvenile delinquents all on their own. All I said, however, was that I was sorry she felt that way.

Old Mr. Martin was the only client who didn't quit.

"I judge people for what they are, not what they were," he said, and then asked if he'd see me at my regular time on Friday, and when I told him he would, he said, "And bring that boy of yours if you can."

The same morning that all the firings happened, Mark had had to leave for a delivery job. It had been on our calendars for a week and he said there was no way he could get out of it. I asked him to stay so we could work things out. He said that Rick was counting on him and he needed time to think anyway. Now, I knew why missing a delivery had not been an option. Then, I'd just accepted it.

Mark packed a duffel with some boxers and a sweatshirt and loaded six cans of Red Bull into a small cooler. Red Bull was his favorite drink. He said that he would be gone four days, five max, and that we would talk about things when he got back.

He barely looked at me when he spoke.

After the reporter drove off, I'd spent half the night trying to explain to Mark what had happened and why I hadn't told him.

What he knew was that my parents had run a cattle ranch and had an unhappy marriage. What he didn't know was the extent of that miserable union and how, when I was thirteen, my father had begun sinking even deeper into his dark silences and my mother had started focusing all her rage and meanness on me.

Whenever I'd done something she perceived to be wrong or selfish or lazy—which seemed like most of the time—she handed me a toothbrush and ordered me to clean the bathroom or the kitchen with it while she stood watch, smoking a long chain of cigarettes that clouded the air with their sharp-edged scent. Later, I would wonder if she had sensed my housecleaning future before I did. Back then, however, all I could do was hate her.

I told Mark I remembered only a few images from the night my mother died. Of me sneaking into the barn after I'd been out drinking with my boyfriend, Matt; of seeing my mother lying in a pool of blood on the barn floor, her mouth open as if she'd been interrupted in midrant; of my dad setting a plate of scrambled eggs in front of me the next morning and of our pasture grass white and brittle with frost.

The psychiatrist my defense lawyer hired said I had something called dissociative amnesia, which is when trauma wipes out sections of someone's memory. It happens to war veterans and victims of trauma and crime. The judge didn't believe her. And my dad wasn't talking, either to say what had happened or to exonerate me: It made me wonder if he despised me as much as he had my mother.

I told Mark I had no recollection of helping my dad bury my mom but that didn't mean I did it. Or that I didn't do it either.

Mark said I should have told him and wondered what other secrets I might have been keeping. I said that was the only one and that I hadn't told him because I was afraid he would hate me.

He said honesty was never a reason to hate someone and went to the couch to sleep.

Part of me wanted him to come home quickly after he left, so he could forgive me. The other part dreaded his return.

Two days after he left and before he said he'd be home, I heard the noisy rumble of a diesel engine around ten p.m. and went to the front window to see who it was. Mark was climbing out of a van I didn't recognize and I could see the slump of his shoulders in the vehicle's interior lights. His hair was wild and uncombed and he slammed the door shut, then trudged down the driveway with his duffel as if he'd been hitched to some invisible weight and now he dragged it behind him. The van gunned its engine and drove away.

I hurried into our bedroom. I exchanged my old, torn Lone Star T-shirt for a nicer one and headed toward the kitchen. I don't know why I thought a T-shirt would make a difference but I did.

When I got to the back door, Mark was just coming out of the garage, which we'd converted into a studio for him. He wore jeans and his UCLA sweatshirt. He looked like he hadn't slept the whole time he was gone. The minute he came into the kitchen, I could feel the old darkness in him—the one that had flared up a few times in our marriage but had been gone for a while.

I started to turn on the lights.

"Don't," he said.

"You're home early. Did the delivery go OK?" I asked quietly.

He didn't answer. Instead, he went over to the stove and turned on the gas burner, so the circle of flame flickered to life. Then he turned it off.

"Mark?" I said.

"I lost them." His voice was shredded, low. "I stopped for twenty minutes, half an hour at the most, and when I got back, they were fucking gone. The bikes, the trailer. Everything," he said. "Plus, my film is dead."

I wanted to take away his pain, to let him know I still loved him—although maybe I would have felt differently if I'd known the real story back then. Instead, I told him he could always get a new job and that maybe we could call his brother, who was a lawyer in Chicago, and ask for a loan to start his movie.

"It's too late," he said, and switched the burner on and fed a folded piece of paper into it. It flamed yellow and then orange. "I can't see a way out. I'm finished. There's nothing else I can do."

The paper curled and disappeared into shreds of black. Mark turned the burner off and went over to the back door.

My heart stuttered. "Wait. Where are you going?"

He opened the door. "Away."

The cold night air pushed its way into the house and I hurried toward him, then grabbed the sleeve of his sweatshirt as if I could hold him in place. "You can't go. Xander needs you. I need you."

He smelled of beer and sweat and greasy food. He shook off my hand. "What's done is done."

Something passed over his face then. Resignation? Fear? Determination? Whatever it was, it sent a chill through me. He tugged up his sweatshirt hood and his eyes fell into shadow. "Take care of our boy," he said. "Tell him I love him." He turned and went down the back porch steps into the soundless night.

I felt as if I were in a speeding car with a canyon yawning in front of me and no way to stop. "Wait," I called, and hurried after him. "We can work this out. We'll get through it. We're survivors, remember?"

"Survivors" was what he had called us when we ran out of money as we traipsed around the country a year after we were married and, once, when we were stranded for eighteen hours in the Rockies after a blizzard shut down the road we were on.

He strode across the back lawn, the neighbor's yard light turning everything pale and sharp edged. He yanked open the Subaru's door and paused, looking over the roof at me. "Survivors also know when to quit," he said, and threw himself into the car, slamming the door behind him.

"You can't quit," I shouted, and ran after him.

Two houses down, a neighbor's dog machine-gunned a series of frantic, high-pitched barks. The Subaru's engine came to life. The tires squealed against the driveway and I sprinted after the car, the concrete cold and hard against my bare feet.

"We can talk about this," I cried as if he could hear me. "Come back."

The car's brake lights tapped red, and for a moment hope rose.

Then the Subaru turned left and accelerated into the night.

19.

—— N O W ——

Three more days passed inside the container. There were no more clouds, no more rain. The sun bathed everything in a bright yellow light while the inside of me turned dark and ominous, like the way the sky feels before an approaching storm. I watched the goats crop a stand of some kind of tall grass and saw Angela hang laundry on a clothesline near the aspens. Once, I caught a glimpse of Mark and Xander going off into the woods with the dog, Shadow, but then nothing. The hours stretched like a river in front of me, my captivity drowning me in a feeling of doom. I tried to set up a routine like there'd been at Goodridge in order to take my mind off what was happening but it didn't do much good.

Just like I did in the old days, I made my bed with tight corners and a perfectly smooth blanket. I did stretches and then strode twenty-five laps up and down the container. I read Mark's book, prowled the space looking for weak spots (could I tunnel my way out?) and sang some of Xander's favorite songs: Toby Keith's

"Should've Been a Cowboy" and Garth Brooks's "The Dance," although that one made me even more sad.

I couldn't schedule meals because of how haphazard Mark's and Angela's lives appeared to be. I didn't know if they were purposely trying to keep me off-balance or if their new lifestyle also meant freedom from mealtimes. I worried about Xander eating enough. One day, Angela arrived with breakfast before I was even awake. The next, it didn't come until late.

Two nights ago, she had brought in my dinner tray, announced its contents like a contestant on one of those TV cooking shows—spruce hen stew with chunks of sweet potatoes and onions from the garden—and asked me if I'd read *Mind, Self, Love* yet and whether I could see what they were trying to achieve.

Her eyes shined with bright eagerness. All I had to do was try, she said. She promised if I stayed for a few weeks with them, I would see that releasing the chains of society and letting my life fill with pleasure would finally allow me to experience joy without the shackles of jealousy and materialism. She said that I'd see divorce was no solution and that I'd never want to go back to the city.

"Pleasure is all we need," she said.

I sat up wearily from the bed. The only pleasure I wanted was to leave. Instead, I nodded and asked about Xander and when I might be able to see him. She said she was trying to convince Mark about a visit but that Mark was afraid I would try to turn Xander against him.

"Mark said that in the last conversation he had with you, he felt like you wanted to punish him for what he'd done by taking Xander away."

"I just said I wanted to try to work something out."

Angela pointed at me and then clapped her hands together once.

"Yes, that's exactly what I told him. I said, 'You have to relax, Mark. This is all new for her. You can't be so rigid and angry.' Kai Huang says, 'Before you can forgive, you have to understand.'"

She paced a few steps and then turned back toward me.

"I'm going to remind him of that. I'll make him see."

When she came back with breakfast the next morning she looked worriedly at my half-eaten dinner and said she was making progress with Mark.

"Just hang in there," she said.

Then, today, Angela rushed in with a tray. There were two Mason jars of water instead of one, a couple of sandwiches, two apples and a bowl of oatmeal. She wore a plaid skirt and some kind of blue velvety top.

"Sorry. I can't stay," she said, and hurried out the door, the bar squealing into place.

For a moment, I just lay on the bed. Why couldn't she stay? I thrust myself up and hurried to the window in time to see Mark striding toward the bridge trail with Rudy and Shadow trailing behind him and Xander hanging on him piggyback. Rudy carried what looked like a basket of food. Apples? Bread? A second later, Angela rushed out of the cabin, hauling a bulging duffel bag over her shoulder, and went after them.

It looked like they were either running from something or to something.

I pounded on the window. "Hey," I yelled. It was too late, however. They'd all disappeared from view. Only the chickens remained.

My imagination, of course, went to the worst place possible. That they'd gotten word that Rick and his partner were on their way, and before the bad men arrived, they were escaping and had left me behind. Or something was wrong with Xander—his heart, his lungs—and they were rushing him to the hospital, which was why Mark was carrying him.

I pounded on the window again. Panic rose, and this time I didn't even try to breathe it away. I rushed to one of the fifty-five-gallon drums and pried off the metal lid and ran back to the window. I lifted the metal circle over my head and began to bang it against the plexiglass.

I pounded and pounded until my muscles grew exhausted and a tiny star-shaped crack appeared, but the window wouldn't break.

I don't know how long it was before I finally stopped, dropped the lid to the floor and crawled into bed.

20.

—— THEN ——

The thing I learned about grief in the months I believed Mark was dead was that it wasn't linear. It was more like a demented boxer who popped up here and there, delivering a punch so hard it was all I could do to stay on my feet.

Sometimes I would be hit with these sucker punches of memory.

I'd be putting on my pajamas or getting into the Subaru when suddenly I would get an image of Mark driving away that night and then of him swan-diving off the bridge into that hard gray slab of water below.

In a horrible article about Mark's death, the *Sacramento Tribune* noted it was a two-hundred-twenty-foot drop from the Golden Gate Bridge to the water. A four-second fall. Go ahead, count it out. I did. It's a lot of time to think.

Sometimes I thought Mark would have liked the adrenaline rush of that plunge into empty space, the same way he whooped while surfing a particularly big wave and once when he bungee jumped off a bridge in Washington State. Other times—the worst times—I would think of him changing his mind midfall, clawing desperately at the air as if there were an invisible ladder he could climb back to safety. Those times, I would have to go turn on the TV to drown out the thoughts, or get out of the car and take deep breaths of air.

Inspector Hardy said Mark had most likely died the minute he hit the water or drowned quickly thereafter because of the injuries he sustained. She told of jumpers with broken backs and legs and punctured lungs. When I pressed her, however, she admitted that a few people had survived the fall but that their bodies had been so broken there was no way they could have swum to shore and hitch-hiked away, like I'd suggested Mark might have done. Besides, she said, there'd been that witness, the ER nurse who'd been driving across the bridge and was so shaken by the fact that she hadn't stopped her car in time to talk Mark down that she'd had to take a leave from her job. The fog had been thick that night, Inspector Hardy said, and the video camera that should have recorded the actual jump turned out to have a failed lens and was awaiting repair.

"Government," Inspector Hardy had said with the resignation of a career civil servant.

She told me I shouldn't pin my hopes on a broken camera and the lack of a body.

"I'm sorry, Mrs. Russo, but that's the reality," she said.

Even so, she promised she would keep an eye out for any sign that Mark might be alive: traffic tickets, social media tags, background checks from prospective employers. I appreciated her thoroughness, even though she didn't have to do it. She'd gotten the assignment—the California Highway Patrol usually handled bridge suicides—because the police officer who'd found our car ran the plates and recognized my name. He told his supervisor, who'd alerted one of his higher-ups, a man both ambitious and vain, who'd then ordered a detective to investigate so he'd be on top of things when the media came to ask about the filmmaker who had committed suicide, leaving his fallen-hero wife behind. Which the media did.

Inspector Hardy had had the bad luck to be at her desk when the order arrived, but I grew to appreciate her thoroughness. She even radioed a Sacramento sheriff's deputy and asked him to drive by our house when I called her in a panic after a stranger accosted Xander in our backyard.

It happened about a month after Mark had disappeared, a week before Christmas, and I was hardly sleeping or eating and I was drinking too much wine every night. I'd also been getting these horrible phone calls, thanks to that first TV crew, who had broadcast a shot of my car with the Liv's Green Clean sign and my cell phone number on it. The callers would tell me that I didn't deserve to be a mother or that Satan was inside me and they were going to come and carve him out with a butcher knife. One man with a thick Southern accent claimed that I was part of some atheist child-trafficking ring and that the baby I caught had actually been destined for the sex trade in Asia. He said somebody should do the world a favor and get rid of me and my family. So, when I stepped into our backyard one afternoon with a jacket for Xander, who was outside playing, and saw a stranger kneeling next to him, I thought the worst.

"Hey," I yelled, and leaped down the back steps. "What the hell are you doing? Get away from my son."

The man looked up. He wore pressed jeans and a dark sweatshirt. His head was shaved and he sported a bushy black mustache.

"Sorry," he said, and stood, raising his hands in surrender. He had an accent I couldn't place. "I was just checking to see if your son saw my dog, Rex. I was visiting a friend down the road and Rex got out. He's brown and black, part Akita." He lowered his hand to a few feet above the ground. "He's about this tall and is very friendly."

I tugged Xander behind me.

"You can see there's no dog here," I said, and pointed up the driveway. "You're trespassing. You need to leave."

The man's eyes were as black as new asphalt. He glanced around the yard.

"Sorry. I didn't mean to upset you," he said. "It's just that I really need to find my dog. I don't know what I would do if I never saw him again. Rex is like my kid, you know?"

Something about the way he spoke made the hairs stand up on the back of my neck. I pulled Xander closer.

"Get out of here. Now," I said.

For a moment he was still and then he said, "OK, sure. I didn't mean to freak you out." He headed up the driveway, turned and gave a little wave to Xander as he left.

"See you, buddy," he said.

"Go," I ordered him.

I followed the man to the corner of our house and saw him get into a black SUV and drive off. The next night, I thought I saw the same vehicle parked four houses away with its engine running. That was when I called Inspector Hardy. I'm sure I sounded slightly hysterical.

She said she would ask the Sacramento Sheriff's Office to send someone by to check our house for the next few nights, and if I saw the vehicle again, I should try to get the license number. Her voice was calm and steady, the way airline pilots sound over the intercom when they tell you to expect a little turbulence as the plane begins to rattle and shake. She told me that dark SUVs weren't especially uncommon in this part of the state and that grief often came out as hypervigilance.

"Try some meditation, Mrs. Russo," she said.

If the vehicle came back, I never saw it.

Nothing in those days seemed right anyway. It was as if I'd moved to a foreign country where car keys were always missing, coffee was always cold and every sunrise was accompanied by a pounding chardonnay headache.

Finally, I roused myself one day in early February, when I went to pick up Xander from school and saw him come out of class wearing a T-shirt streaked with dried spaghetti sauce, a pair of swim trunks and mismatched socks. For a moment, I wondered who had dressed him and then realized that I had and that the reason for the outfit was that there hadn't been a single item of clean clothes anywhere in the house.

I went home and started a load of wash right then, pulled on a pair of rubber gloves and began to clean. I worked through the night, emptying trash, scrubbing the kitchen and bathroom tile, sweeping the floors and bagging Mark's clothes to take to Goodwill. The next day I mowed the lawn and went to the food pantry, where I picked up a box of groceries. I poured the last bottle of wine down the sink.

I still felt like I was sleepwalking through life. Like the baby falling and Mark jumping from the bridge were just part of a terrible dream in which I'd saved one person but lost another. The fact I soon discovered—that after I'd paid our property taxes, there was barely enough money to make the March mortgage payment—woke me up to the reality of what Xander and I faced.

I thought about calling Mark's brother to ask for a loan, but when I'd phoned to let him know his baby brother had committed suicide, his reply was that Mark had always been the dramatic one in the family and that he hoped I wasn't expecting him to help pay for a funeral because they were a waste of good money as far as he was concerned.

In the end, I never had a memorial for Mark. I didn't have the energy or the money to plan one, and besides, who would have come except the media, who'd salivate over the mother burier mourning her bridge-leaping husband?

Instead, I chopped my hair short and found a job with Tidy Clean maid service for eighteen dollars an hour—if the owner, Dolores, had recognized me, she didn't say anything—and I began paring back on expenses.

I cut off our cable TV, stopped watering the lawn, got most of my groceries from the food pantry and canceled garbage pickup, instead distributing my trash each week into two or three of my clients' bins. Sometimes I even snuck our laundry in with the sheets and towels I washed at my clients' houses so I could save on electricity and detergent. I also sold some of Mark's things—his old motorcycle, two surfboards, his bike, one of his cameras; still, the bills piled up and I began to get threatening letters from our mortgage company. Losing our home seemed inevitable. I couldn't even sell the place because it was underwater after we'd refinanced it to pay for a new roof and the expenses that insurance wouldn't cover for Xander's therapy.

There was also no way I could work two jobs to make up for the loss of Mark's income because what would I do with Xander, especially when summer came? Stash him under the counter while I worked a night shift at a 7-Eleven? Let him sleep in the car while I stocked shelves at Walmart? I'd wake up thinking about those things, which made my heart pound and made me wish for the thousandth time that I'd been braver and told Mark about my past. More than once, I considered going to that grief group Inspector Hardy had talked about, and yet all I could think was that my misery didn't need company. It was crowded and noisy enough on its own.

The months passed that way, a haze of work and money worries and sadness and taking care of Xander. At least he seemed to be doing OK. After the second story came out, the same moms who had suddenly wanted playdates after the Catch apparently told their kids to stay away from Xander. It didn't take long for Xander's teacher to call me in to report a number of students were refusing to sit by Xander, which was causing a disruption in class. She said perhaps I should keep Xander home for a while or find a school that was a "better fit" for him. She was an older woman with watery blue eyes and gray hair scraped into a tight bun who probably should have stopped teaching a decade earlier. When she leaned in and said she was only suggesting this for Xander's own good, I told her that she was lucky to have a sweet and kind boy like Xander as a student and that maybe she could learn a lesson about acceptance from him instead of being such a hateful and lazy bitch. That didn't make anything better but I didn't care.

I found a different school for him and Xander settled into his new kindergarten with a young, energetic teacher who seemed to adore Xander, and with mostly working-class moms who didn't have time to do lunch or organize playdates and who treated me as if my problems weren't that much different from theirs. I finally told him his father was dead after his teacher took me aside and said Xander had asked her if she could mail the Earth Day card he'd made to his daddy, who was on a long trip.

She handed me a book about explaining death to your child, and said kids could handle more than we thought they could. I sat Xander down that night and told him his father had been very sad and had had a bad fall and gotten hurt so that his body didn't work anymore but his love and spirit would always be with us.

"Like Benny?" he asked.

Our neighbor's tabby, Benny, had died after being hit by a car a few weeks before.

"Yes. Like Benny," I said.

"Are we going to dig a hole for him to sleep in?" he asked.

My throat closed.

"Maybe someday," I said. It was all I could get out.

Two days later I picked him up from school and he told me that he knew where his daddy went.

"He drove to heaven and he's staying there with a guy called Jesus and then he'll come back," he said.

I guessed some kid in his class told him about heaven. I probably should have corrected him, but he seemed so confident in his conclusion and I was so exhausted, I didn't.

Instead, I trudged on, the quicksand of my life slowly swallowing me until one day, I knew, I would just give up and let everything take me.

Then, early in summer, the text arrived.

21.

——— N O W ———

Mark and Angela and the boys came back. It turned out Angela had wanted to attend a talk given by a famous herbalist in Valdez and Mark needed to buy tires and spark plugs for the old rototiller and a new alternator for the Subaru. They'd decided to make a family day of it and take the boys to eat ice cream and watch sea life. The reason they hurried was they didn't want to be late for the talk, and the duffel Angela had carried contained a wall hanging she'd made and hoped to sell at one of the art galleries there.

I didn't see them come home. I spent the day trying to talk myself down, banging on the window with the metal lid in an attempt to break it and then lying back down before doing it all over again. At some point, I found a loose nail in the floor and spent an hour prying it up to see if I could use it to lift the bar across the container doors (it was too short). I ate one of the sandwiches, sipped some water and fell into bed, anxious and bloody fingered. When I awoke in the middle of the night and saw a light on in the cabin, I started to cry with relief and then realized I still didn't know if Xander was OK.

Angela told me where they'd been when she came in with breakfast and I felt myself sag with release. She looked at the uneaten sandwich and apples and the small crack in the window.

"I thought you left me here," I said lamely.

"We would never do that," she said, and set my breakfast on the steamer trunk. "We love and care for you, Liv."

I looked out the half-open container door and thought again about shoving my way past Angela into the fresh air. But without the key and my car, the wilderness was as much a prison as Goodridge had been, and without Xander, what was the use? Mark would just get angry, herd me back inside and clang the door shut. I needed a plan.

Angela lowered herself into the upholstered chair and gestured toward my breakfast. "Frittata with goat cheese and dandelion greens," she announced, and said that on their drive from San Francisco to Alaska, Mark had told her my story. Now that I was here and we'd talked, she said, she realized how much alike we were.

Both of us knew what it was like to feel abandoned, she said, and we'd each grown up without love.

"Intimacy is how we heal. Intimacy is what brings us together," she said, and began her story.

Most of her childhood, she said, had been spent in a little town in eastern Utah where pickups outnumbered cars by five to one and where haying season meant kids stayed out of school to help with the cut.

Her dad was nineteen when he married Angela's mother and twenty-six with two children when a distracted teenager in a pickup truck broadsided her mother's car as she pulled out of a Walmart with a trunk full of groceries.

At twenty-seven, still deep in grief over her death, Angela's father married his first wife's younger sister—there weren't a lot of options in the town—and she began to crank out babies, three in five years, and also resent the presence of Angela and her brother, whom she called lazy and disrespectful. The truth was that although Angela and her brother called their aunt/stepmother "the Witch" behind her back and made it a point to disobey any order she gave them, the real reason their father's new wife was bitter toward them was that they served as daily reminders of her older, prettier and slimmer sister, of whom she'd always been jealous. It didn't help that Angela's father sometimes compared her to his first wife.

When Angela turned sixteen and began to bear a startling resemblance to her late mother, the aunt/stepmother convinced her husband to farm Angela and her brother out for a summer to her older brother, an ex–Army sergeant. She said her brother was a bachelor but would know how to straighten out two children she believed were sullen and rebellious. Angela's father—who was tired of a house full of crying babies, a nagging spouse and two older children who stubbornly refused to call their aunt "Mother," as she demanded—agreed. The brother lived in a single-wide trailer just outside of the town of Brilliance, Utah, which had a population of 1,087 and was a two-hour drive from where they lived.

According to Angela, her uncle's idea of straightening them out was to make them do chores—cleaning out the junk that had accumulated under his trailer, whitewashing the stones that outlined his yard and raking circles into the dirt—while he sat in a lawn chair and got drunk. If he thought they didn't work hard enough, he reduced their supper to crackers and water. If they talked back, he duct-taped their lips shut. A month into their stay, she said, he came out to the couch where Angela slept and put one hand over her mouth and the other underneath her nightgown. After that, Angela slept out in the sagebrush, changing locations each night. Then, one day, she said, the uncle told them he was going to visit a friend in Colorado and do a little fishing. According to her, he told them he'd be home in five days and left twenty dollars on the table.

Eight days later, Angela called her father to tell him that their caretaker had left and that they were out of money and food and wanted to come home. Angela's father, however, said that as much as he wanted them to return, it wasn't a good time. Their aunt/step-mother was suffering from terrible morning sickness and the two youngest children had strep throat. He mailed them forty dollars and assured them their uncle would come back and they should be patient. Over the next weeks, other envelopes with cash in amounts ranging from thirty to a hundred dollars appeared but never their father—or their uncle. Sheriff's deputies were called but they said unless there were signs of foul play, an adult was able to go wherever he or she wanted without needing to tell anybody.

"Maybe he just found a new place to stick his fishing pole," one of the officers said, and winked at his partner.

The deputies told Angela's father he needed to retrieve his kids or they would notify Child and Family Services. Neither he nor the cops kept their promise. Their father made excuses: He had gotten a new job and was working six days a week; his wife was suffering from a bad case of nerves; the car had blown the head gasket and needed to be repaired. Within two months, Angela and her brother had turned feral. They skipped school, slept in until noon each day, ate junk food and stole pills from their neighbors, including a forgetful old woman who had a bad back and a doctor who happily resupplied her with OxyContin whenever she ran out. When Angela's brother was fourteen, he hitchhiked out of town, intending to go to LA. A few days later, Angela convinced a truck driver she met at the Pilot truck stop to take her west with him. She ditched the trucker in Salt Lake City when he demanded a blow job in exchange for breakfast, and she spent two wasted years in the capital city, smoking heroin and selling herself to middle-aged men to get money. She discovered Kai Huang while living with a dozen other misfits in a remote canyon outside of town where she learned about herbs and how to weave. She quit the drugs and moved to California.

"I never felt safe or loved or good enough until I met Mark," she told me. "He was the first person to make me feel worthy and I suspect it was the same with you."

Her story made me see her in a different light and I felt sad for what she'd had to endure. How could a father pick a jealous wife over his children, and what would it do to a child not only to lose their mother but to be sent off to live with a drunken abuser? Tears brimmed in Angela's eyes when she was finished, and I let her take my hand for a moment. It surprised me how close she'd come to the truth about me and Mark. Meeting him had been the thing that allowed me to finally believe it was possible for someone to love me.

"I'm sorry about how you had to grow up," I said.

Angela squeezed my hand and then let go. The skin on her neck was blotched red. "I'm not the only woman who was raised under the thumb of the patriarchy, who had her voice silenced," she said. "Your father silenced your mother's voice and yours too. Just like the world does every single day. The men who rule us, the fat-cat politicians and righteous-sounding preachers, are afraid of the power women hold, so they try to leash us with rules in an attempt to possess us. They want us to be the virgin whore, then the submissive wife and finally the devoted mother who wants nothing more than children and home. They convince us we need to be married, to be faithful, but all that does is make love wilt and die. But if you let love be free, then it will grow. It will be abundant."

"But that's where I'm different," I said. "I think monogamy, loving one person completely, is actually freedom."

"I'm not saying monogamy kills love. I'm saying that the insecurity, power struggles and jealousy that usually come with monogamy kill it. If you don't consider something 'cheating,' then it doesn't bother you. 'Let the river flow and it will bring you what you need' is how Kai Huang puts it. That's why I want to help you. I want you to be happy. I want Mark to be happy. I want you to live with joy."

I asked her how I could see this so-called joy if they kept me locked up.

"Just read the book, and when you do, Mark will see that you're trying and trust you again."

"What about letting me see Xander?"

Angela looked away. "I'm still working on it."

"And what about Rudy? Mark called him his 'son.'"

She stood and picked up the remains of my breakfast. "That's a question to ask Mark, not me." She started to leave, then turned. "You have to trust me, Liv."

22.

—— T H E N ——

Trust wasn't something that came easily to me and yet I had trusted Mark. I trusted his promise that he would always come home (until he didn't). I trusted that I knew him (I hadn't). And when the text arrived with those two important words—three words, actually—I trusted in fate, which was another mistake.

It was early June and the weather was warm but not too hot and I was cleaning Jason Oberland's pigsty of a town house when the phone pinged from the back pocket of my jeans. Jason Oberland was a copilot for a private jet company who, according to what I'd had to clean, ate only pepperoni and bell pepper pizza, smoked like a fiend, drank cheap vodka, dabbled in light S&M and apparently had never learned what a dishwasher was for. Once, I found a dead mouse in his shower. If he'd been a private client, I would have quit.

I pulled out the phone, expecting to see a note from my boss, Dolores. She was always sending texts to let me know a certain client also wanted their oven cleaned or that a pet had left a mess on a regular's bedroom rug, and could I take care of it on my way home?

Instead the text was from a number with a 907 area code and had no name attached.

Order ready. Pic up ASAP. Batteries flour coffee
sugar plus Red Bull. Cant hold.

I frowned. What the hell?

I'd canceled my phone and started using Mark's cell, both to save money and also stop the threatening phone calls, a move that had accomplished both, and I might have ignored the message, figuring it was a mistake, but the mention of Red Bull stopped me.

I imagined Inspector Hardy's calm voice saying she was 99 percent sure that Mark was dead and me thinking, *Doesn't that mean there is also a 1 percent chance he isn't?* I checked the time: four forty-eight p.m.

I had less than forty-five minutes before Xander's day care would start the countdown clock, charging ten dollars for every minute you were late after five thirty. If I didn't get to work, I would end up owing more money than I made that day. That was the hamster wheel of day care for low-wage moms like me: work so I could afford child care, or stay home and let the government buy me food and pay the rent, so people could call me lazy and unproductive.

I decided Jason Oberland wouldn't notice if I skipped cleaning the guest bathroom. I set aside my mop and dialed.

The woman's voice on the other end of the line was rough-edged, like she was a smoker or a whiskey drinker. Or maybe she was both.

"Barclay's. This is Pam."

"Yes, I'm calling about your text? The order you're holding? The one with the Red Bull?"

I don't know why I was putting question marks after everything.

"Oh yeah, sorry about that, hon. I know you come in regular and that bad rain we had probably stuck you in, but fishing season's here and I got merchandise stacked higher than a moose's backside." She barked out a laugh. "I wish I could tell you that you could wait but this place can't hold no more."

I took a deep breath. "And where exactly is this place?"

It was her turn to sound confused. "In town. Where else would it be, sweetie?" A bell tinkled in the background and the woman called out, "Be right with ya, Tanner."

"I meant, what town?"

"In Cohut." I could feel her frown over the phone. "Wait. Ain't this the lady that lives up off Tenmile River?"

I didn't answer her question. "Could you have sent the text to a wrong number?" I asked instead.

"I suppose it's possible. My fingers ain't that nimble anymore. Let me check." There was a rustle of papers. Then: "Nope, this is the phone number I got for the account. Don't got no name with it, though. Just account number seven-seven-five. That's what we do with our regulars. A phone and a customer number."

"Is there an address?" I pressed.

"We don't deliver, if that's what you're thinking."

I could tell she was starting to lose patience with me.

Another bell chimed. "Hey, Fred. Coffee's just about ready," she called. Then to me: "Look, if you don't want the order, just say so and I'll put it out, although that fancy Peruvian coffee of yours is going to be a hard sell."

I felt suddenly dizzy, as if I were standing at the edge of a high cliff. If there was one thing Mark insisted on spending money for, it was good coffee, and if you added in the Red Bull, well . . . Three words—Red, Bull, coffee—that was all it took.

"Look, I'll be honest, Pam. That's not my order," I said. "I live in Sacramento and I'm trying to find my husband and the number you texted is his and I wonder if you'd mind calling me when the woman on Tenmile River comes to pick up the stuff, or maybe get her address."

There was another long pause, a hum of male voices in the background.

"Sorry, lady. I've made it a habit to never chase after no-good men and you should do the same." There was a click and then silence.

For a moment, I couldn't move. I looked at the time. Thirty-eight minutes left before the countdown clock started. I Googled "Cohut."

According to what I found, Cohut was a tiny town in south-central Alaska with a population of 263 and hunting and fishing tourism as its main industry. My mind raced ahead to the fact that I knew only one person in Alaska and that was Alvin Jones, the subject of Mark's movie. I knew because Mark had once flown to Anchorage a few years ago to make an appearance with Alvin at some conference about veterans and PTSD. The organizers showed Mark's movie and then he and Alvin answered questions. If I remembered right, Mark also visited Alvin's farm but I couldn't recall where it was exactly or how long Mark had spent there, only that Mark said the land had healed Alvin.

The rational part of me said it was just a coincidence that someone in the huge state of Alaska, where I knew only one person, had ordered Red Bull and good coffee, which my husband and thousands of other people drank. The other part said it was fate that the rains had come and the clerk had sent the text about Red Bull and coffee and that I'd started using Mark's phone and seen it. I thought if it was fate and it meant Mark was alive, then maybe I could fix what had broken us.

If it wasn't fate but coincidence—an explainable surprise like the fact that lots of people craved big jolts of caffeine—then I would only be reigniting the foolish hope that I'd worked so hard to extinguish.

Yet there were things I had discovered as I cleaned up Mark's belongings and tried to sort out our affairs. At the time they had seemed odd, but after the text, I added them to the list of fate's signs. For instance, I had found an autobiography written by a hermit living in the interior of Alaska with sections about meat storage and vegetable growing in high northern latitudes highlighted in yellow. There was also a credit card charge for $135.37 from an outdoor-gear store near Reno on the day before Mark had disappeared. Inspector Hardy said the purchase was for a pair of hiking boots, which made no sense. Why would you buy new shoes if you were going to wear them to jump off a bridge, forcing your widow to pay the bill? Unless doing so was planned as another small punishment for her. And how come I never located the boots in Mark's duffel or in our car? If memory served me right, Mark had been wearing flip-flops when he left that night.

I glanced again at the time and quickly scrolled through Mark's contacts. I thought there might be an easy way to answer the question of whether the call was fate or coincidence. Mark was one of those people who always erased his texts and recent-calls list, so I had no evidence he'd been in contact with Alvin before he supposedly jumped from the bridge, but I could phone. I found two numbers for Alvin.

The first was disconnected. The second rang through to Alvin's aunt, Miriam, in Atlanta; she said, sure enough, Alvin's farm was located off Tenmile River, although she hadn't heard from him in a while—ever since he had gone off to Thailand to marry a girl he met on the Internet. She was sure that, yes, Mark had paid a visit to the farm last year because Alvin had mentioned it just before he left.

I had to grab Jason Oberland's kitchen counter to steady myself.

When she told me she was pretty sure Mark had been there on November twentieth because that was three days after her cataract surgery, my legs noodled and I was glad I was hanging on to something.

November twentieth was five days after Mark had jumped.

I asked Miriam if she was sure about the date.

"You don't forget something like that, dear," she said. Her voice was soft with age. "I can see so much better now. I've even taken up driving to the grocery store again."

It turned out I was late to pick up Xander and had to pay sixty dollars in late fees, almost half of what I'd made that day, but I didn't care. I settled Xander down with a toasted cheese sandwich and apple slices and dialed Inspector Hardy.

Even as I laid out the clues for her—the visit to Alaska five days after Mark had supposedly jumped; Mark's friend living on a river near the store where the Red Bull and Peruvian coffee order waited (about fifty miles away, Miriam had said); the hermit book; and my misgivings about the shoe purchase—she sighed and agreed to check, even though she said those things didn't necessarily point to someone hiding out in Alaska. Mark could have left his number at the store during his earlier visit, she said—and half the shift workers in America probably relied on Red Bull and/or coffee to get them through the night.

I gave her the address that Miriam had supplied and Inspector Hardy reluctantly agreed to send someone out to check. A week later, she phoned back to say a state trooper had gone to the farm and found no sign of a man living there, except for a pair of size thirteen work boots, which were too big to have been Mark's. He said there was a woman at the place, and she said she was caretaking the farm for Alvin Jones until he got back. The trooper said he thought she was a lesbian. In addition, Miriam had grown flustered when Inspector Hardy called her and said she might have misremembered the date. It might even have been the wrong year. She told Inspector Hardy she was growing scatterbrained.

"I'm eighty-five and sometimes things flit out of my mind like a butterfly," she said.

"I'm sorry, Mrs. Russo," Inspector Hardy told me. "I hope you don't mind me saying this, but I think it's really time to move on."

Except it's hard to move on when your heart is screaming at you not to. Besides, there was this dream I'd had a few months after Mark's jump. In the dream, I was sleeping and heard a loud bang and went to the front porch and there was Mark in a camouflage jacket and pants, saying, "Surprise! If you wanted to find me, all you had to do was look."

The dream had seemed so real that when I startled awake, I jumped out of bed, threw open the front door and felt surprised the porch was empty. When I recounted the dream to my client Mr. Martin, who'd lost his wife, Nell, to pancreatic cancer two years before, he said he'd dreamed that his wife had come to him and said, "Knock off your moping, George," which was something she would have said. When he told his counselor at the VA about the vision, however, the man said dreams like that were simply signs of regret and longing.

I thought Mr. Martin's counselor was probably right, so I didn't rush off to Alaska like I wanted to. When the bank mailed me a formal foreclosure notice at the beginning of August, however, I took it as the final sign that fate was sending me in a new direction.

I told Dolores I was quitting, packed up a few things and left. Either I'd find Mark or I'd let the bank have the house and start a new life in Alaska, where, I'd found out in my research, there were decent jobs, good pay, excellent doctors and, most important, people who didn't care about your past.

As it turned out, accepting something as fate actually meant you gave up control of your own life. I saw now it was a stupid thing to do.

23.

——— N O W ———

A cage does things to those inside it. Have you seen the way a leopard will pace in a zoo? The way bars will make prisoners turn meaner than before they'd been sent to jail? That's because being confined gives your brain too much time to travel every dark road inside it.

I tried to follow the routine I set up and yet somehow my mind always wandered back to Mark's betrayal, to the night my mother died and to how I was now trapped in a box in the wilderness. The thoughts made my head throb and caused terrible dreams that disrupted my sleep. I could smell the musk of my body and feel my hair hanging thick and oily against my skull. My appetite disappeared, and for the past two days I'd only sipped at the water Angela brought.

She looked worried each time she appeared and pressed herbal teas on me but I refused them. Finally, the container door groaned open one morning and Mark came in. He'd tied back his golden hair with a piece of leather and his blue eyes crinkled with concern. He crossed the container.

"Angela says you're not eating."

I was lying flat on my back on the bed. "I'm not hungry."

He looked at the untouched bowl of lentil stew from the night before. A fly crawled happily across its dried surface and he waved it away. "You can't keep doing this."

I pushed myself slowly into a sitting position. "Why? Because then you'd have a guilty conscience?"

"No, because I love you," Mark said.

I was too tired to be the fox, to pretend I believed he loved me at the same time he claimed to love another woman. I gestured at the container walls. "You certainly have an interesting way of showing love," I said.

He dropped his head. For a moment, the only sound was the buzzing of the fly, which had returned to its congealed meal.

"You're right," he said finally, lifting his gaze to mine. "This isn't the kind of love we wanted. This is damaged love, a love wounded by secrets. Both yours and mine." He dropped into the chair next to the bed and steepled his fingers under his chin. "Kai Huang says, 'Real honesty requires that you know the depth of your lies.' Angela said you've been reading the book she suggested."

Over the days I'd been locked up, I'd read a few chapters of *Mind, Self, Love*, which preached the rejection of man-made rules and the pursuit of pleasure as a way to freedom. It sounded so simple and yet it also made me wonder how the world would function if hedonism was our only god. Wouldn't our constant pursuit of pleasure mean we would ignore others' suffering because it didn't bring us happiness? Wouldn't we neglect chores like laundry and dishes and descend into messy chaos? How would our children learn to face adversity if decadence was all they knew?

I waved the fly away. "There's nothing else to do in here but read."

"I know you're upset but there's a way to end this." He smiled at me, the dimple in his left cheek appearing like a small burst of sunlight.

"And what's that?"

"To open our souls to each other. To stop hurting each other and finally be honest." He leaned forward. "Let's do it. Right here, right now. Go ahead, ask me anything."

"It's too late."

"It's not too late," he insisted. "Can't you see I want only the best for you and Xander?" He took my hand. "I can't stand to see you suffer. You're my heart, my warrior. I want us to be a family again."

I pulled my hand from his and stared into his eyes. "OK, then. What about Rudy?"

I don't think it was the question he'd expected and I could see his mind working. He rubbed his chin and sat back in the chair.

Rudy, he said finally, was the product of a brief union between himself and a woman he'd met in Africa while filming the documentary with Alvin. The two of them had been in a coffee shop in Marrakech, waiting for the right papers to start their journey, when the woman, Diana, had walked in and taken a nearby table. She wore a red sundress and hiking boots, and it turned out she was from Juneau, Alaska, and on a solo backpacking trip around the world. She ended up traveling with them for three months before she decided to move on.

Mark said he would have gone on not knowing about his son except, when Rudy was four, Diana's parents had tried to take the boy away from her. They thought her lifestyle—always on the road or living rough in the woods—was too dangerous for a child. They wanted to adopt the boy and so Diana had contacted Mark and asked him to sign a paper claiming his parental rights and refusing the petition to adopt. A DNA test had followed. Before the matter could be resolved in court, however, Diana's father had a stroke and her mother dropped the case.

"I would have told you but Diana is a very private person," Mark said.

"How could you think it was all right not to tell me?" I asked.

Mark sighed. "I know. I should have told you and I'm sorry I didn't. But now that you know, we can move on, right? Kai Huang says honesty's wounds are quickly healed."

"Where is Rudy's mom now?" I asked.

"On a trip," he said. "I've always dreamed of having my boys together."

"Then you should have told me about him."

"You're right. Being honest and free means there's no need to lie anymore. No need to hold tight to things that don't work. Wait until you get to know Rudy. He's been a wonderful big brother to Xander."

"And how can I get to know him when I'm in here?"

"By trusting us. By agreeing to give this life a chance without running to court or the police. The key is in your hand, not ours."

It was my opening and I took it. I couldn't fight anymore.

I looked him in the eye like the girl at Goodridge had taught me. *Liars look away; liars blink,* she said. Even though the prosecutor and his psychologist claimed that I was good at hiding the truth, I became a decent liar only when I was in prison.

"You're right," I told Mark. "I need to try. We need to be open with each other. Not closed off."

He grinned.

"I guess I can stay for a while and see what you're talking about. If it doesn't work out, though, if I can't live like you do, then I'll leave. But I won't call the cops or file for divorce and we'll figure out a way for Xander to be here with you too. Maybe I'll stay in Alaska so that can happen."

"It will work. I know it." Mark leaned over and kissed my cheek. "Once you see what we're building here and know true freedom, you won't want to go anywhere else."

I tried not to flinch at the feel of his lips, the same ones I'd seen him lock passionately with Angela's out in the garden or in the doorway of the cabin a few times. I asked if he could trust me enough to let me outside to stretch my legs and also get a shower. I made myself look repentant the way my lawyer had advised when I stood before the judge at my sentencing.

Mark said he would consult with Angela, since all decisions had to be mutual.

"This is the greatest news," he said.

24.

—— T H E N ——

My trial was nothing like you see on TV. It happened in a small room with wood paneling and a stern-looking judge with a crew cut who sat behind a large oak desk on a raised platform. There were several rows of folding chairs for family and friends but nobody sat in them. It was just me and my lawyer and the prosecutor, who wore a dark suit and pointed at me a lot, even though the judge hardly looked up from reading whatever was on the desk in front of him. The prosecutor called witnesses who described my mother's wounds, the blood they'd found on my sneakers, my hair clip next to her body. He even called the youth pastor at the church, who said I'd come to him before my mother died and complained about her anger and how she treated me.

"She recounted that she was upset because her mother made her do chores and slapped her once when she didn't say, 'Yes, ma'am,' after being asked to take out the trash," the youth pastor testified. He was a slender thirty-year-old with soulful brown eyes. "She also said she thought her mother was addicted to diet pills, which was why she was always angry. I told her that I knew Helen, Mrs. Crocker, to be a lovely, upright woman who walked in the path of the Lord and that I'm sure she was only trying to make sure her daughter walked the identical path. In the same way, I knew Mrs. Crocker would never abuse her God-given body with pills."

He stared at me. My lawyer had made me wear this collared blue dress that made me look like one of those Jehovah Witnesses who come to your front door; it made me feel as if everything were happening to someone else. "I also reminded Miss Crocker that the Bible commanded children to be obedient and respectful of their parents but she remained defiant. She said that if that's what God said, He didn't have a mother like hers and that she hated her mother and would do anything to get away from her. I'm not surprised by what she did."

The youth pastor made it sound like I was happy to have helped my father bury my mother in a dung pile after he killed her. And yet I could remember almost none of that night.

More than once I tried to get my memory to come alive. There's nothing worse than having a blank space where a period of time should be. I lay in bed, closed my eyes and tried to replay that night in my head: my boyfriend, Matt McCauley, and me in his pickup. Him saying he was thinking of moving to Nevada, where his mother lived and where he could be on a better football team and practice motocross, and me saying I didn't care, even though I did, and him giving me a sloppy kiss and saying maybe I could come and visit him. Both of us were drunk. Him more than me.

I pictured myself sliding out of his pickup, which idled at the end of our long driveway, since I'd told my parents I was going to study at my friend Carol's house instead of going with Matt to the reservoir to drink beer, which was what we had done. I remembered feeling the cold air on my cheeks and knowing it was over between Matt and me and thinking our ending had always seemed inevitable, even when we'd started dating the year before. I pictured myself weaving up the rutted driveway, knowing that I'd drunk more than I'd planned to and, if I went into the house, my mother would know I was drunk, and deciding that I would go to the barn, where there was a sink, and splash cold water on my face, and then the next memory was of seeing my mother's body lying on the barn's concrete floor.

Then nothing again until the plate of eggs the next morning.

My attorney called to the stand the psychiatrist who'd diagnosed me with dissociative amnesia. She told of patients she'd examined who had lost whole years of their lives: one a woman whose boyfriend had tried to strangle her, and another an old man who, after seeing his beloved dog beaten with a baseball bat by his neighbor, had shot the neighbor but couldn't remember doing so. She said I had a classic case of dissociative amnesia brought on by the sight of my mother dead on the barn floor.

I could tell the judge didn't believe her, especially after the prosecution called their own expert, who said that, after interviewing me, he determined that I was emotionally unstable and prone to fabrication, which meant, basically, he was calling me a liar. I watched the judge roll his eyes when my psychiatrist testified, and I knew I was in trouble.

If my lawyer had called me to the stand, which he hadn't, I would have told the judge that I was telling the truth and how it was like somebody had taken a big eraser to those hours. Also, if I had taken a shower after the crime to destroy evidence (which is what the prosecution said I did), why hadn't I also thrown my bloody, manure-streaked shoes into the burn barrel and lit them on fire? Or how had

I managed to go to all my classes the next day and even pass a history test if I had known what I'd done? Most important, why had I helped my dad bury my mother, like the prosecution said I had? All I could think was that when I showed up in the barn, my father had decided to make sure I was ensnared in his crime so I would keep quiet about what I'd seen. It sounded so diabolical, and as I listened to the witnesses, I thought that my father must have hated me too because you wouldn't do that to someone you cared about.

I wasn't surprised when the judge found me guilty. My lawyer's defense wasn't that I was innocent but rather that I'd been so afraid of my father killing me too that I'd done what he said and helped him get rid of my mother's body. Even I could see the weakness in that argument. All I would have had to do was outrun my father—which I could have easily managed, since he suffered from a bad hip—and make my way to a neighbor's house to call the cops, or run and wake up Slim in his bunkhouse.

Even now I would sometimes try to think back and figure out the reasons for my father's hatred toward me, and the thoughts that I must have been thinking as the manure fell on my mother's face, and the motive a child could have had for doing that to their mother. Even if I didn't remember what had happened, I thought, I probably deserved what I got.

25.

───── N O W ─────

The late-August air was cool but the sun warmed my back. I was next to the chicken coop, digging a narrow trench into which I was supposed to place leftover lengths of aluminum roofing in order to keep predators like my fox from burrowing their way inside.

Mark and Angela had come into the container this morning grinning like game show hosts with a million-dollar prize. They said they'd decided to let me out and were thrilled I'd agreed to observe their lifestyle. For a moment, I wondered wildly if that meant I would also have to be privy to their lovemaking or maybe they would want me to join them. Instead, I swallowed the thought and thanked them for the opportunity. It was mortifying to say.

Mark said Kai Huang believed there was also pleasure in work, and as such, he hoped I would join them in their labors around the farm. What else could I do but agree? He suggested I reinforce the chicken coop fencing while Angela checked the spring, which seemed, worryingly, to be drying up. He said he was going to take the boys down valley to see some old-timer about possibly bartering for a Smith & Wesson pistol.

"We need to beef up security even more now that you and Xander are here," he said.

I felt sick at the thought of needing something deadly in order to stay alive.

Angela touched my arm. "Don't worry. It's all for the best."

Breakfast in the cabin felt normal and yet not. Angela made biscuits with wild mushroom gravy and served coffee while Xander cuddled next to me at the table. It was exquisite to have his warm body cupped against mine and my throat closed at the thought of how I'd brought him to a place with bears and guns and killers, not to mention a father who locked up his wife.

"Rudy teached me to get eggs," he said, and cupped his small hands to demonstrate. "You have to be gentle, Mama. Like this."

Mark grinned. "You see how happy he is?" he said.

I didn't trust myself not to tell him that was because Xander didn't know his father was a liar and a drug smuggler, so I busied myself with my coffee.

After breakfast, everyone scattered and I was alone with the work. It turned out to be a harder chore than I'd expected, since, under an eighteen-inch layer of soft brown soil, there was a thick vein of rocks and gravel. I kicked the shovel into the earth, heard the clink of metal against stone and stabbed the shovel again. A blister was already forming on my thumb.

Birds sang from the trees. The sky was so blue it almost hurt my eyes. The place was like a postcard, and any other time I might have simply sat and soaked up its beauty. Now, however, I just wanted to leave.

My plan was straightforward—although it was so full of holes and variables that I almost couldn't call it a real plan. First, I would have to locate my keys, my wallet and the cell phone, which Mark and Angela had taken, and then wait for the right time when Xander was around and everyone else was gone in order to make my break. Then I would have to hope there was enough gas in the car, remember the route here and pray it didn't start raining and turn the roads into a muddy soup.

I wondered if there were programs in Alaska where I could get money for fuel; if I could find a food pantry; and whether I could make it back to California or if I should go to Anchorage, change my name and get a job there. I felt dumb for ignoring the signs that should have given me a warning: the time Mark had thought a gray sedan was following us and he'd driven a circuitous route home and then tried to laugh it off later by saying his boss's paranoia about the government was rubbing off on him; or how he'd suddenly insisted that he would handle the budget and bill paying, claiming it was one less thing I'd have to do even though I'd done it in the first years of our marriage.

I slammed the shovel point into the dirt.

I saw the hole under the fence where the fox had tried to dig her way into the coop, and I thought how a female fox was called a vixen and how the same word meant a fierce and quarrelsome woman. Was it because when a woman outsmarted a man, like the fox had done to the dog, the only thing a man could do was to call her combative so he wouldn't have to admit to her cleverness?

I glanced over my shoulder, set down the shovel and hurried into the house.

Mark's room was the twin of the one in which the boys slept. There was a double bed with some kind of big, primal-looking animal skull mounted on the log wall above it. A nicked pine dresser was on one side of the room with a tall armoire near the door and four or five cardboard boxes stacked in the corner next to it. Quickly, I opened the dresser drawers, running my hands through Mark's T-shirts and boxers, through Angela's underwear and camisoles. It felt strange to touch my husband's lover's intimate things. Still, I searched. No wallet or keys or phone so I could try to call for help even though I doubted I could get a signal out here. I pushed my hands into the pockets of the coats in the armoire, rifled through the small stacks of folded jeans, camouflage pants and Angela's skirts.

I heard a bark. My heart jumped and I ran back outside.

When Angela found me a few minutes later, I was digging away at the soil. Her gaze ran over the work I'd done and I could tell that she approved.

"I could use a little help up at the spring," she said. Shadow came up and sniffed at my shin. Could dogs smell deceit?

"Sure," I said, and slapped the dirt from my hands and followed her.

We went into the woods at the far edge of the garden and began to climb a shallow gully that cut up the hill. We were following a line of old galvanized pipe, skirting around boulders and stooping under low-hanging branches that clawed at my hair. The forest here was dark, almost smothering.

Angela moved slowly, picking her way up the slope, and I followed. Water dripped from small duct-taped sections of pipe where I guessed it had cracked during hard freezes. I thought of the clever way water came into the cabin and wondered whether Alvin had devised the setup or the previous owner had done it. What happened when winter came? I promised myself I wouldn't be around to find out.

We stopped finally in front of a fifty-five-gallon drum like the ones in the container. It was positioned about three feet below a small concrete alcove set into a rocky bank. The alcove was wet and covered in moss. Ferns peacocked their fronds around our knees.

"This is our spring box," Angela said. "The water goes from there into that pipe and then into the barrel, which provides a little more pressure for watering and such." She pointed to a round gasketed opening at the bottom of the barrel. "The other part of the pipe goes there but it looks like the output hole is partially blocked. Alvin said we were supposed to clean the drum after the spring melt but we didn't get around to it. I think there's a layer of silt, so the water can't get all the way through."

"And you want me to help you dump it?" I asked.

The rocky slope dropped away below our feet. It would be easy for the heavy barrel to become unbalanced and knock a person down, breaking a bone if they were lucky and fracturing a skull if they were not, and I thought, *What if I push Angela right now? What if she tumbles down the hill and breaks a leg and I run back to the cabin and wait for Mark to come back with the boys?* I'd follow him around until I saw where he hid my keys. Then, when he wondered where Angela was, I'd pretend I didn't know, and when he went to look for her, I would run to the car with Xander.

But what if, instead of a broken leg, she cracked her skull? What if she died? Could I live with that? I thought again of that baby smashed on the sidewalk and knew I couldn't.

"Liv?" Angela said.

"I'm sorry. What did you say?"

"I said what I need is for you to help me empty the barrel. If we can rock it back and forth, get some of the water to spill out, then we can dump the rest of it more easily." She smiled. "Two is better than one, right?"

"Sure," I said, ignoring the barely veiled hint that two wives might also be preferable to a single mate, and took my place on the other side of the barrel with her. The container was dark with water. The spring trickled softly behind us.

We worked together, grunting with effort. Five minutes later, the barrel was empty and on its side, and I was on my knees pulling out handfuls of smelly, dark silt. After that, I rinsed my hands in water from the spring and we put the barrel back into place, refastened the bottom pipe, put the lid back on and screwed in the top pipe before opening the valve from the spring.

Water thrummed into the barrel.

Angela put her hands on her hips and said that, with luck, she'd be able to start watering in a few hours. "I'm trying to get in a last crop of daikon radishes. They're antiviral and anti-inflammatory. Lots of vitamin C too. Now, if I just had an answer for those stupid deer . . ."

As we headed back to the cabin, she said that she'd planted garlic and chives around the perimeter of the garden to try to deter the animals and that someday, when Mark and she could afford it, they'd build a fence. I told her about the stinky spray my mother used to douse the edges of her garden—egg, milk, dish soap and hot pepper sauce—and she said it was worth a try.

We walked carefully down the hillside, finding our way over mossy boulders and slippery duff. I made sure to thank her for her support in getting me out of the box. Flattery was one of the few weapons I had. Even so, I wondered why she'd helped me. Was she the gentle peacemaker she seemed? Or was it something else? Some motive I couldn't see?

I didn't have time to come up with an answer. We were back on flat ground.

She turned. "Mark said you wanted a shower. Let me show you how it works. I'll make you some tea after."

The shower was glorious.

I stood naked outside on a wooden platform with the afternoon sun filtering warm through the aspens around me. A black solar bag, heavy and pear-shaped, hung from a pole above my head. I turned on the spigot and let the sun-heated water slide over my lips and down my breasts and between my legs. I washed my hair with the lavender soap Angela had given me, and scrubbed the dirt and sweat from my skin until my flesh was red. I let the slight breeze dry my skin. I looked toward the cabin and saw Angela in the garden, turned in my direction. Was it my imagination or had she been watching me?

26.

―――― T H E N ――――

I don't remember my mother ever saying, "I love you," or even hinting at any affection for me. From the earliest age, I felt her resentment like a heavy blanket on my life. It was as if my birth had simply added another burden onto her already hard existence. By the time I was a teenager, her disdain for me was full-blown.

She'd begun going to a new church, one that preached a strict adherence to the Bible, and around the same time found a doctor who prescribed her diet pills. She grew pinch faced and rabid with the Lord.

She raged against sinners, against my father, against the weather and against the bank that held our mortgage. Mostly, she raged against me. One morning, when I was fifteen, she decided to teach me a lesson I wouldn't forget.

I'd just started dating Matt then. He was on the football team, drove a shiny Ford pickup and was beginning to follow in the footsteps of his father, who drank too much. I didn't see it at the time, however. All I understood was that a boy I'd considered the most popular in my class was paying attention to me.

My mother saw it differently, believing I was the one arousing lust in a vulnerable young man. Once, she caught me coming out of school with my shirt tied so my midriff was exposed. She accused me of being a harlot, and when we got home, she threw the shirt—my favorite—into the burn barrel and lit it on fire.

When my mother told my father what she'd seen, he looked up from his pork chops and green beans.

"Matt McCauley isn't worth anybody's time, let alone yours," he said.

My mother got up from the table. "Why can't you ever support me?" she cried. "You're as bad as she is."

"Sit down, Helen," my father ordered. The quietness of his command gave it a sharp edge.

"Don't tell me what to do," my mother said, and took her plate and slammed it into the sink. The crash sounded like cymbals at the end of some stirring symphony and she stormed from the room.

My father sat still for a moment and then turned back to his meal.

The next morning, I awoke to find my mother at my bed, holding her sewing scissors.

She leaned over me. "'Likewise, women should adorn themselves with respectable apparel, with modesty and self-control,'" she recited, "'not with braided hair and gold or pearls or costly attire but they should array themselves with what is proper for women who profess godliness—with good works.'

"One Timothy, chapter two, verses nine to ten," she added triumphantly.

I turned to see a big hunk of my hair lying on my pillow and ran to the bathroom, where I saw that, while the right side of my hair hung down past my shoulder as it always had, the left side ended just below my ear.

When I screamed, my mother came into the bathroom and set the scissors on the counter.

"We're going to church. Now finish the job," she said.

But I didn't.

Instead, I tucked what was left of my hair under a hat, and after we sat down in the second pew from the front, a spot my mother had claimed as ours, I yanked the hat from my head so everyone could see her handiwork.

I smiled when Janice Parkinson, the sheriff's wife sitting behind us, gasped.

My mother's lips went tight, and that afternoon she made me clean the house from attic to basement while she stood over me inhaling one cigarette after another.

Everything got worse after that. The more she yelled and insulted, the more I rebelled. Like I said, I was a stubborn child. Yet, even as I hated her, I found myself craving her approval, which she refused to give, no matter how hard I worked.

A few weeks before her death, I had that conversation with the youth pastor that the prosecutor later used against me, along with the revelation that I was spotted arguing loudly with my mother at Midtown Market.

Sometimes I'd remember a story I'd read online about a helicopter that had crashed into the ocean while leaving the Bahamas one night. Of the five people aboard, two had survived the initial impact. One, a forty-year-old businessman, had had the presence of mind to grab an inflatable life vest as they went down. The other, a twenty-seven-year-old software coder, had not. She clung, white-faced and paralyzed with shock, to a piece of hard-shelled carry-on luggage that had somehow floated to the surface of the choppy sea. The businessman had yelled at her to swim to him and they would try to make it to shore and yet she didn't move. In fact, she seemed not even to hear as she drifted into the darkness. He yelled once more, then glanced toward a few lights he could see in the distance. He thought of sharks in the black water and decided it wasn't worth risking his own life to save a woman who wouldn't even help herself. He began to swim. And I would think, *Aren't I just like him?* Even if I hadn't done what the district attorney said I'd done, hadn't my selfish and stubborn ways been part of the problem in our family? Hadn't I helped stoke the flames of my mother's anger with my rebellions and bad behavior, so it grew hotter and eventually caused my father to kill her? Would she have been alive if I'd been a better daughter?

27.

──── N O W ────

For all Mark's talk about uncovering secrets, there still seemed to be plenty of them. For instance, I didn't know how Mark had managed to hide the money he'd made from smuggling so neither the IRS nor I knew about it, or how he had crossed the Canadian border without his passport. He said that those were minor details and that I was missing the point about the honesty he talked about. In filmmaking and photos, he said, honesty was laying bare the human soul for the world to see and nobody needed to examine the editing, the tiny story shifts made in order to reveal the greater truth.

Instead, as we worked in the garden or went out harvesting berries for Angela to make into fruit leathers and jams, he would lecture me about how some indigenous societies understood that capitalism corrupted and about how white children abducted by Native tribes and then returned to their families would often escape back to their kidnappers because the way the People lived—by sharing everything and not holding one person above the others—was superior to the settlers' ways. The happiest peoples, he claimed, were those who didn't rely on capitalism and who didn't regulate sex or force rules on society that made a person have to be dishonest in order to love the way they chose to love.

And yet, a few days after I'd been let out of the container, I discovered more dishonesty, and it wasn't simply a matter of editing.

It happened as Mark was playing a game with Xander and Rudy that involved stacks of spruce cones and rocks. I was just coming out of the container after getting a sweater to ward off the chill. I was no longer being locked in and yet I couldn't stop a twinge of anxiety whenever I went inside. I kept imagining the doors slamming closed and the bar clanging into place behind me.

As I came back outside, I saw a figure, a woman, emerging from the bridge trail. She was tall and athletic-looking, dressed in camo pants and a black turtleneck, with a large knife in a sheath at her belt. She wore hiking boots and her blond hair fell in a single thick braid down her back. A green pack hung from her shoulders and she held a fancy metal bow loosely in one hand. I recognized her immediately.

She was the woman in the photo I'd found in Mark's studio.

Mark looked up and I went to him. "Who's that?" I asked even though I suspected who she was.

"That's Diana," Mark said. "Rudy's mom."

"I thought you said she was on a trip."

"She was. She's a guide. She had back-to-back clients. I didn't expect her back home for another day."

"'Back home'? Why didn't you tell me she lived here too?" My voice rose so it was too loud and too sharp.

Mark's eyes darkened. I could see a little part of him close off from me.

"How can you even begin to think this is OK?" I asked.

Most cheating husbands had one mistress. Mine had two.

The muscles in his jaw worked and I knew I'd gone too far. "You can either accept what is, Liv, or keep trying to fight and destroy yourself," he said.

I shoved down what I was feeling, which was anger wrapped in a coating of fear. I didn't want to be locked up again. "I'm sorry. You're right. I was just surprised. I shouldn't have said that."

"I thought you were trying to open up," he said.

"I am, really. It's just a lot to take in, you know."

I watched Diana stride toward the cabin with long steps. Her chin was strong, her back straight.

"We'll talk about this later. Maybe what you need is time to think," he said, and looked pointedly at the container.

Panic bubbled up inside me. "I'm sorry," I said, but he had already turned to the boys.

"You guys will have to finish the game without me."

He marched across the garden and intercepted Diana as she got to the cabin's front door. They both stopped and he leaned toward her, spoke a few words and pointed at me. She turned to look and I saw her eyes were the same pale blue as Rudy's. A moment later, she and Mark disappeared into the cabin.

I realized that I wasn't the only one watching. Angela had stopped picking bugs from the kale in the garden and stared after the pair, and little Rudy had dropped the rock he was holding and done the same. After a moment, he shoved his hands in his pockets, mumbled, "I gotta go," and disappeared into the woods.

Xander was the only one who hadn't noticed the scene. "Wanna play, Mama?" he asked. "It's called Crack the Stack and Daddy invented it. Rudy gots four points." He hopped up and down on one leg in excitement.

"Sure," I said, because what else could I do? Now I'd have to grovel and apologize and hope I could repair the damage I'd done, so Mark would let down his guard again. And yet I didn't think I was the only one affected by Diana's arrival. I'd seen Angela's spine go straight and something flit across her face when Mark and Diana went into the cabin.

I wasn't sure what it was but I stored it away for later.

I hurled the stone. The spruce cones jumped and scattered.

"One cracky-stacky point, Mama," Xander cried.

Three nights later, I snuck out of the container.

Mark's threat had made me worry he planned to lock me in again, and so I tried to appear as if I'd accepted this new truth even while I wondered how, if there were no rules, punishment could be part of this life. After dinner, I even quoted Kai Huang to Mark about jealousy and selfishness not being needed if love and pleasure were plentiful. He said that jealousy was natural in a capitalistic system and that the longer I lived here, the more I'd be able to overcome those feelings and that he would be more patient with me. It was a matter of reading and reflecting on the self and letting go of material things. He said he would help me with that so I could find the happiness he had.

"This really is the only way to truly be free," he said.

I don't know if he thought it would make me feel better but he told me he'd never planned for Diana to be part of this life. He'd asked Alvin to email Diana from the computer at the market to tell her where he was—he didn't want Rudy to lose track of him—and she'd showed up about four months ago, after Alvin left.

I thought, *You emailed her but relied on some poem for me?*

Mark said that she'd gotten a job as a hunting and fishing guide and that she'd thought that Rudy could use some time with a father figure. Her last boyfriend, a trapper, had punched Rudy in the stomach after Rudy had let a fire go dead, causing the cabin's pipes to freeze, and she'd realized none of the men she'd been with had been good for the boy.

She'd stayed in the other bedroom with Rudy first but quickly moved into Mark's bed. He said she was strong and independent—maybe a little too independent—but that I would come to see she wasn't a threat to our relationship.

I started to say, *What relationship?* Instead, I said I would try.

When it was time for bed, I worried he would follow me to the container and lock me inside but he simply closed his book, said good night and followed Diana into his bedroom. Angela watched them, the knitting needles stilling in her hands.

Now I slipped outside and paused to let my eyes adjust to the shadowed darkness. It must have been around three a.m. I hoped Shadow wouldn't hear me. I turned right, willing my footfalls into silence. I walked just inside the tree line. Every nerve was on high alert.

Having lived in the city for so long, I'd forgotten how to walk in the night, and I flinched at the dark outline of a boulder that resembled a crouching man, and snagged the toe of my shoe on a tree root, causing my back muscles to spasm and then tighten. I slowed my steps, trying to follow the trail that led to the bridge. Stars netted the dark sky.

Once, after I'd locked myself out of the Subaru at a client's house, I'd gone to a hardware store, had a spare key made and hidden it in a small magnetic box in the front wheel well. I'd never had to use it again, so I hadn't remembered it was there until yesterday, when Angela had said something about unlocking my heart to love. I still hadn't found my keys and wallet or the phone, but after Mark's threat, I was even more determined to leave. How could he expect me to become a carefree co-wife with two other women, or sit around waiting for someone to arrive and kill us all?

If I could find the secret key, I would hide it until Xander and I could run. I would drive and pray I didn't get lost or run out of gas and end up stranded in the wilderness. I would do whatever it took to get us away from vengeful drug dealers and a husband I didn't recognize anymore. I felt like that guy whose arm had gotten stuck between two boulders and had to decide between dying or sawing off the limb. Both staying and leaving were dangerous.

Halfway to the bridge, I thought I heard something move in the forest, a slight crack of wood, and my first thought was that it was the bear. Fear flashed like lightning and I crouched, my palms pressed against the soft, cool earth. Wasn't that what you were supposed to do if a bear approached? Submit? Or were you supposed to make yourself big and talk to it?

The woods fell silent after that. I waited a few long moments, my heart pounding, and finally began to move again.

I crossed the bridge—it was a lot easier when I couldn't see exactly what was below—and hurried to my car. A small blue pickup was parked next to it and I guessed that Diana had taken it to her guiding job, which was why I hadn't seen it when I first arrived at the farm. It was probably the same truck Angela had used to pick up Mark from the bridge and drive to Alaska. I knelt by the Subaru's front wheel and ran my hands over the spot where the hidden key should have been. I gave myself a silent cheer when my fingers found the little box. I pulled it from the car and slid the lid open.

The container was empty.

I wanted to fling the little key holder into the river in frustration. Instead, I put the magnetic box back in its place and hurried back to the shipping container before anyone could realize I was gone.

The next evening, however, when I pulled back the covers on my bed, the key holder was there.

My hands began to shake and I shoved the key holder under my pillow. It was a long time before I slept.

28.

—— T H E N ——

One day on the ranch, I rode out to the east pasture with my father to see about a sick cow. It was one of the few times he allowed me to go with him as he worked. My father was no one's romantic image of a rancher. He didn't ride horses or wear chaps or sport a cowboy hat. He rode an old ATV and wore ball caps that tractor and feed companies gave away to promote their products. At the time, my mother was trying to convince him to switch from Hereford cattle to Black Angus since there was more demand for the meat and thus it brought higher prices. In fact, she was pressing him about it that morning. My father refused to switch.

"I'm not doing it, Helen" was all he said.

I knew it was a battle my mother wouldn't win. Only a few weeks before, I had watched my dad nod his head earnestly as some cattle agent described how Herefords were a hardy breed that had not only easily adapted to the open range but were also roped to Texas history, with famous ranchers like Charles Goodnight and Christopher Columbus Slaughter promoting the animals. In my father's mind,

Herefords were the most handsome and practical of the popular cattle breeds. My mother got angry and called him a dumb hick that morning because he refused to budge.

I was thinking about this while I sat behind him on the ATV. It was summer and I was about twelve years old. An acquaintance of his from the next ranch over had called during my mother's ranting to say he'd been out riding fence and seen one of our cattle in what looked to be distress at the salt lick near Dog Creek. My mother said she was going into town to get her hair done.

"Take her with you," she said as if I were a piece of rotten meat that needed to be removed from the house.

My father didn't say anything. He just opened the screen door and nodded outside into the pale yellow morning. I pulled on my boots and ran after him as he retrieved his tools from the barn—a six-foot length of garden hose with the ends cut off, a metal speculum and a bottle of some kind of medicine—and when I asked him what it was for, he said something about the cow likely suffering from free-gas bloat, and we set out. He wasn't the kind of person to call a vet for something like that.

The ranch was mostly flat, green where we irrigated it and brown where we didn't. The soil was red, and a rust-colored cloud spiraled up behind us as we traveled the trail to the east pasture. I saw a flock of wild turkeys and a couple of mule deer. We crossed Dog Creek over an old flatbed railcar the previous owner had laid down for a bridge.

Like always, my father didn't say much when we found the cow, her tongue hanging out as she panted and one side of her bulging unnaturally. He just mumbled that I should stay where I was. Like always, of course, I didn't listen.

I watched as he lassoed the cow and tied her tight to a fence post while the rest of the herd milled worriedly some distance away. He retrieved his tools as the cow began to let out painful and frightened cries. As he approached the animal, I slipped from the ATV and tried to sneak around his back side. I wanted to get a closer look at what he was about to do.

The cries of the cow coupled with my curiosity were probably why I didn't hear it but my father did.

Suddenly, he was a yard or so away from me with the shovel that was usually strapped to the ATV in his hands. Before I could even register what was happening, he was swinging that shovel viciously at the ground.

I looked down to see the headless body of a five-foot rattlesnake writhing in the dust. Only my father didn't stop. He kept chopping that snake until it was in a dozen pieces. His eyes had gone narrow and hard and his breath huffed as he slashed.

It was the only time I ever saw him actually be violent and I thought it was mostly born of the fight he'd had with my mother that morning but also a little bit of my disobedience.

I wondered later if he looked the same way when he killed her.

29.

——— N O W ———

I'd just finished raking the chicken coop, tugged off my work gloves, and was resting on the small bench in front of the cabin when Angela came around the corner of the house. She wore a long plaid skirt, a cotton blouse and sturdy boots as if she were playing the role of some nineteenth-century pioneer woman.

"There you are," she said.

She sat next to me. Her eyes looked emerald in the sunlight. She smelled faintly of soil and the lavender soap she used. The air was cool and still.

"This is nice, isn't it?" she said.

I grunted a reply.

Then: "Do you ever think about how you'll die, Liv?"

Over the past three weeks I'd been here, she'd been pestering me with questions like that. *When did you know you were in love with Mark? What was the best day of your life? What one thing would you change about your life if you could?* It was as if she wasn't satisfied with just crawling into my husband's bed. She wanted to crawl into my head too.

I put up with it for the most part. After all, her questions had led to my discovery that Mark's three lost days in the desert hadn't been with his film school buddy but with Angela. She said it was where Mark had been introduced to the idea of "the chains of monogamy and capitalism and the wisdom of spirit." Still, her barrage of questions made me tired. I looked over at Xander and Rudy, who were playing on the wrecked snow machine on the edge of the clearing.

"I don't think about death. I prefer to think about life," I lied.

The truth was, even as a kid, I thought a lot about how I would die. You don't live with a vicious woman who regularly threatens you with physical violence and not imagine you'll wind up with a nasty end.

"You're so wise," Angela said, and hooked her arm through mine. "Even with what happened to you, you can still see the good parts of life. Maybe when I'm older, I'll be able to do that too."

I resisted the urge to yank myself away from her and her little insult. Rudy and Xander were now sitting on the snow machine, waving sticks in the air like swords.

She smiled, then said, "I know you and Mark are still working things out, but when you're ready, I can teach you the tantric sex position Mark likes best. It's guaranteed to make you come at the same time." She squeezed my arm. "You'll be amazed at how powerful it is."

I didn't want to think of Mark and Angela locked in some sex position, howling out their climaxes together like wolves. I shoved myself from the bench and started across the garden.

"I'm only trying to help," Angela protested after me. "I just want you to feel fully, the way Mark and I do. Closing yourself off from the unknown only denies yourself pleasure, you know."

I kept walking.

"Wait, Liv," she called, and hurried after me. "I'm sorry. I didn't mean to upset you. I just want what's best for you. To be your friend and a helpmate to you." She was like an empty bucket that could only be filled with others' approval. "Don't shut me out."

"I'm not. I just need to do some laundry."

30.

—— N O W ——

Autumn arrived, the mornings suddenly turning sharp with chill. Squirrels chittered from the trees as if to warn us about what was to come, and fewer birds seemed to call from the branches. The golden leaves on the aspens began to lose their hold. They fluttered to the ground like bright butterflies.

The harvest was underway. Angela and Mark dug potatoes and gathered squash. The boys and I picked buckets of highbush cranberries, which Angela made into jam, and Diana came home from a guiding trip with a quarter of venison a client had given her. The first frost arrived, painting the ground white and causing me to dig out another wool blanket for my bed. There was an undercurrent of urgency in everything we did. Winter was approaching and I thought, *I have to leave before the snow or I'll never get out of here.* Whenever I could, I searched for my car keys, although there weren't many opportunities.

Rudy took care of the goats and tended to Shadow, making sure all had water and food. I let Xander help me feed the chickens and collect eggs and also do the wash. He loved punching the clothes up and down in the washtub and running through the damp clothes and bedding as they hung from the line near the aspens. He begged every day for the "how-many" game. I was using rocks to teach him basic addition. The only good part of being here, I thought, was having free time to spend with him, not to have to rush off to work or to warehouse him in day care.

Diana went off on another guiding trip and Angela seemed to relax. She knitted me a colorful beanie to wear and hummed as she worked.

After my escapade searching for the hidden key, I told myself I needed to be more methodical about my escape and I began to squirrel away food: a few slices of venison jerky here, a couple of apples there, a jar of canned green beans I thought wouldn't be missed. I also stole an old rusted gas can I found underneath the boat and hid it in the brush near the bridge. I couldn't just rely on good luck to survive.

Meanwhile, Mark began courting me as if he thought he could somehow woo me into his love rectangle now that I'd convinced him I'd decided to stay. Lying had become my default mode and it felt like lugging a heavy pack that never allowed you any rest. I wondered how spies did it for months and years.

I'd tuck Xander into bed, say good night and head for the container, only to have Mark appear a few minutes later with mugs of tea and a book. Sometimes he'd also bring me a pretty stone or a piece of bright moss he thought I'd like.

He'd start a fire in the little stove and I'd sit on the bed watching. He worked the blaze with confidence, making a small tepee of sticks, adding tinder and blowing gently to urge the flame into a full-on fire before he added a split log or two. The orange glow from the fire lit his face.

After, he would throw himself into the upholstered chair as if it were the most natural thing on earth to be here with me while two other women waited in the wings. I wondered how the other women accepted it and decided they had fallen under his spell just like I had for so long. I'd never recognized Mark's need for control until now.

The ability to hold sway over others seemed to come easily to him. He had some undefinable quality that made people want to be near him, to feel some of his talent and light rub off on them. Once, we'd gone to a house party in the Hollywood Hills. The rooms were full of beautiful women and powerful men, and yet it wasn't long before a group of them began to drift toward Mark as he held a tumbler of Scotch and stood in a corner in jeans and a button-down shirt. Soon, they were laughing at his stories and leaning their bodies toward him as if they were desert wanderers and he were the water they needed. Even those titans of industry and beauty swooned in the face of his attention.

I had been no different. I had never questioned the tightness of his hold on me.

On the nights he came into the container, sometimes, in spite of everything, tiny embers of those old feelings would stir. He'd sip his tea and his blue eyes would meet mine, and I would have to shove down the old memories and remind myself that his strength required my weakness. Then I'd harden myself.

He'd crack open the book he'd brought and read to me about the loss of the ancient ways of connecting to the earth or about the quashing of pleasure. Other times, it would be poetry: Yeats, Frost,

Whitman. Sometimes when a line of poetry struck him, he would lift his head and smile.

One night, he took out a worn copy of Walt Whitman's *Leaves of Grass* and began to read.

"'Give me nights perfectly quiet, as on high plateaus west / of the Mississippi, and I looking up at the stars; / Give me odorous at sunrise a garden of beautiful flowers, / where I can walk undisturb'd.'"

His voice was steady, warm.

"'Give me for marriage a sweet-breath'd woman, of whom / I should never tire; / Give me a perfect child—give me, away, aside from the / noise of the world, a rural domestic life.'"

He stopped and his eyes crinkled with a smile and he asked if I remembered the night Xander had been conceived.

I did.

We had been lying naked on a sleeping bag on top of a mountain near Mono Lake. The stars were like confetti in the sky and a warm breeze was blowing in the scent of coyote bush and sage and he pointed out Taurus and Gemini and Ursa Major. Those stars made me feel small and yet connected to something big.

"It was pretty magical," I said, because it had been.

"What if we . . . ?" he began.

"What if we what?"

"What if we had another child? You and I. Wouldn't that heal us? Wouldn't that prove how much we love each other?"

He looked so sincere, and yet how could he actually believe I would agree to that?

I waited a moment and told him that was a big decision and I needed to think about it. I didn't want to be locked up for saying the wrong thing. I still hadn't located my stuff.

The fire in the small woodstove crackled and hissed. The days were growing shorter, so darkness came earlier now. The lantern on the shelf cast a small halo of yellow light around the two of us. Mark closed his book and came to the edge of the bed. He leaned over and kissed my cheek and I could smell his scent: cedary perspiration, a hint of sap and woodsmoke.

"Don't think too long, babe. You know how blocked you can get."

He straightened and I watched him go.

You son of a bitch, I thought.

And yet his request had given me an idea, a plan B, which I needed because so far plan A had been pretty much a failure.

Even while Mark and Angela talked about how wonderful life was when you lived with pleasure as your goal, I could see cracks in their facade. Sure, the garden yielded sweet carrots and tender potatoes, and the water ran cold and pure. And of course we all slept well after a day of hard work and Diana kept us supplied with protein: strings of fish she had caught in the river, a small buck she had killed as she drove back from a guiding trip in the Chugach Mountains. But there were fissures in their lives that they seemed either to ignore or not to notice. Two nights ago, for instance, as Mark sat on the couch, Angela had pulled off her sweater, revealing the ivory camisole she wore, and put her hands on his knees so her breasts hung soft and pale in front of him.

"How's the most handsome man in the world?" she said.

"Tired," Mark said, and didn't look up from the book he was reading.

Angela waited a beat and then huffed herself upward and put her sweater back on. When I looked over, I saw a smile flit across Diana's lips and she shook her head as if she had witnessed a spoiled child get what she deserved.

And for all the freedom and mutual decision-making he

preached, Mark was still the one in charge: the benevolent lord in command of his castle. I noticed Angela pout a little if she didn't get her way, and more than once when he gave Diana an order, I saw her walk away as if he hadn't said a word.

I thought maybe I could use those cracks to shatter Mark's little utopia and make him see that a life centered on pleasure didn't always bring happiness; that no amount of preaching could banish jealousy and insecurity from the human heart, which meant that hurt was a natural by-product of this life of his. If I could make him see how we were picking at one another and fighting for attention and nobody was truly happy, how could he insist that Xander and I stay? How could he believe his little experiment had succeeded? And if I could help that process along by sowing a bit of discord here and there, so much the better. It was the only weapon I had.

Or if that didn't work, perhaps I could enlist Angela's help by playing on her need to be loved. If I could make her believe that I was a threat to Mark's attention, she might see a benefit in me leaving and help Xander and me escape. I didn't care what their guru Kai Huang said. We are all selfish creatures in the end.

After Mark's visit that night I knew where to start.

On the wall in the kitchen was a picture calendar I'd noticed when I began spending more time in the cabin. It had notations about the weather and crop planting written in looping handwriting I guessed belonged to Angela. There were also strange, runic-looking marks that I came to realize indicated which woman was sleeping with Mark and which woman was in the second twin bed in the boys' room. In addition, certain dates were circled in red with a small letter A inked next to them. They went back four months, to right around the time Diana had arrived, and from their regularity

I was pretty sure they marked Angela's fertile times. The next one was in three days.

Find out what someone wants and you'll always have a weapon against them, was what my mother had believed. She had been a master at brandishing words to divide and conquer, and as much as I didn't want to think there was any of her in me, I'd learned at her knee.

So, when I was outside later, helping Angela build a makeshift root cellar for our harvest—three metal drums from the container sunk into the ground—and she started up with her questions (What was Mark's family like? Why did his brother hate him?), I said, "I have a question for you. How would you feel if I got pregnant?"

The shovel stilled in her hands and she asked if Mark and I were together now. When I told her, "Not yet," she seemed to relax and said Mark had promised to tell her when we were.

"To put you on the calendar," she said quickly when I frowned.

"Oh, sure," I said.

She dug out another shovelful of dirt and asked, just as I'd hoped, if I'd always wanted more children. I told her I hadn't, since we couldn't afford another special-needs child (the truth), but now I was considering it (a lie). I said Mark seemed to want a child right away to prove his love and commitment and yet it was too big a decision to be made quickly. When I told her she and Mark were wise to wait to have a child, she frowned.

"Mark said we wanted to wait?"

I pretended confusion, saying that perhaps I had misunderstood. Maybe Mark had meant that since I was older, I didn't have time to wait, and because she did have time, I needed to make my decision quickly. I let that sink in for a moment.

"Of course, that doesn't mean he doesn't want a commitment with you," I said. "I'm sure he does. It's a matter of timing, not how much he loves you."

I almost felt bad for what I'd done. Angela looked like a puppy that had been kicked. But I had to drive a wedge into the crack if I wanted to leave. I couldn't stay here. Not with a possible assassin on our heels. Not with a husband as twisted as mine was now.

Later, I went to the river to gather willows for baskets Angela wanted to weave, and I saw Diana across the river on the opposite bank. She stood on a rocky shelf about six feet above the water with an arrow nocked in her bow. She moved over the steeply sloped rock face as if she were floating, and she seemed intent on something I couldn't see.

If Angela was like my shadow, Diana was the indifferent sun. She barely acknowledged me, speaking to me only when necessary: to warn me to stay away from a stinging plant called devil's club near the bridge trail, or to tell me my sneakers were ridiculous to wear in this territory before she tossed me a used pair of her hiking boots. She was self-contained and aloof, like some goddess who roamed her own world and cared little for those beneath her—including her son, I thought. Guiding season was almost over, so she now spent her time with us, hunting and fishing for the icy months ahead. She said that every sign pointed to this being a bad winter and that game seemed scarce. The moose and the Dall sheep that should have kept us fed for most of the dark months seemed to have mysteriously moved out of the area. She said it was because of climate change.

She left the cabin early most mornings with a sandwich and a thermos of coffee and came back in the evening dirty and tired and generally empty-handed. The only things she managed to find were a few ducks and some spruce hens. She also had a snare line that she ran. It gave us a supply of rabbits, which I thought Angela appreciated as a kind of revenge for all of her plants they'd destroyed.

Now I watched Diana pause and rise slightly. Her arm pulled back on the bowstring. For a moment, it seemed as if the forest held its breath, or maybe it was just me. Then the arrow flew and there was an explosion of dark feathers halfway up a spruce. She lowered her bow and looked at me. A slow smile lifted the corners of her mouth. I didn't know what that meant.

31.

—— N O W ——

If there was one thing I'd learned, it was that the universe never respected the plans you made. What happened a week after I'd seen Diana at the river flipped everything upside down, even plan B.

First, Angela came back from a supply trip to town, saying she had news. She always rented time on the public computer at Barclay's whenever she was in Cohut.

"Anything from Alvin?" Mark asked.

"An email," she said quickly. "He said something had come up—a residency problem, I think. He said he needed to deal with that and then he would mail us the deed. Who knows how long that will take?"

Mark swore.

Apparently, Alvin was supposed to send a deed for the property but hadn't, making Mark wonder if his friend was trying to cheat him. Alvin, he said, had left the farm toward the middle of December last year, before Diana and Rudy had arrived. He'd acted strange in his last few days here. "He could barely look me in the eye and then he just hightailed it out of here one day when I was gone getting medicine for one of the goats. He didn't even say goodbye, just told Angela he'd send the deed and left" was how Mark told it.

"But there was something else, something bad," Angela said. She unhooked the bulging backpack from her shoulders and dropped it to the dirt.

She'd done a computer search for anything related to Mark or the motorcycle shop and found a small article in the *Sacramento Tribune* about a former resident who had drowned while swimming in the ocean near Puerto Vallarta, Mexico. The victim was identified as Joe Ramirez, formerly of Sacramento. He had been the shop's bookkeeper.

According to the article, Ramirez had quit his job and moved across the border before the drowning happened. His wife claimed that her husband's death wasn't an accident and that he had been an excellent swimmer. Authorities were investigating.

Mark's face went pale. He said he and Joe had surfed together at Ocean Beach a couple of times and he would never have drowned. "He must have found out what was going on."

For a moment, I felt weightless with the news. Another person killed?

Mark said the death was proof of what he suspected: that things might be even darker than he'd imagined.

"Rick's partner is the really bad one," Mark said. "He's not the kind of guy who will give up either. This is not good news. I need to think."

He strode off before I could ask for more details. Angela said we needed to get the supplies she'd brought into the cache, which was one of the wooden buildings I'd seen when I arrived at the farm. Inside were shelves filled with canned salmon and trout; boxes of powdered milk, sacks of beans and jars of surplus peanut butter from the food pantry truck that came to Cohut once a month; homemade jams and bags of flour and rice. The floor was packed dirt. Evening was falling and I told Angela it felt dangerous to stay here.

"It's even more dangerous out there," Angela said. "Mark and I agree. It's better that we're here, that we stick together."

All I could think was that my need to leave with Xander was even more urgent.

That night, Mark came back from a walk through the forest to the main road and presented us with a plan. He had already ripped down the sign at the road, he said, and now he would build a locked gate across the driveway and set up an alarm system that incorporated an air horn and a small trigger stick hidden beneath one of the stone steps to the bridge. And just in case Rick or his partner came a different way, he would dig a series of what he called spike pits on the three or four trails—animal and man-made—that led through the thick woods and brush to the cabin. These were to be deep holes lined at the bottom with sharpened sticks and camouflaged with thin branches and dirt or leaves. He said he'd learned the trick in Africa when he and Alvin came across a small settlement being terrorized by a man-eating lion. When hunters couldn't kill the beast, the villagers had resorted to spike pits and finally destroyed the animal.

I told him that with the boys around, those kinds of things were dangerous. He said he would show Rudy the locations and mark the spots with stacks of three small stones that a stranger wouldn't notice but would let Rudy know to be careful. Xander, he pointed out, never went anywhere without one of us.

I asked about Shadow and he said dogs were smarter than

humans and would sense the pits and go around them. I told him I thought we should come up with a different plan.

"Don't you want to be safe?" he asked.

What I wanted was to get away from here. What I wanted was to take Xander and sneak away in the night without a lantern or a flashlight to give us away, and how could I do that with dangerous holes and alarm systems and locked gates? Now I would have to find not only the keys to the car but also the key to the gate, and we'd have to leave during daylight.

Later, we were eating dinner—a vegetable stew—and I thought of the drowned bookkeeper and the doomed motorcycle tester and I pushed my half-empty bowl away. The image of my mother's body on the barn floor came, and I imagined how it would be if some gunman burst out of the forest, then killed all of us. Or what if he shot us adults and then left Xander and Rudy alive, but then they slowly starved to death because there was nowhere for them to go for help?

I pushed myself up from the table.

"Are you all right?" Mark asked.

Angela stopped eating. Diana and Rudy were shoveling food into their mouths like they always did, as if it might be their last meal.

"No, I'm not all right," I said. "We can't just stay here like sitting ducks, not after what happened to Joe."

Xander looked around the table. "I don't see ducks."

Mark set down his fork. "It's just a saying, Xan, and we're not sitting ducks. We've got a plan and it's solid, and we've lasted this long without anybody finding us."

"But what if they do?"

"Then we'll be ready for them."

"Leaving here means we're exposing ourselves unnecessarily,"

Angela said. "What if we got stopped by the cops for some reason? And how would we support ourselves if we didn't have the land or our animals?" She got up, came over and hugged me from behind, squeezing hard. I could smell garlic and onions on her hands from when she'd prepared dinner. "You've been working hard, adjusting to a new life. You're just stressed, that's all. We've got this handled."

"Please, sit," Mark said. "You're scaring the boys."

Which was the only reason I sat back down.

Mark finished his stew and looked around the table. The light from the candle cast a feeble circle of brightness against the darkness outside. Xander was already yawning.

"I think what we need is some good news," Mark said. "What do you think, Diana?"

She shrugged.

"We were going to wait, but, well, I just can't."

Angela looked perplexed.

"Drumroll, please," Mark said, and thrummed his knuckles on the table. "I just found out yesterday. It was a big surprise but a happy one, for sure." He smiled and waited half a beat. "Diana is pregnant. You're going to be big brothers, boys."

Xander sat up straighter. "How big will I get, Daddy?"

"As big as you want, son." Mark laughed and pulled Xander onto his lap.

"I don't understand. How could . . ." Angela's voice trailed off. She looked from Mark to Diana.

"It just happened," Diana said. "Apparently, I missed a few pills." She looked away. "It is what it is."

"What it is, is a sign of the abundance to come," Mark said. "I told Diana that we'll all be a village for this new life, that this child will be lavished with all our love."

185

Angela turned to Mark. "But you said it was my turn. I'm the only one who doesn't have a kid."

I wondered about the conversation she'd had with Mark after my talk with her.

"Like I said, Angie, this is a happy surprise."

"But it's not fair." She stood. "How come everybody comes first but me? How come she gets a baby and I don't? It's my turn, not hers, not Liv's."

"The winds of change are blowing, Angela. Be a windmill, not a wall," Mark said calmly.

"She doesn't deserve it. She doesn't even care about the kid she has," Angela shouted.

"This child will belong to all of us," Mark said.

"How could you be so mean?" Angela cried, and grabbed her coat, then flung herself out the door into the night.

"She thinks she can control me," Mark said.

"She's such a child," Diana said.

Mark asked Rudy what he thought.

Rudy bowed his head and kicked at the table leg until Mark told him to stop.

An hour later, after I'd put the boys to bed, Angela came back and apologized for her outburst. Her cheeks were pink with cold and she quoted Kai Huang. "'Want is the root of unhappiness,'" she said. "I need to work on that."

"'Growth comes when we confront our weaknesses,'" Mark said.

They were aphorism vending machines. Drop in a subject and a saying spewed out.

"Good girl, Angie." Mark got up from the couch, where he'd been reading, and hugged her, and she leaned into him. "Don't worry. Things will work out."

After that, she asked how far along Diana was, and when Mark said, "Six or seven weeks," she said, "A May baby. Diana will need minerals and protein. Lots of eggs, beets, kale and tea for the baby's development."

I thought how hard it was going to be to break Mark's spell on her.

Later, Mark came into the container to ask if I was OK. I'd been quiet at the announcement. "Stunned" might be a better word.

"I hope you don't think that this rules out a baby for us, because it doesn't," he said. "We'll figure out a way to add onto the cabin and maybe we can buy another goat and ramp up the cheese business. Or Angie could start making more of her wall hangings to sell to tourists in Valdez. The gift of another child is a reason to celebrate, not to worry."

"Did you forget that someone is trying to kill us?"

"'If we let fear be king, we will always have to bow before it,'" he said. Another Kai Huang quote. "We need to be ready. We need to prepare. But we must also continue to live with pleasure and freedom. Otherwise, what are we doing here?"

"That's what I want to know. What are we doing here? Why did you stay at that job when you knew how dangerous it was?"

"I was careful."

"Not careful enough."

He stared at me for a moment as if deciding whether to challenge me. Then: "Don't worry. I've got things handled."

I shook my head. "I'm not cut out for this."

The chair creaked as Mark shifted. "Do you mean you're not cut out for defending us or for this beautiful life of love that we've created? Because if it's that you're not cut out for this life, then you should leave. Right now. If you somehow think that I can't protect you, that you'd be happier without me, without this life, then be my guest. But Xander stays. I won't let you take him."

My heart pulsed in my ears.

"That's not what I meant."

He cocked his head at me. "Then what did you mean, Liv?"

I could see him waiting to spring his trap, to snare me in the choice: to say I wanted to have his baby or to leave Xander behind. Although he had never said it out loud, I knew he believed he was smarter than me. He'd gone to college. I'd never even graduated from high school.

I reversed course. "I just meant I'm not quite where I need to be yet." I made my voice sound humble and repentant. What I actually thought was: *His ego and confidence are his weaknesses and I will use them to get out of here.*

"I guess I need to work harder. Get over my insecurity," I said.

Mark cracked his neck the way fighters do. A quick snap of the head from side to side. "That's all right. I forgive you. You're still learning. I have to remember that." The sudden shift of his emotions was unsettling. "I'll just have to guide you better. Enlightenment isn't easy but it's always worth it in the end."

He stood.

"I'll try to do better." The words were bitter in my mouth.

"That's my girl," he said.

32.

―――― N O W ――――

A cold-fingered fog gripped the valley, making the world feel hard-edged and threatening. Biting winds cut through the little rust holes in the container walls within which I slept, and I had to keep the stove going to stave off the cold. No assassin arrived. I thought of our house in Sacramento.

By now the bank had probably changed all the locks and let the lawn grow tall and weedy. Mold probably grew in the bathroom and spiders moved in dark corners. I imagined a broken front window, a stale smell filling rooms. My neighbors probably shook their heads whenever they drove by and thought, *What do you expect from such a troubled woman?*

I missed everything about that house.

Angela had to make a trip to town to buy duct tape, in order to repair a frayed electrical wire in the cabin, along with getting some yeast for bread making. While she was there, she stopped to use the computer at Barclay's; she told us later that she'd found Joe Ramirez's obituary, which said that he'd died of a stroke brought on by high blood pressure and that the authorities had closed the case.

Mark said that proved nothing. It was easy to slip something into someone's drink to cause someone to go unconscious, he said.

Our days filled with labor.

We canned vegetables and fish and stored the jars in the cache. We duct-taped the electrical wire and a tiny hole that had opened in the pipe from the spring, and patched the roof where it had begun to leak. Mark was working furiously on his pits, trying to get the holes dug before the ground turned hard—and before Rick or his goons arrived. Even with the news about Joe, Mark was sure he was still being pursued. His paranoia grew and spread, filling him with a nervous kind of energy that put us all on edge. I'd see a light in the cabin in the wee hours of the night and catch him prowling along the perimeter of the clearing at dawn. Dark circles formed under his eyes.

Angela told me Mark had apologized after the night of the pregnancy announcement, promising her the next child after Diana delivered. On a human level, I should have been glad for her happiness. She was, after all, as much a victim in this as I was. She was a wounded soul who had been taken in by Mark's charms and seduced by his attention. However, I knew I needed to sow discord if I wanted to escape, so I said I was surprised by that, since Mark had told me again that he wanted me to get pregnant as soon as possible.

I could see her brain working, trying to resolve the two versions of Mark's promise.

"He's so generous. I'm sure he wants the best for both of us." Her smile was wobbly, though.

Diana was right. Angela was a child.

That night, Mark came into the container. He'd washed his hair and shaved the stubble from his face. He told me he'd been thinking about what I'd said and thanked me for making him aware of how he needed to be a better teacher. I wondered what he was up to.

He dropped into the chair next to the bed and said he realized he needed to make a bigger effort at communication if we wanted to grow. He asked if I remembered the night we'd met, and when I said I did, he told me how beautiful I'd looked. Not like the vapid twigs who filled Hollywood and New York City but like a painting by Gauguin—exotic, strong, free from convention, he said.

"Let's be like that again. Our souls stripped bare."

I didn't think that was what had happened the night we met. The only thing stripped bare was our lust. Still, I nodded.

"I want us to open up to each other. We need to listen if we want to understand," he said. "It's the only way we'll heal."

I thought of his earlier deviousness, how he'd hidden his other life from me. Still, I decided to play along.

"All right, you first," I said. "Tell me why our life in Sacramento made you so unhappy."

A frown creased his forehead. "I wasn't unhappy. I loved you and Xander. I think it was more a question of expanding my mind, of finally seeing the reality of who I was rather than what others told me I was."

His fingers were cracked and swollen from work and he kneaded them for a few seconds before he went on. "I never told you this, but once, when I was fourteen, I overheard my father talk about 'his sissy-pants son' winning a photo contest. I'd taken a shot of a snail climbing the side of an empty water glass, and he says, 'What kind of art is that? Next, he'll be taking pictures of dog turds,' and his friends laughed. I'd been really proud of the photo and he just made me feel stupid and worthless. I started skipping school and smoking dope and got sent to this therapist, who helped me see it was my father's own insecurity that made him mean. My old man would have had a heart attack if he had known what he'd paid for." Mark chuckled. "Anyway, I did a lot of work to get over the hurt he caused and I got out of there, but I think there's still a bit of wounded space inside me, so sometimes I hurt others even though I don't mean to. I've managed to clear my head but I'm sorry I caused you pain."

The lantern hissed on the shelf above us. I didn't know what to say. His confession was the first time I'd heard that he'd doubted himself.

Mark cleared his throat. "Now you tell me something."

"Like what?"

"Like prison, maybe. How did you get through that?"

I could have told him about the constant noise and how you had to try to be invisible in there in order to survive and how much being locked up again had scared me. Instead, I told him I kept myself busy with sewing and attending classes and reading books from the library.

"You're so strong," he said. "I've always loved that about you."

He came and put his arm around my shoulder, squeezing me to him. He was warm and solid, and for a moment I let myself relax against him. I thought touch, of all the senses, was the hardest to live without. Even when I pulled away, I could still feel the heat of him on my skin.

We talked for another hour that night, and over the next four nights we did it again. He didn't talk about Kai Huang or the other women. He didn't tell me how I had to love his new life. We talked about Xander and Africa and Edward Weston, whose photographs he admired. He began to feel like the old Mark.

"You're so amazing and beautiful. You know that?" he said on the fifth night, and leaned over and kissed me.

He pulled back, smiled and touched my cheek.

"Thank you for sharing yourself," he said. "Thank you for opening up."

Which might have been why I didn't stop him a few days later.

I was about two hundred yards from the cabin, limbing a fallen tree for firewood, when he came toward me. The fog had disappeared and the sun warmed the ground, so it smelled like baked bread. He'd been working on one of his pits and his shirt was off and he carried a shovel over his shoulder. He looked handsome, like an actor in a movie.

"I wish I had my camera," he called as he approached, "because I would photograph you in this moment: powerful and free, an ax in your hand. Like Artemis, goddess of the hunt." He drew closer. "Do you know how sexy you look right now?"

"I wouldn't call this sexy." I was sweaty and flecked with dirt and blond chips of wood.

He stopped in front of me and smiled. "This is exactly how I always pictured us. You and me in the wilderness, unchained from society, living free in a paradise, drowning in pleasure."

A squirrel chattered from the trees. He took another step forward, put a hand behind my head and pulled me to him. His lips were soft on mine, his breath warm.

I should have seen the trouble coming. And yet I didn't.

He released me.

"You felt it, didn't you? Do you see how alive you become when passion is unlocked?"

The sunlight turned his eyes turquoise. "I guess," I said.

"I've seen you watching me."

"I just . . . ," I started. I could hardly tell him that was because I wanted to find the car keys and escape.

He took the ax from my hand and set it aside. "I know you've always pushed down your feelings but I can see them emerging. These past few nights, I've seen them break free. I've seen passion building, doors opening. It's time to bathe yourself in pleasure. Drink it in, dance with it. Let yourself go. Just feel."

He kissed me again. This time his lips were more insistent. I felt his arousal through his jeans.

A sliver of worry rose. I pulled back. "I've got to finish this log."

"It can wait," he said, and tugged me toward him again.

His lips were on my neck and then on the lobe of my ear, the places he knew I liked. "Don't close off your feelings," he murmured. "I know they're there. Give in to them. Open the gate to passion."

"Mark, stop. What if Angela or the kids come by?" I said.

"They won't," he whispered, and cupped my behind with his hands.

"I just want to love you. I just want us to be one again," he said, and lifted me up, then tumbled me to the ground. Not in a violent way. More slow motion. Gently.

"Babe," he moaned.

His torso pressed against mine, causing a small rock to poke sharply into my back. His hand found its way to my hips. "Let yourself be free. Let yourself feel," he said, and unzipped my jeans.

My heart raced and I pushed against his shoulders. I couldn't catch my breath.

He must have mistaken panic for arousal—or he didn't care—because he murmured, "That's it, baby," and slid his finger beneath my underwear to touch the spot where he used to make me come.

And here's the thing. When a man with whom you've made love so many times is having sex with you, even if it's not what you want, there's a part of you that wonders if you're the one who has it wrong. That maybe you sent out some kind of signal. Or that you led him on by letting him kiss you.

He shoved down my jeans and underwear. Then he was inside me.

I didn't move. A single cloud floated white in the blue sky. The rock dug sharply into my skin.

I waited for everything to be over.

After he was finished, he helped me to my feet, told me how much he loved me, kissed my cheek and was gone. I went to the river, where I shucked out of my jeans, squatted in the cold water and scrubbed myself until I couldn't feel him anymore.

That night at dinner, he seemed more animated. "All our dreams of freedom are manifesting themselves," he said.

Across the table, Angela looked first at him and then in my direction. I wondered if she'd seen us.

Diana shoveled food into her mouth in the way she always did. "What's going to be manifesting itself is a big fat storm," she said between bites. "The weather box is calling for sixty-mile-an-hour winds, ten inches of rain, mud flows. It's going to be a mother."

The cabin had a square little battery-powered radio that issued forecasts from the National Weather Service.

"There's no storm that can destroy our will," Mark said. He reached over and patted the back of my hand.

I managed to hold it together during dinner and while I read *The Swiss Family Robinson* to the boys after I'd tucked them into bed. I'd found the book under the sofa, where it had been substituted for a broken couch leg, and Rudy had taken to the story with a fierceness that made me wonder if his mother had ever read to him at all.

I begged tiredness afterward and went up to the container and waited in the darkness, my insides vibrating with tension, to see if Mark would arrive. When he didn't, I crawled into bed fully dressed. A few minutes later, I lost it. I began to shake, both from shame and from violation. I threw off the covers and went outside. The moon was a sliver in the sky, the trees dark and foreboding.

Spruce needles poked my bare feet and I welcomed the pain. I stepped to the edge of the garden and looked at the night sky. Tears welled and I began to cry. I felt so alone, so exhausted by the effort it took to tightrope the lies, the threats, the need to escape. What if I never was able to leave?

I don't know what time it was when I finally fell asleep.

I grew bolder after that. I had to.

33.

─── N O W ───

The trees around the bridge trail swallowed Mark, Angela and Xander. The wind was out of the southwest. It blustered through the trees and made the chickens nervous. Angela said animals knew when a storm was coming, which was why they needed to make an emergency drive to Cohut to buy sacks of feed for the hens and some hay for the goats, fill the propane tanks and deliver some goat cheese to the new owner of a nearby hunting lodge before the storm hit. Mark was going in order to help balance the big load on the small truck and drive the rutted track home so the vehicle's springs didn't break. He would stay hidden in the truck while they were in town. He wore a ball cap pulled low over his eyes and a sweatshirt hood tugged over his head. Angela said she'd pick up a set of winter clothes for Xander and a warmer jacket for me at the mobile pantry, which was supposed to be in town the next two days.

Diana had gone hunting. Who knew where Rudy was?

I was the only one who seemed to worry about Rudy. He reminded me of Mowgli in *The Jungle Book*, a wild child who walked the edges of the civilized world. His eyes were always watchful, his face always dirty, his words spare. Often, he disappeared into the forest for hours before he returned with his "treasures": tiny white squirrel skulls or sharp-edged stones that resembled arrowheads, and once a small brown bottle embossed with the words PETE'S LIVER AND KIDNEY TONIC. CINCINNATI, OHIO. Sometimes I'd find him perched high in a spruce tree, silently watching as if he were scouting for trouble or danger. However, he was kind and gentle with animals— and with Xander—and I appreciated how he'd helped Xander with his sometimes uncooperative feet and fingers, telling Xander to try to walk in his footprints, which Xander did, his feet straight and true for those few moments. I wondered why the therapist I'd paid hadn't thought of that and what Rudy's life must have been like with a mother who was so often on the road or living with men who abused him. Perhaps her parents had been right to want to take him away from her.

I waited until everyone was gone and then headed for the cabin. I'd scoured most of the house for my keys and wallet (I'd discovered the gate key on a nail under the sink), but it was hard to find an excuse to be in Mark's room. I closed the cabin door behind me, looked once out the window and hurried in.

I was immediately struck by what I hadn't noticed before: the tangible evidence of Diana and Angela, which was everywhere. The strange skull and horns above the bed and a deer-hide coat hanging from a nail on the wall for Diana. A woven throw tossed across the foot of the bed and a few pairs of earrings scattered on top of the chest of drawers for Angela. It felt a little like the way dogs marked their territory and I wondered if that was what each had done.

I went through the dresser drawers first. Nothing. I searched inside boots and dug through the clothes in the armoire. I looked under the bed and felt above the doorframe in case the Subaru key was there. I turned next to the cardboard boxes. The first was filled with clothes: moth-eaten T-shirts, worn jeans and a faded New Orleans Saints sweatshirt, size XL. The next held blankets, the other towels. The final box was filled with things like candlesticks, a dented kettle, a rusted hunting knife, a drill bow, and an Army canteen.

At the very bottom were a few photos: a serious-looking Alvin with a bunch of guys in dusty combat uniforms; Alvin jogging past colorfully dressed women in Africa somewhere; him as a teenager standing solemnly on the front porch of a run-down farmhouse. I hoped he had found happiness in Thailand with his girlfriend. He was a good man.

I put the photos away, shoved my hair out of my eyes and leaned my head back in exasperation, which is when I saw it: the corner of a wooden box on top of the tall armoire. It was too high for me to reach, so I opened the armoire's doors, put a foot on one of the shelves and reached, praying the whole thing wouldn't fall over and crush me.

I wanted to shout with relief when I opened the box. There were my keys and my wallet with my driver's license, my credit card and Xander's birth certificate, which I'd need if I wanted to cross the border. The phone and the charging cord were in there too. Somebody must have retrieved the cord from my car.

I stood for a moment and just stared at my salvation. "Thank you, universe," I said.

I started to empty the box but thought better of it. If, for some reason, Mark or Angela opened the container tonight and found everything gone, they'd figure out what I was up to pretty fast. In the end, I climbed back up the armoire, shoved the box into the spot where I thought it had been and stepped down. I would retrieve it later when the time was right.

"Hey!" said a voice.

I whirled. "Rudy," I said, and put a hand to my chest, "you scared me."

"You're not supposed to be in here," he said.

I smiled and closed the armoire doors. "It's fine, Rudy."

"No, it's not," he said. "This is my dad's room and we're not supposed to come in unless he says we can. That means you too."

His pale eyes bored into me.

"Why are you in here anyway?" he said. "Dad ain't even home."

I thought fast. "I was looking for a heavier jacket to borrow. It's getting cold again."

His face held something I couldn't read. "I seen you in here before," he said. "You was looking in the drawers. If I tell my dad you was looking through his stuff again, he won't like it."

He was right. Mark wouldn't like it.

"I wasn't doing anything wrong. I just need a jacket," I told him.

He scowled and crossed his arms over his thin chest. "I think you was doing something," he said.

Desperation rose and I said, "You know, Rudy, if you tell your dad and he gets mad, I won't be able to read *The Swiss Family Robinson* to you anymore and then what will you do? You can't read, can you?"

I regretted the words as soon as they were out of my mouth. He was just a boy.

He looked like he'd been slapped.

Before I could apologize, however, he turned and slipped away as quietly as he'd arrived. The click of the front door latch was the only notice of his leaving.

I tried to tell myself the threat was necessary, and yet my cruelty had come so easily it made me feel ill. Was meanness in my DNA after all, having come down the line on my mother's side? The family story had it that after a neighbor had called my great-granny poor white trash, she'd taken a pair of shears to their clothesline, leaving ribbons of cloth writhing in the breeze like snakes.

Was I just like them?

The image of my mother lying dead on the barn floor flashed again and yet this time it was different. Instead of freezing to a single frame as it usually did, the scene played on: my mother's hand twitching against the concrete barn floor, my dad's voice faint in my ears. The room spun for a moment. Had my mother been alive when I helped my father bury her? Were her last moments spent trying to claw her way out of a mountain of waste?

The image faded, and even though I tried to get it back, it wouldn't come. I know people say they're haunted by their memories but I think not remembering is worse. If you don't know what you did, how can you feel remorse or forgive yourself or absolve those who hurt you?

It seemed strange that the new memory had surfaced at that moment and I wondered whether the boy had sparked it or if it was somehow related to what had happened in the forest with Mark, the shame I felt.

A gust of wind rattled the cabin roof and I hurried outside to tell Rudy I was sorry.

He was nowhere in sight.

I went back to the woodpile and began splitting logs for the woodstove and hauling them into the cabin in advance of the weather that was coming. The sky had turned leaden and angry-looking and I tried not to think about what I'd done and instead began to plan my escape.

Mark and Angela came back just ahead of the storm. They lugged two full propane tanks and sacks of grain, and Xander wore a secondhand orange jacket and a pair of blue snow pants. He also carried a plastic pirate sword and swiped it across the air to show me its power, and he said he was going to use it to "kill bad guys." Mark and Angela looked grim. On the drive back, the radio had announced warnings from the National Weather Service. The storm had intensified and turned our way. Wind gusts of a hundred miles per hour were expected over the mountain peaks and flash flooding was possible. Already, the wind had picked up, causing the spruce to sway like angry hula dancers.

The tempest unleashed its fury an hour later.

Angela was rushing to secure the chickens and goats and Mark was bringing in more armloads of firewood when Xander looked up from the little battery-powered radio that served as our chief contact with the outside world.

"Hey, where's Rudy? This is his favorite song."

The rain drummed against the front window.

"Didn't he go with you?" Mark asked Diana.

She'd just come back from a hunt and was standing near the stove, drinking a cup of Angela's tea.

"I needed to cover a lot of ground," Diana answered, as if that were enough explanation. She glanced out the window. "He knows he's supposed to get back before dark."

"That's only an hour away," I said. I felt sick at the thought that I was the reason Rudy was out there. "What if he's lost or he hurt himself?"

"He'll be fine," Diana said. "He's been through storms before."

"Christ, Diana. He's a ten-year-old kid and this isn't just a storm," Mark said.

His voice was hard and a smile flitted across Angela's lips at Mark's anger toward Diana.

Mark went to the hooks by the door and shrugged back into his jacket. "Do you have any idea where he might be?"

"He's not lost. He's got Shadow," Diana said.

It was the first time I'd noticed Shadow was gone too.

"It doesn't matter if he has the dog," Mark snapped. "He's out there and I'm going to look for him. Christ."

"I've seen him go up by the spring," Angela said. "There's a little cave there. Maybe he holed up when the rain started."

Mark grabbed the rifle and a headlamp and opened the door. The rain slanted sideways, thrumming against the cabin walls.

"Try the river too. Under that big log," Angela called after him.

"I can't believe this," he said, and slammed the door behind himself.

Outside, the light was fading.

I turned to Xander. "Where does Rudy like to go, Xan?"

He looked up. "He likes to be with the goats."

"Where else?" I asked.

Xander shrugged. "Maybe the river. Maybe Flamiko March."

It took me a moment to realize what he meant. Flamingo Marsh was the name the Swiss Family Robinson had given to a boggy spot where they cut their arrows.

"The meadow," I said, and threw on the wool jacket Angela had brought for me from the charity shop. "I'm going to look for Rudy," I told her. "I think I know where he might be."

"He'll be fine," Diana said.

I almost didn't find Rudy. I was slogging my way around the perimeter of the meadow, the hiking boots I wore sinking into the dark mud and the rain stinging my face when I caught a flash of white just where the grass met the edge of the forest.

"Rudy?" I yelled.

On the way here, I'd tripped over a fallen log and landed on one knee, the jolt sending a stab of pain up my leg and into my brain. Part of me wondered how badly I was bruised and another part said that I deserved whatever I got for hurting a child. I limped forward.

The glimpse of white turned out to be Shadow, who bounded into the grass before turning around and running back into the woods. As I got closer I could see a crude A-frame shelter a few yards into the forest. It was small, made of spruce branches and bark piled over a brown tarp. I squatted in front of the opening and peered into the dim interior.

"There you are," I said.

A small fire flickered weakly in a grotto made of flat stones, the smoke filtering out through an opening in the back wall. Rudy sat cross-legged on the packed dirt in front of it. He was wet and trying not to shiver. "Go away," he said.

He'd made a small bed out of spruce and cedar branches and constructed a shelf crowded with a half-burned candle, a dented pot, a cigar box and a mug I recognized as having come from the cabin, along with a row of his treasures: small stones and feathers and the old tonic bottle. The hunting knife he always wore hung in a sheath from the peak of the shelter.

I told him that everybody was looking for him, and he shook his head as if he recognized the lie. I asked if I could join him and he said, "No." I squatted in front of the tiny hut and told him that I was sorry for what I'd said and that he was right that I shouldn't have been in the room. I said if he came back to the cabin, I would read ten pages of *The Swiss Family Robinson* to him, twice what I normally did, and also help him learn to read if he wanted. Shadow came and looked over my shoulder. The rain drove itself against my back.

A shiver rumbled through Rudy and he turned to me. "But what was you doing in there?"

I started to lie but stopped myself. There was something in his eyes. Something that said he'd been lied to too many times. He was an innocent. A kid with a mother who wasn't mean like mine had been, just indifferent. I wasn't sure which was worse.

"I was looking for something I lost," I said finally.

He stared at me. "Car keys?"

I couldn't help the exhalation of breath that escaped me. "Rudy, you can't tell," I began.

"Don't worry," he said. "You ain't the only one who don't want to be here."

34.

—— N O W ——

We emerged from the cabin the next day to see the destruction that Mother Nature had wrought. Trees lay crisscrossed on the ground, a half dozen windows in the greenhouse had been shattered, there was a hole in the aluminum boat from where it had been blown against a sharp boulder and, worst of all, a good-sized aspen had smashed through the roof of the cache.

Mark swore as we stared at the soup of fish, flour, peanut butter, jam, rice and broken glass on the muddy ground. The only things left undamaged were a single jar of blueberry jam and a twenty-five-pound sack of beans that had been set in a corner on an upturned bucket. Mark tried to sound upbeat, reminding us of the vegetables we'd stored in our little root cellar. What was left unsaid, however, was that they weren't enough to sustain six people for an entire winter.

"We'll just have to get to work," Diana said. "We'll hunt and fish and beg if we have to."

I thought, *Xander and I won't be here, so it won't matter.*

Rudy wandered into the mess, picked up a broken jar of peanut butter and scooped a finger full of it into his mouth.

"Oh my God, what's wrong with you?" Angela said, and slapped his hand away from his lips.

His eyes widened at the sudden pain but he didn't say anything. He dropped the jar, turned and scurried off, disappearing into the forest.

Angela watched him run and looked at us. "He's like a rat, always sneaking around, always eating," she complained. She had no patience with him.

"Don't you touch my son again," Diana said.

"As if you care about him," Angela snapped.

"Just stop it," Mark said. "We've got work to do."

That afternoon, I snuck a change of clothes and a sweatshirt for Xander out of the cabin under my jacket. I stuffed them into my duffel and added a few of my clothes and a wool blanket, along with the food I'd gathered. I shoved it under my bed. There was no moon that night, so I had to risk the lantern when I crept out of the container and headed for the bridge. I intended to hide the duffel tonight, and tomorrow I would wait until everyone was occupied, grab the wooden box with the keys from Mark's room and sneak away with Xander.

Trees dropped their stores of raindrops on my shoulders and twigs snapped under my feet as I moved. I hurried forward, hoping the roads wouldn't be too muddy when I left and praying I could find the route back to town. Finally, I arrived at the river. What I saw stopped me like a punch to the gut.

A large cedar had fallen in the storm, knocking over one of the bridge's anchoring posts. The cable holding the span sagged, causing the walkway to twist drunkenly over the river.

I dropped my head into my hands and tried to breathe away my despair, but it was no use.

35.

─── N O W ───

I followed Diana to the river, my footsteps sounding like little fire-crackers going off against the quiet padding of her feet. She carried a pack, a fishing rod, her bow and a quiver of arrows. She was going to teach me to fish, and while I fished, she would hunt for game as a way to replenish our food stores. I thought of the bridge and then of the Robinson family, who'd been trapped in a cave on the island for three days by a fearsome thirty-foot boa constrictor. I felt the same way.

Mark was trying to repair the footbridge, although, he said, with-out a winch, doing so would be close to impossible. Angela, mean-while, had taken on more chores, including winterizing the coop, so the chickens wouldn't get their usual break from laying, which might have seemed heartless to anyone who wasn't facing the prospect of running out of food.

According to Mark, the only way to get from the farm to town without the bridge was a five-mile trek to a place where Tenmile River ran wide and shallow, so you could carry supplies across it.

Then you'd have to hike four miles back to the vehicles. In the winter, when the river froze, however, there was a spot you could cross that was a mile and a half away with a mile or so trek to the car. Xander seemed to be stronger—maybe it was from all the fresh air or simply from his spending so much time playing with Rudy—but sometimes his breathing got bad or his little heart would flutter like a bird in a cage and he would have to lie down until he felt better. Which meant there was no way he could walk nine miles and I would have to carry him part of the way, which I couldn't do for very long. Not if you added the supplies and clothes I'd have to bring along. Even if the river froze, a two-and-a-half-mile hike through a thick forest and brush might still be too hard.

Diana's voice interrupted my thoughts.

"If you're going to stay here, at least learn to walk without sounding like King Kong. Any game within a half mile is already gone."

I focused on the word "if." Had Rudy mentioned my search for the keys?

"I'll try to be more quiet," I told her.

We came to the fishing spot, which was about twenty-five yards downriver from the small beach where I'd cut willows for Angela. Diana said that even though it was late season, the river was still good for graylings and possibly rainbow trout. I was to catch as many fish as I could and Angela would can them. We had two dozen quart-sized Mason jars left. Even I could see, however, that that amount wouldn't be enough and that for all Mark's talk of being tough and living with what the land gave us, we were in trouble.

"You won't be a good fly-fisher but I can teach you enough to get you serviceable," she said, and set about the lesson: the choosing of the fly based on what insects were about, the four-count rhythm, the mending of the line, the light flick to set the hook. Diana caught a twelve-inch grayling, a blue-gray fish with a sail-like fin, within a few minutes. The fish felt slippery and unsettling in my hands and I tried not to let my squeamishness show as she had me knock it over the head with a rock, run a line through its gill and stake it in the stream. Diana said graylings weren't picky eaters, so that was in my favor.

"You've got a nice lay down, a good feel for the drift," she said after she watched me for a while, and I felt inordinately proud.

She studied the sky.

"Conditions should be OK for a couple of hours. Then head back." She crouched near her pack. "Tell the others I'll be back before dark."

She was hoping to get a moose, although, she said, she hadn't seen sign of them around—or maybe she'd find a deer if she was lucky. She had what was called a subsistence permit. I didn't know what that was.

The river rushed over boulders and eddied in calm pools. Diana dug into her pack and retrieved a metal water bottle and set it on a flat rock. "First rule, never go anywhere without water," she said. "Second rule, always carry one of these."

She stood and tossed me a small black canister, which I fumbled and dropped. I retrieved it from the ground.

"What's this?"

"Bear spray. The directions are on the canister. Hook it to your jeans."

A ripple of worry ran through me. "Is it safe?"

"Unless you spray it into the wind. Then it'll come back and hit you instead of the bear."

My neck prickled at the thought of coming face-to-face with the grizzly that roamed the area. I'd glimpsed him early one morning on my way to the outhouse. He had come out of the woods near the spring line; he had a massive head with strips of shaggy fur that hung from his haunches. He looked unkempt and dangerous. I'd held my breath until the bear disappeared into the willows.

Diana hefted her pack and quiver of arrows onto her shoulders, picked up her bow and started to leave.

"Can I ask you a question?" I said.

She stopped and turned her head.

"Why did you want Mark to keep Rudy a secret from me?"

A raven croaked from somewhere high in a tree. Diana looked across the river and then back at me.

"I didn't," she said.

I carried her answer with me over the next days as Mark urged us on with hunting and fishing and pit digging. It was like I'd swallowed a dark stone that sat heavily inside. What else was he still lying about? The days grew shorter and I noticed the small reductions in our meals: the tinier portions of meat in the soups, the slightly shrunken loaves of bread, the rabbit stews that were mostly potatoes and carrots. I thought of the Donner Party, who had pushed on despite every sign of bad things to come and eventually destroyed themselves.

At night, Mark pored over his books: *Mind, Self, Love* and others about survival and the dangers of big government. There was no more poetry. He began to lecture us about how our troubles were nothing against what was happening in the world and that we needed to harden ourselves against the temptation to give up.

"Our society is so afraid of letting people have their own power, of letting us find our passion and reject the chains of capitalism, that they try to take away every pleasure we have. Think of Prohibition; think of the war on drugs. If we'd made drugs legal, the government wouldn't have done the corporations' bidding and sent gang members back to El Salvador and guns to Nicaragua and labeled Mexico a dangerous place so we could exploit people with low-wage jobs that allowed companies to get rich. I didn't understand it before but I see it now. I was a slave to greed. Once we sever ourselves from this sick society, however, and become our own saviors, we will have abundance."

Xander piped up, "I want to do a bun dance, Daddy," and Mark laughed.

"We will, Xan. I promise," he said.

I had a hard time following his lines of thought. They seemed to lead only to the places he wanted them to go. Angela, however, parroted what he said. "Abundance will come to us," she repeated over and over.

Diana, meanwhile, began to range farther in search of game. We celebrated when she came home with a beaver she'd shot. The meat was full of fat and therefore even better for us than the leaner meat of rabbits, which we'd been relying on. Once, she came home with a porcupine, although we had to throw the meat away because its liver turned out to be spotted with disease. The long days exhausted her, however, and she often fell asleep right after dinner. Her eyes looked sunken and her skin pale. Angela fussed over her and said pregnant women needed more vitamins and minerals; she pressed Diana to eat more kale and drink herbal tea.

Angela, for her part, seemed to grow even more needy. As Mark sat on the couch, she would stretch like a cat in front of him, lifting her arms so the smooth white skin of her belly showed or bending into yoga-like poses so her behind pressed like a peach against the fabric of her skirt. She'd run a hand across his chest and make suggestive remarks. Most of the time, he ignored her.

"Baby, what's wrong?" she would ask, and Mark would say that he was tired or that it wasn't her day and, once, that she needed to stop acting like a "cheap stripper."

She came up to me after that and asked if I knew what was going on with Mark and if I was sleeping with him.

"I thought maybe you guys hooked up and all his energy was going to that." Her eyes were filled with hurt. "How can I have a baby if he won't touch me?"

I lied and told her we hadn't had sex and kept quiet about the fact that Mark had been coming into the container and that I'd been making up excuses to keep him away from me: a headache, a pulled muscle in my back or heavy bleeding, although the truth was that, while I'd had two light periods here, my menses were now MIA.

Each time, I could see irritation flash across Mark's face, which was then replaced by a kind of forced patience. As if he was trying hard to be the enlightened person Kai Huang urged his followers to be but couldn't quite do it.

"If you don't let pleasure in, your body gets out of balance. That's why you're sick," he said after I complained about a scratchy throat.

I mumbled something about needing sleep instead and he left. Angela brought me cups of turmeric-laced tea and put a warm poultice on my throat. Three nights later, he was back.

"Angela says you're better."

"I guess I am."

He sat on the edge of the bed and studied me. "What's wrong? You don't seem happy to see me." His tone was playful. His eyes weren't.

"Of course I'm glad to see you." I was sitting cross-legged on the bed. There was a fire in the stove.

He ran a hand up my thigh. I tried not to flinch. "What is it, then?"

Something scraped against the container and I decided it was the wind.

"It's just that I can't help thinking about Angela and how much she wants a child." I'd come up with this idea a few nights ago.

"And?" His hand stopped.

"And Kai Huang says all our needs are supposed to be equal and I feel like, well, maybe she's being left out."

Mark's eyes narrowed.

I hurried on before he could speak. "It's just that she said you guys missed her fertile day, that you were up here helping me with the stove and then you went back and fell asleep and you're spending so much time with me and not her. It's making her unhappy, and you know what Kai Huang says about standing in the way of others' happiness."

"Don't be the dam on other people's rivers of joy," Mark mumbled.

"Exactly. I know it's not the time to have three babies."

He started to open his mouth and I held up my hand.

"We need to add on to the cabin and fix the bridge so we can get supplies, and with three babies, we're not going to be able to keep up with the planting and the animals."

I could tell the same thoughts had already crossed his mind.

"I can't be happy if Angela's not, so I think you and I should wait. Let Angela get pregnant first. I know that means abstinence for us, since I don't have any birth control here, but I can't feel pleasure at her expense."

Mark studied me. I laced my fingers together in my lap so I didn't fidget and give away my nerves.

He swore under his breath. Something about stubborn women. But I think it was because he knew I'd worked him into a philosophical corner: Deny my arguments and he was denying his precious book. He stomped out of the container into the night. The next afternoon, he took the sled, a duffel and the rifle and headed off on the long hike to the car and town. He said that he was the only one who could manage the trek now that Diana was pregnant, and that he'd be careful and get in and out of town as fast as he could.

"We also need grain. If the chickens starve, then so do we," he said.

That night, when I came into the container for bed, I found a single owl feather laid out on my pillow. In Kai Huang's stories, the owl was a bad omen.

The feather felt like a threat and I thought maybe that was why Mark had left it there. Quickly, I opened the container door and buried it under a few inches of dirt and leaves.

36.

———— N O W ————

I took my rod and stepped into the cold river. I wore jeans, my wool jacket and Diana's hip waders. Mark had been gone for two days, and this morning Diana found blood in her underwear. Angela said that spotting was normal during the first trimester of pregnancy and that rest was her best option. Diana said rest was no option when starvation was hard on our heels and insisted on going out to hunt. I said I would fish.

The breeze hushed through the trees and water tumbled over and around the boulders in the river. I walked downstream to a deep spot near an overhanging rock where I'd had success before, although Diana had said the water was almost too cold to fish anymore. I chose a fly I thought would work and cast my line over the slow-moving water; then I watched the drift. Nothing. I cast again and again. It was like meditation.

Somewhere nearby, a hermit thrush sang its "oh holy holy ah" refrain. The sun slanted rays through the spruce branches as if Mother Nature were posing for a calendar photo. Twenty minutes later, I caught a nice grayling. I thought how it would make a good soup and said a silent thank-you, clubbed it over the head, strung it on a line and staked it in the water.

I still wondered why Mark had chosen to keep Rudy hidden from me. He would have known that I wouldn't have objected to his having had a child before he met me or to his sending money to the boy when he could. I think it was more his need to control his narrative, to write our lives the way he wanted them to be. When I looked back, I realized that all our big decisions had been made by him and that I had always played the role of a good wife by going along with whatever he said. I was so worried I'd lose him.

Maybe that Kai Huang guy had been right about needing to free yourself from the thing that's most precious to you.

A raven flapped overhead and I moved a few yards downriver to a spot that felt promising. I'm not sure how much later it was—I'd caught another grayling and staked it with the other—when I saw movement on the opposite bank. I squinted into the trees and saw a flash of brown just before everything fell silent. A moment later, the grizzly came out of the brush above a rock face that sloped into the water. He was huge, filled with a menacing power that seeped from strong muscle and thick bone. My heart thumped and I stilled, hoping he wouldn't notice me. He stopped, sniffed the air and then started down the rocky slope to the river as easily as if he were stepping off a front porch. We were about fifty yards apart—a distance, according to Diana, a brown bear could cover in a few seconds. I took a step backward.

I reached for the bear spray I usually had on my belt, but remembered too late that I'd left it behind when I grabbed my fishing gear from the container. I could picture it sitting on the floor where I'd set it down to sort through the fly box. I cursed my stupidity and continued to move backward slowly, keeping my eye on the bear.

Fear fluttered like a small bird in my chest.

The bear waded into the water.

I thought of the graylings I'd caught and the fact that I probably reeked of fish, and I quelled the urge to run—Diana had said that running was the worst thing you could do with a bear. I set down my pole and again backed up slowly, trying not to trip or move too fast, one foot behind the other.

The grizzly's eyes were dark, like death.

I knew the bear's path and mine would intersect if I tried to get to the willow trail to the cabin, so I edged backward down the narrow beach, feeling for obstacles with my feet and hoping I didn't fall. There was a sharp bend in the river ten or twelve yards downstream and I thought if I could just get around it, I might be OK.

The bear was halfway across the river, swimming now. His gaze seemed to laser in on me.

I knew it was my imagination but it seemed like he was taking my measure. How easy would I be to kill? Would doing so be worth the effort?

I readied myself as I moved backward, keeping my eyes on the animal.

Water dripped from his fur as he came out of the stream. He sniffed the pole I'd left behind.

Take the fish, I urged silently. *Forget about me.*

I stepped backward. This time, however, my foot disturbed a smooth, melon-sized rock, causing a loud clack. I hissed in a breath.

The bear's head rose.

I stopped dead. A chill ran down my spine.

There was a moment when it seemed as if the world had narrowed to only this moment, this place.

"Please," I whispered. I wasn't sure whom I was talking to. God? The universe? The bear?

I waited. So did the bear.

Finally, his head dipped and he padded toward the fish I'd staked in the stream.

I turned and began to walk toward the bend in the river, moving quickly but not running, looking over my shoulder every few seconds. One of the fish was in the bear's mouth and he was pawing at the stake as he tore it from the line.

The bend was six feet away, then four, then two. I rounded it and scrambled over the broken rocks and driftwood logs scattered along the shore. A few yards farther, a huge slab of dark stone dropped steeply into the water and blocked my way. I climbed up the embankment into the woods instead.

I sensed a presence behind me and the hairs on my neck prickled. Panic took over now and I began to run. Twigs cracked under the waders that covered my feet and branches tore at my hair.

The ground rose upward and I clambered over trees that had fallen in the storm; then I detoured around a stream gully and headed in the direction I thought was home. I heard a branch snap behind me and stumbled forward through stabbing branches and whipping brush. The ground rose more steeply now. My foot slipped and I felt the sharp tug of a ligament in the knee I'd hurt before. Sweat dripped into my eyes. Finally, I had to stop.

There was nothing except my breath and a thick silence that filled my ears. I looked up. And realized I was lost.

I turned in a slow circle, seeing nothing but slanting hillside and dark forest, and I cursed myself for forgetting the bear spray and for running off like a crazy woman. I searched for a glimpse of something familiar: the peak that looked like a Shriner's hat, the meadow. There was nothing but choking brush and trees. I wished for a machete, then thought that if I was making wishes, I should wish for something better: a helicopter to haul me out of there; a hunter with an ATV who would drive me to the cabin and then maybe help Xander and me escape. My throat was dry. A blister was forming on my heel.

I thought of the stories of people who'd set off on a day hike in places like the Grand Canyon or Glacier National Park and hadn't come back, and of the ranger in Arizona who, after heading out on a trail in the park where he worked, had never been seen again. I thought of Xander growing up without me. In this place.

I shoved back the sob that rose from my chest. I would not cry. Crying helped exactly nothing.

Moss wrapped the tree trunks in cloaks of green. The dirt was rich and fertile-looking, fed by death. Everything—animals and plants—dying and decomposing over the ages so that others could live. The more time I spent in the wilderness, the more I saw that life required death. Was that how I would end up: food for mushrooms, for scarlet paintbrush?

I took deep lungsful of air. Somewhere above me a woodpecker hammered out a staccato beat. I looked up and found him three-quarters of the way up a lightning-struck spruce; he was a handsome brown bird with a black collar. His insistent knocks felt like some kind of message, nature's Morse code. *Even a small bird has power,* it seemed to say.

I watched his pecking and told myself not to give up, to toughen my resolve just the way he was doing against that hard tower of wood. I heaved another breath and stumbled forward up the forested hillside; the waders were damp with my sweat. Finally, the woods seemed to open and I felt a slight breeze. Ahead of me, at the very top of the hill, was a clearing with a huge, thick-trunked spruce in the middle of it and there, nailed high on the tree's side, was a faded orange-and-black metal sign. The first indication of civilization. I hurried toward it.

ATTENTION, it read. TO WILLFULLY DESTROY, DEFACE, CHANGE OR RE-MOVE ANY GOVERNMENT SURVEY CORNER OR MONUMENT OR TO WILL-FULLY CUT DOWN THIS WITNESS TREE MARKING THE LINE OF A GOVERNMENT SURVEY IS PUNISHABLE BY A FINE OF $250.00 OR SIX MONTHS' IMPRISONMENT OR BOTH.

The threat and capitalizations seemed oddly old-fashioned and yet welcome, because apparently they had deterred anyone from messing around with what was going to save my life. For there, in the right corner of the sign, the date "7/21/72" had been scratched and, on the left side, the single word "south."

Relief bubbled up inside me. Alvin's land was laid out like a tilted rectangle with its shortest side abutting national park land. I'd studied the parcel before I set out for Alaska, and knew all I had to do was walk north and I would find the cabin.

The tree might have borne witness to winds and time and boundaries but it was now a witness to my survival.

I leaned my forehead against its rough bark.

A breeze rustled the spruce and I straightened. Something bright was in the branches. I stepped closer, my tired legs stumbling over the uneven ground, my knee reminding me again of the twist I'd given it. Hanging from a branch was a Saint Christopher medal on a tarnished silver chain. Beyond it was a fire ring made out of blackened stones with a larger rock set nearby on which someone could sit to warm themselves.

I wondered why the medal was in the tree and who had left it. Some wanderer like the guy who had died in that old school bus up north? A hunter who'd camped here and forgotten it? The fire ring looked old. I didn't spend too much time thinking about it. I hurried north, past the circle of stones, and came to the edge of a steep hillside. Below me in the distance was the cabin. A thin ribbon of gray smoke curled from the chimney and dissipated quickly in the wind. Laundry flapped on the line. I looked toward the river and realized I'd run in a great sweeping circle and that if, instead of climbing, I'd stayed along flatter ground, I would have arrived at the cabin.

A faint zigzag trail led down the hillside to my left and I followed it until it joined another trail that then branched into a larger track that I realized ran from the meadow to the cabin. I hurried in that direction.

I wasn't going to tell anyone about what had happened. However, Diana found my gear by the water when she came back from her hunt, and when I explained the reason at dinner that night, she said, "You may have been lucky but you were still a fool."

Angela said, "That's not nice, Diana."

"Neither is dying," Diana snapped, and stood. "I'm going to bed."

The next day I found a small tarnished brass compass in my jacket pocket. I wondered if that was her way of apologizing.

37.

—— N O W ——

It was strange that I'd never noticed the Witness Tree until it saved me. Now, however, I couldn't help but see it every time I was outside. Its crown towered above the trees around it, reminding me of the Saint Christopher medal in its branches. Finding it felt like an omen somehow.

According to the legend, a child came to the saint and asked to be carried across a rough river. The big and muscular Christopher agreed, but as he crossed the waterway, the child grew heavier and heavier until Christopher began to sink beneath the water and nearly drowned. The child turned out to be Christ himself and he was burdened with the weight of the world.

What if, like Christopher, I believed too much in my own strength and will? What if I tried to cross the frozen river with Xander and we fell through the ice and drowned?

I told myself Saint Christopher's story was basically a holy fairy tale but doing so didn't help. I felt a weird sense of dread whenever I looked at the tree.

Mark had been gone four days on the trip to town and we were all waiting for him to come back with supplies. Angela fretted that he'd been gone too long, and she asked Diana to go look for him. Diana told her Mark was a grown man and he would be fine. The next morning he walked into the clearing. A huge duffel hung from his shoulders. Behind him was our log sled heaped with supplies from town. The lines around his mouth seemed deeper. His lips were chapped raw from the cold. He'd brought forty pounds of flour, a twenty-pound sack of rice, five pounds of coffee, a forty-pound sack of chicken feed, a freshly filled propane tank and two cases of Red Bull.

"Really?" Diana said when she saw the drink. "You know how expensive that crap is."

He dropped the sled rope, shrugged the duffel off his shoulders and bent over, his hands on his knees. "You want to do the hike the next time? Be my guest," he said between huffing breaths. "I wouldn't have made it without that."

She stared at him, refusing his challenge.

"How much money do we have left?" Angela asked as we unloaded the food into the cabin and put the chicken feed in a metal drum near the coop.

"Enough," he answered.

The way he answered, however, made me think he was either lying or hiding something.

"When the river freezes, you'll need to go to Valdez and apply for welfare," he told Angela. "Tell them that you're single and that you live by yourself." Mark looked away. "It's just to get us through the winter," he said.

I knew how much it must have bothered him to have to rely on a government he despised when his goal was to be self-sufficient and live off the land. I'm sure he saw it as a defeat.

Angela came to me later and said Mark had hurt her feelings when he picked her to apply for welfare as a single, unmarried woman when Diana was unmarried too and could have gotten more money because she had a child and was pregnant. "If I were a mother, he wouldn't make me go against what we believe," she said.

I told her I was sure Mark asked it of her because he trusted her most and not because he loved her less than Diana.

Her eyes filled. "You're the only one who has my back, who insisted Mark try to give me a baby. You're the sister I've always wanted." She took my hand. "Whatever you need, you just ask me, OK?"

I thought that when the time was right, I might.

In my mind, however, life was a race between winter and Angela's womb. I needed the river to freeze before we found out whether she was pregnant. Pregnant meant I could no longer stave off Mark's attention. Not pregnant meant I might be able to stall for one more month but that was it.

I knew I needed to get stronger.

I hefted log rounds and carried them out of the woods instead of pulling them on the sled. I scrambled uphill to check on the spring instead of walking. I did surreptitious squats and push-ups at night. I gobbled whatever protein Diana managed to snare—rabbits mostly but also squirrels—and snuck more strips of venison jerky up to the container to have when Xander and I made our escape.

And yet I could not stop what happened next.

Mark had finished his spike pits, only to realize the focus on our defenses meant we'd neglected our firewood. He said we'd need a minimum of five cords to get through winter and we had only two at most. He was going to build a lean-to with wood from the damaged cache in hopes of helping the green wood dry enough to burn, and decided we would devote four full days to chopping wood.

Angela and Diana took the ax and crosscut saw while I heated water for laundry and worked with Xander on his occupational therapy drills: picking up small pebbles I scattered on the floor, stacking six wooden blocks Mark had carved out of spruce for him and sorting the laundry into whites and colors for washing.

His little face frowned in concentration but already I could see the improvement in his coordination. I wondered if I had worked less and spent more time with him in Sacramento, he might have been further along.

"Good sorting," I said of the laundry piles he'd made, although a light blue washcloth and one black sock had ended up with the whites.

"Now let's throw everything up in the air," he said.

"Let's throw them into the wash water instead," I told him, and got up from the floor, a wave of nausea running through me. I'd felt slightly sick all morning and told myself it was too much exercise and not the thing I'd begun to worry about.

Three hours later, as Xander and I hung the wash on the line, we heard Angela's shouts.

According to what Angela told us afterward, she'd been chopping down a thirty-footer while Diana used the saw to limb a nice half-dead spruce that might have yielded drier wood, when something went wrong. Angela said she yelled, "Timber." Diana said she didn't hear anything and Angela said she watched in horror as the branches of the falling tree snagged a nearby spruce. The deflection was enough to bounce the tree to the left, toward Diana. Angela screamed. Diana looked up, saw the tree headed for her and leaped aside. The tree slammed into the ground, the trunk missing Diana by less than two feet. The tree's lower branches, however, knocked her flat.

Angela pulled the stunned and bleeding Diana from the tangle of needles and limbs. Diana was alive, although one of the tree's branches had sliced her arm so badly, Angela could see bone. Angela ripped off a piece of her skirt and bound the wound tightly; then she loaded Diana onto the sled.

Mark heard her cries and carried Diana into the cabin. Xander ran and hid in the back room at the sight of all the blood and I went after him. Rudy disappeared.

I heated water and Angela cleaned the wound with it and stitched the cut closed. The injury, however, left the fingers on Diana's right hand numb. Angela said she was sure Diana would get her feeling back. Still, it was a huge blow for us. Diana could no longer pull a bowstring or set her snares and Mark was a terrible shot.

Mark said it was Angela's fault. Diana said, however, that it had been an accident.

"We were in too much of a hurry," she said.

"You could have been killed," Mark said, and looked sternly at Angela.

Two days later, Diana lost the baby.

First came the cramping, then the rush of blood, which stained the sheets and soaked into the mattress on which Diana lay in Mark's bedroom. Curled in the dark room like an injured animal, she refused food and told Mark to leave her the hell alone.

He came into the living room, his face set and hard. We were using lanterns since we'd diverted the power from the solar panel to light the coop and make the chickens believe it was summer so they would keep laying. The lanterns gave off harsh white light.

Angela looked up from the couch, where she was darning socks, and told Mark that Diana would feel better in a week or so and not to worry. According to her, a midwife she'd befriended had said miscarriages were nature's way of taking care of a problem fetus. A vein in Mark's temple pulsed but I didn't think Angela noticed because she went on about how the female body had an intrinsic knowledge that any weakness would undermine the strength of a tribe and thus rejected what was fragile or damaged. It was an ancient understanding, she said. Survival of the fittest.

"Just shut the hell up," Mark told her.

He grabbed his coat and the rifle and slammed out the door into the bone-aching cold. I knew he thought the same thing I did: Angela was inferring that maybe nature had erred with Xander's birth and that his weakness might endanger us. The kettle of water on the stove whistled and I got up to start the dishes. Angela trailed me, wringing her hands and explaining that she'd only wanted to make us not feel so bad about the loss of the baby.

"Besides, there's another child destined for us," she said.

I stilled, my hand on the kettle. Did she know my period hadn't come? Did she suspect what I was refusing to acknowledge?

She went on. "Even before Diana lost the baby, I felt my fertility rising, a new heat in my womb. I think my body is recognizing a new power. That happens, you know. In times of crisis, if the alpha female in a wolf pack can't breed, a lower wolf steps in. Then she becomes the alpha. She rises to the top and the other wolves will hunt to feed her."

"We're not wolves," I said.

"I know you think I'm crazy but that's Mother Nature's way," Angela said. "Survival of the species. That's what drives her. Even when she seems cruel. A mother bear, for instance, will eat her new-born if she can't feed it or it's deformed. Some plants have to be de-stroyed by fire in order to propagate. Destruction becomes necessary for creation."

"Be quiet," I snapped.

"It's true, Liv."

"Maybe it is, but I don't want to hear about it." I got out the dish-pan and dumped the hot water into it, then added cold water from the pipe.

Angela wrapped her arm around my shoulders. "I'm sorry. I didn't mean anything by what I said. Xander is a beautiful spirit, a special little boy, and we all love him. I was just trying to give us a little bit of hope in these dark times."

She kissed me on the cheek. Then: "You'll see. Everything will be fine."

38.

—— N O W ——

I headed out on the snare line, bundled in thermals, jeans and my wool jacket. A dusting of new snow lay on the ground and my nostrils were pinched with cold. Diana had recovered from the miscarriage but her injury kept her from hunting. With fishing no longer an option, she had taken me into the woods, taught me how to set a snare and walked me through her line. I carried a burlap sack for what was dead and one of her hunting knives for what wasn't, although the one time I'd found a live rabbit in a snare I'd laid the sack over its head to hold it in place while I unlooped the wire from its hind leg. Then I watched it hop off with a mixture of regret and relief. I hoped Diana never found out.

Dull sunlight filtered weakly through the broken clouds as I walked. The thermometer outside the cabin registered nine degrees. I oriented myself to the Witness Tree and hiked on. The bear spray was on my belt and the little compass was in my pocket and yet, slowly and almost without knowing it, I'd started not needing to rely on it. I found myself being able to read the land and the sky, to feel the slight shift in the air as weather approached and to tune my ears so I heard the quick movement of small game. I saw hares that had been brown in summer begin to turn white as winter approached, and birds flying low before storms. Once, I watched a hawk drop out of the sky to snag an unsuspecting squirrel and I began to understand how the slow and weak became prey for the strong. How survival depended on awareness and readiness. I started to see nature as a teacher but only if I slowed down enough to actually receive her lessons.

I pushed myself as the forest and animals did: gathering strength for winter, noticing details, sensing the change in relationships. I had to. Not only because it was the first week of December and freeze-up was underway but also because I could no longer deny the truth. Every night I lay in bed and willed the blood to come.

I'd done the same in high school when I realized with growing dread that my thickening waist wasn't the result of too many pizza slices in the cafeteria but because my period hadn't come. At the time, I'd been more afraid of what my mother would do than the fact that I might become a single mother or have to marry Matt, who'd just been suspended from school for arriving drunk to class. I imagined her making me confess in front of the whole congregation and sending me to some home for wayward girls, or making me wear a red A like Hester Prynne in *The Scarlet Letter*, which, unfortunately, had been part of our English reading list that year. One day, I got so desperate I jumped off a ten-foot-high stack of hay to the barn's concrete floor in an attempt to start the bleeding. All I got for it was a pair of stinging feet. Finally, I told my father and he drove me to a clinic and silently signed the papers for the abortion. He looked at me differently after that but I didn't think he ever told my mother. It was the thing between us, the snuffing out of something.

Now the consequences of being pregnant seemed even more dire. Only this time I pictured a tiny version of Xander nestled in my womb and knew I could no more end its existence than I could end Xander's. My only option was to escape before I got too big, and then figure out how I would survive with two children.

I shoved the thoughts from my mind, finished checking my line (empty) and hurried south to scout the river. Would it be frozen enough to let me cross?

Instead, I found Rudy.

I was weaving through the trees above the river when I saw him. He was a small dark figure in the middle of a stretch of ice that ran from one side of the river to the other. He held his arms out like he was a tightrope walker, and he slid his feet as if he were skating. His trail led to the far bank and it appeared he was returning from wherever he'd been, although he was headed slightly upriver now. What the hell was he doing?

I started to call out and then stopped myself. Even though he seemed to have forgiven me for my threat and he leaned against me as I taught him his letters and their sounds, I wasn't sure he wouldn't tell Mark I'd been wandering far from the cabin. Yet I couldn't leave him alone. What if he fell through the ice and there was no one there to save him? I hunkered down behind a split-trunked tree and watched.

Even from fifty feet away, I could see the determined look on Rudy's face. His eyes squinted into the gray December light and his white-blond hair stuck up in matted chunks. Angela had tried to cut his hair last week but he'd skittered away like she was an executioner about to lop off his head. She called him a spoiled brat.

Again I wondered about the things he'd seen in his ten short years. From his watchful ways, I guessed that getting punched by that trapper had not been the worst that had happened to him.

Finally, he reached a tiny pocket of beach just below the spot where I crouched, and I let out a breath. He fished something out of his jacket and seemed to study it. Then he gathered a few twigs and made a small tepee on the sand. I started to sneak away but something held me. He located a clump of moss, stuffed it under the twigs and lit it with what was in his hand, a silver lighter.

Where had he gotten that?

He watched the flame for a moment, then pulled a small leather pouch from somewhere under his coat. He opened it and laid out a red stone, what looked like a black knight from a chess set and some kind of military medal on a red, white and blue ribbon. Next came a white square of paper that he carefully unfolded, revealing a crinkled photograph. He set a rock on it to hold it in place. His little fire jumped and spit.

He pulled his hunting knife from his belt and stabbed it into the sand.

Then Rudy began to dance.

He stomped his feet, threw his head back and yipped into the sky. A raven flew past, croaking out a complaint. Or maybe it was a warning.

Puffs of white rose from Rudy's lips as he twirled and leaped and shouted a cry that sounded like "Poke the hay" or "OK hay." It made no sense.

I watched him dance and pound his chest, and I thought how powerless a boy like him must have felt against a world that had been so cruel. I began to feel like a voyeur, so I turned and moved quickly back onto the trail through the woods. I could hear his faint cries as I left.

Two hundred feet farther, I spotted what looked like a thread of gray smoke rising from behind a distant ridgeline. I stopped and told myself that it was a hunter trying to warm himself against the cold and not an assassin. Mark and Diana would occasionally see signs of hunters around. And yet I felt a sudden chill. If it was Rick or his partner and I could see his smoke, wouldn't he be able to see ours too? I watched for a few moments and decided Mark's paranoia was rubbing off on me. What assassin would build a fire and give away his location? And since the smoke came from behind the ridge, wouldn't our fire be hidden from view? In the end, I didn't say anything to Mark. Besides, how could I have explained why I'd wandered so far from my trapline?

Diana looked up as I went into the cabin, her gaze falling to the empty burlap sack in my hand. She was at the stove, frying a couple of eggs. "You were gone a long time to come back with nothing," she said.

"I got a little turned around, that's all," I said.

"Christ," Diana said, and shook her head.

Mark was at the table, whittling. He set down his knife. "Turned around how?" Ever since his trip to town, he seemed even more jumpy.

"Just turned around," I said.

Diana dumped the eggs onto a plate and carried it to the table. Fifteen minutes later, the cabin door opened and Rudy came in.

"And where have you been?" Mark asked.

"Nowhere," Rudy said.

I thought of his strange dance.

Mark looked at Rudy's pants legs, which were wet and spackled with mud. "What did I tell you about wandering off?"

"I didn't go off." Rudy stared at the floor.

"Look at me, Rudy," Mark ordered.

Slowly, Rudy raised his head.

"What if the bad guy comes? What if you're out there and he finds you and hurts you? What if he makes you lead him to us and then hurts all of us? Haven't I told you that we're safe only if we stay together? Haven't I said that our world is the only one we need?"

"I guess," Rudy muttered.

I thought again of the smoke I'd seen behind the ridge.

"Stop mumbling," Mark said.

"Let him be," I said.

Mark looked directly at me. "We all need to watch out for one another and stick close, OK? No more wandering off our property. No more getting lost. We need to be more disciplined, more careful in our ways."

For a worrisome moment, I wondered if Mark had followed me or somehow found out where I'd gone. "I'll try," I said.

Angela uncurled herself from the floor where she'd been playing Candy Land with Xander.

"Who wants tea?" she asked.

39.

———— N O W ————

The next day I hurried to the river where Rudy had crossed, so I could test the ice. About ten feet from shore, a faint crack sounded beneath my boots. I looked down and saw a thin zigzag line spreading out from where I stood. I turned and shuffled back to shore as quickly as I could, my heart pounding so hard I felt dizzy. *Not today,* I thought, *and probably not for another week.*

Maybe never, said the dark voice inside my head. The only good news was that there were no more signs of smoke and no assassin had arrived. Also, I'd snared a rabbit, which, I hoped, would distract Mark and Diana from my lateness. When I got back to the cabin, however, the boys were outside hurling snowballs at the ruined boat, and Angela was inside on the couch, knitting furiously.

The cabin was cold.

I frowned. "Where are Mark and Diana?"

Angela's needles clicked double time. "They left. There was an argument."

According to what Angela said, she'd gotten into an argument with Diana over a pair of porcupine quill earrings that she suspected Diana had taken. Diana had called her a crazy woman and Mark said that Angela needed to stop acting like a diva and that one's possessions had no meaning in a community where everyone was supposed to share anyway. The two had left to look for game—Diana tracking and Mark with the gun—and the last thing Mark had said was that we wouldn't have to be so worried about starving if Angela had not caused Diana to get hurt.

I pulled the cold, stiff rabbit out of the sack and said, "Maybe this will help."

Angela sniffed and said I was the only one who didn't blame her for what had happened. She set aside her knitting and took the rabbit while I stirred the embers in the stove, put the last two logs inside it, cracked the door so it would draft and went outside to retrieve another armload of wood. Xander and Rudy were making a snowman now and Xander danced with excitement as Rudy packed snow into a white ball. I told Rudy not to let Xander stay out too much longer and he said he wouldn't.

I went back into the cabin and tumbled the wood to the floor, tossed one more split into the stove and began to pull off my boots. I'd been too long in the cold. My toes felt more like stone than flesh.

Angela came over and began to stack the splits next to the stove. "I think she let herself get hurt so Mark would see me in a bad light. I think she did it on purpose."

I told her that sounded pretty extreme.

"Then you don't know her," she said.

I rubbed my feet and held them toward the flames while Angela muttered on about how Diana had showed up at the farm like some kind of queen and how Mark had mooned after her and then she, Angela, had become a second-class citizen. That wasn't how Mark had described Diana's arrival but I didn't argue with her. I was fine with stoking that particular blaze.

Finally, the fire roared with heat and the room began to warm. Outside, Rudy called out something.

"Shoot, I forgot the bread," Angela said, and retrieved a towel-covered bowl from the floor near the stove, where it had been left to rise. "Look what she made me do."

She took the bowl to the counter. "Did Mark tell you why Diana came here?"

I told her what Mark had said about her wanting a father figure for Rudy. Outside the window, a scattering of snowflakes drifted out of the sky.

"I think that meant she was running out of men to destroy." Angela clunked the bowl onto the counter, grabbed the cutting board and dusted it with flour. Her voice rose. "She's an evil, nasty woman. She should be in jail, not here." Angela slapped a hunk of dough onto the floured board. "As far as I'm concerned, she got away with murder."

I looked up. "What? Are you saying Diana killed someone?"

Angela began to knead the dough savagely. "Maybe. Probably. She had this boyfriend, an ex–Army sniper, and she was living with him and Rudy somewhere near Grand Junction. He was a mess, PTSD, drugs, and he tried for a while to work as a mechanic but got fired and they decided to go into the mountains. To heal, is what she said."

She punched and folded the dough.

"A month later, she and Rudy show back up in Grand Junction, only the boyfriend isn't there. Later, some backpacker finds a fresh grave and it turns out it's the ex-sniper. There's evidence of a bullet wound to the chest."

My toes burned as circulation began to return. "How do you know that?"

Angela didn't answer. "So, when the cops come to Diana," she continued, "she tells them that nobody could stop a man from doing what he intended to do anyway and that she'd given him a burial in a pretty and peaceful place. But she's so cold, you know, so the cops keep investigating and the landlord tells them how Diana and the sniper would have these violent fights and that once he'd seen the sniper with a knife cut on his cheek. In the end, it gets ruled a probable suicide."

She looked over her shoulder and gave a last punch to the dough.

"I think if she didn't kill him outright, she talked him into doing it. She's a snake. If you ask me, she got away with murder. I don't understand why Mark lets her stay. She hates you too, you know."

I thought "hate" was a strong word for how Diana treated me. It was more that I wasn't even worth her notice.

Before I could ask more, the cabin door flew open and Xander burst in with Rudy trailing behind him. The snow flurried now, the pale flakes twirling from the sky like tiny ballerinas.

"We're hungry," Xander announced. He shrugged out of his coat, tugged off his gloves, ran over and dropped everything in my lap.

Rudy's hair was wet and his lips chapped with cold. He took off his gloves and set them by the woodstove to dry. Angela said she had some leftover lentils and turned to the refrigerator. Xander wrinkled his nose.

Rudy wandered into the kitchen, where the kneaded dough lay on the counter. He sniffed and pressed a finger into the soft, yielding surface.

"Hey!" Angela turned. "Get your dirty fingers out of my bread."

Rudy paused as if he might obey. Then his hand darted out and he grabbed a chunk of dough.

"You little shit," Angela cried as Rudy barreled out the door, his slight figure streaking past the cabin window and then out of sight.

Xander's eyes grew wide.

"He's such a brat," Angela said, slamming the refrigerator door closed and going over to inspect the damage. "Diana lets him run wild. I try to discipline him but it's no use. He's going to wind up in jail or writing manifestos like Ted Kaczynski unless somebody does something."

I thought of his strange dance, of his secret little hut in the meadow and of how hard he was trying to learn to read.

"He's a good kid. He's just had a tough life," I said.

"That's not an excuse. Look at me. Nobody gave me any breaks." Angela slammed the dough back into the bowl. "I won't raise my child the way she does. He or she won't wander off all the time. I'll be an excellent parent and Mark will see how committed I am and then he'll have to love me even more than he loves her. Everything will turn out the way it's supposed to."

I wasn't sure if she was talking to me or to herself.

"Is there cookies?" Xander asked.

I told him there weren't but I would get him some blueberry fruit leather, and I rose from the couch. As soon as I stood, however, I felt such a wave of dizziness that I had to sit back down.

"Liv?" Angela said, and hurried to me.

I told her I was OK and just needed a glass of water but she insisted I lie down. She knelt next to me. In the dim light of the cabin, her eyes looked like tarnished gold. She lit a lantern and ordered me to stick out my tongue, peered into my eyes and put her fingers on my wrist while she counted a pulse.

I heard her suck in a breath and then frown.

"You'd tell me if something was going on, wouldn't you?" she asked. She leaned in so close I could smell the herbal tea on her breath and the slight sour tang of mildew on the red sweater she wore.

"Of course," I said, and looked her in the eye the way a good liar did.

She held my gaze and I felt myself falter.

"I'm fine," I said, "just tired."

That night when I went to bed and lifted the covers to crawl in, I found Angela's porcupine quill earrings laid out on the sheet. I sucked in a breath and looked around as if whoever had left them might still be there. I stuffed them under the chair cushion so I didn't have to see them. Still, I felt their presence for most of the night.

40.

—— N O W ——

Things grew more tense after the argument over the earrings, even though I snuck into Mark's bedroom and dropped them under the bureau so it looked like they'd fallen instead of being stolen. Diana hardly spoke to any of us and I caught Angela watching me in a way that was almost creepy. It wasn't like before when she had been trying so hard to be my friend and asked me all those questions. This was more like she wanted to see below my skin in order to study the workings of my heart, my mind, my organs. Did she know what I was hiding? Did she suspect my plans to escape?

As for Mark, he seemed frustrated by even the smallest things. He complained about the bread being overbaked and reprimanded Rudy for spending too much time away from the cabin. But who could have blamed Rudy? The cold and darkness of the season gave us all cabin fever. Only Xander seemed immune. He played Candy Land and listened to music on the little battery-powered radio. His cheeks were pink and his breathing strong.

Twice, Mark announced he would accompany me on my snare

line. He tromped silently after me with the pistol in a holster at his hip and I prayed that whatever I caught would be dead, so I didn't have to use the hunting knife to dispatch it. Both times, the snares were empty. I began to feel his distrust like a noose around my neck and I decided to delay my next trip to check the river ice to let things settle a bit.

Meanwhile, the goat milk production began to fall off and some critter chewed through the solar panel wire to the chicken coop and the hens spent a freezing night before we discovered it. Two of our best layers died. We made a pot of chicken stew with them. We had a six-inch snowfall followed by dry and super-cold temperatures. The previous winter had been a lot milder, Angela said.

Mark and Diana tracked a bull moose to the far edge of our property. Mark took the shot but managed only to wing the huge creature before it crashed into the woods and disappeared. We were eating vegetable stews, eggs, rice and beans with the occasional hare.

"Why are you reading that crap to the boys?" Mark said one night when I took the lantern and the copy of *The Swiss Family Robinson*, which we were rereading, and started to herd Xander and Rudy off to bed. "You should read them *Wildcraft* or *Take Shelter*," he said, "something useful."

Rudy stopped walking, his fists curling. He looked like a tiny soldier about to go into battle.

I put a hand on his shoulder. "Sometimes escape is just as important as learning how to tan a deer hide," I told Mark. "Let them have a few minutes of imagination."

"Oh, so you're saying they need to escape." He was at the table, sharpening our hunting knives. "Is our life suddenly wrong to you?"

I wanted to ask if by "suddenly" he meant two years ago when he had started screwing Angela behind my back and smuggling drugs and believing in some self-help fable, but I didn't. "I'm just saying not everything has to be a lesson. Besides, the story helps them fall asleep and you know how Xander needs his rest."

Diana lay on the couch with an elbow thrown over her eyes. She didn't move. "For God's sake, let her read the book to them. It's not going to hurt anybody."

"It's not going to help anybody either," Mark muttered, but he let us go.

The next day, I went off to my snare line, intending to sneak away and check the ice. Just as I started for the river, however, Diana appeared. She was so quiet I didn't realize she was there until she was almost upon me. Her blue eyes were unreadable in the somber gray of the winter sky. A brown wool scarf was wrapped around her neck.

"Why are you following me?" I asked. I was too rattled by her sudden presence to pretend this was just a coincidence.

"I'm not following you. I've got better things to do." She pointed. "You ought to reset that snare. It's too high. No wonder you can't catch anything."

I could tell she was frustrated by her inability to hunt and I remembered the story about the ex-sniper. Was it the chase or the killing she missed? I went over and reset the snare while she watched.

"Good enough," she said.

I told her I needed to get back to clean the ash from the woodstove in the shipping container where I slept.

"The farm is that way," she said, and cocked her head toward the north.

"I know that," I said.

"Well, you were going the wrong way before."

"I was just going to check that section over there. Maybe set a new snare." I held her gaze steadily.

"All I'm saying is that you should pay attention to where you are and what there is around you," she said. "There's plenty of things here that can hurt you if you're not careful. And you aren't going to catch anything over there. It's too swampy." With that, she was gone.

Later, Mark found me near the woodpile, my arms loaded with splits for the stove. His cheekbones were sharp from lack of food. He was always the last one to serve himself at mealtimes, allowing first the boys and then us women to fill our plates. It was the first really selfless thing I'd seen him do since I came here.

"Angela got her period," he said.

It sounded almost like a threat.

He looked into the evening sky. It was barely four thirty in the afternoon and yet the day was already dark. A rising moon poked from behind the Witness Tree hill.

Mark said he wasn't even sure he wanted a child with Angela. He said he still couldn't forgive her for what had happened to Diana and he blamed her for the loss of Diana's child as a result. Diana, he said, had told him that it was Angela who selected the tree to cut even though the wind was all wrong for chopping that one down.

"Now we're all paying for her stupidity. I won't reward her with what she wants for that."

The cabin door opened then and Angela came out.

"Soup's ready," she said.

Her voice was cheerful and yet her eyes were not. I wondered if she'd overheard what Mark said.

"I'll make us some blue cohosh tea afterward. It'll help us all have deeper, more restorative sleep," she said.

Mark had been suffering from bouts of insomnia and the shortened days were playing havoc with all our circadian rhythms.

"Can we talk more later?" I asked Mark.

"There's really nothing to discuss," he said, and took the splits from my arms and we went into the cabin.

That night I had a dream about my mother. In it, she was at the stove in the ranch kitchen, frying a batch of potatoes. Instead of her usual jeans, however, she was wearing a shiny red cocktail dress, and when she turned around, I saw she was hugely pregnant.

"Stick a fork in it. It's done," she said, and smiled. Then she grabbed a paring knife from the dish drainer and stabbed herself in the belly.

41.

—— NOW ——

The next day, Mark and Diana fell ill. Diana woke up with a sledgehammer-like headache, which was quickly followed by vomiting and diarrhea. Mark succumbed next. Angela said they must have picked up some kind of bacteria on their last hunting trip—a sip of feces-tainted water or contact with the stool of an infected moose or beaver—since none of the rest of us were sick. Angela tended to them with herbs and fluids, emptied the makeshift toilet she'd put together with a lidded bucket and sand, boiled all our sheets and towels and heated water for sponge baths. Her energy seemed limitless.

Since I knew no one would follow me, I took the ax and snuck off to check the river crossing Mark had talked about. My plan was to chop a hole in the ice and measure its thickness. If it was safe, I would pack up Xander and head out tomorrow while everyone was occupied by illness. We would cross the frozen river, circle around through the woods to the Subaru and make our escape. The only problem was figuring out how to snatch the wooden box with the keys, wallet and phone from the armoire while Mark and Diana were in the room. I thought I would either ask Angela to make some of that cohosh tea and sneak in while Mark and Diana slept, or I'd pray they would be well enough to come to the table and have a small breakfast while I slipped into the bedroom. Angela said they should be ready to eat a soft-boiled egg or a bowl of plain rice soon.

The ice was about three inches thick, so it seemed like it might be strong enough. Or not. If it were just me, I would have done the crossing. Xander's still unstable feet, however, meant he couldn't make it across like Rudy had, and I would have to carry him, along with our duffel, which we needed. Without food and warm clothes, we might not survive our escape. I stared across the river and thought of the Saint Christopher medal and how Christopher had almost drowned because of his belief in his strength. I decided to wait two more days and hope for cold weather to thicken the ice. Still, my spirits lifted. Finally, the universe had decided to give me a break.

"You look happy," Angela remarked that night when I sat down to a dinner of bean soup with her and the boys, and I had to compose my face.

"I'm just relieved Mark and Diana are getting better and none of the rest of us got sick. Maybe tomorrow there'll be a rabbit in one of my snares and I can make a nice stew with dumplings."

"That would be lovely," Angela said. "Protein is so important. You've turned into quite the hunter, you know. Mark always said you hated any kind of violence but it turns out you're as bloodthirsty as the rest of us." She chuckled.

I set down my spoon. "That's not funny."

She frowned. Then: "Oh my God, I'm so sorry. Your mother. I forgot." She had the decency to at least look a little contrite. "I just meant that none of us knows what's really inside of us. It's only when

we're tested that we're able to do things we never thought we'd do."
She touched the back of my hand. "You're a perfect example of that,
my beautiful warrior sister."

I pictured again my bloodied mother on the barn floor and
shoved my half-eaten bowl of soup away.

"I said I was sorry," Angela said.

I stood up from the table and turned to the boys. "You guys want
to play Go Fish?"

"Don't shut me out, please," Angela said to me.

"I'm not shutting you out." I knew I needed to placate her. I
couldn't have Angela trailing me like some needy teenager while I
was trying to leave. "I just don't want to talk about what happened."

"Of course," Angela said quickly. "It's just that we should honor
pain and not run from it."

I was about to tell her I was sick of her stupid sayings and then
realized it didn't matter. In a few days, I might never see her or hear
her voice again.

Xander jumped up from the table. "I want to Go Fish."

Rudy, whose eyes had followed every move of the interplay between Angela and me, scrambled away from the table. "I'll get the
cards."

It turned out I didn't have to bring up the cohosh tea to Angela.
The next afternoon, Mark and Diana emerged wan and stale-
smelling from their room. Angela settled them on the couch with
blankets while she stoked the fire and put on eggs to boil. The boys
were outside throwing sticks for Shadow and I said I would change
the sheets on Mark's bed.

"That's thoughtful of you," Angela said.

It wasn't, but there was no need to tell her that.

I slipped into the room, first cracking open the window to air out the muggy funk of illness and then getting a new set of sheets from the armoire. I yanked off the bedclothes, glanced out the door and listened. Angela was telling Mark and Diana about the bacteria-fighting properties of honey and oregano oil. I closed the door halfway to block the view from the kitchen and hoisted myself quietly onto the second shelf in the armoire. I ran my fingers over the top of the furniture piece, searching for the box with my things. At first, there was nothing and I felt a flutter of panic. Had Mark moved it somewhere else? I pushed myself onto my tiptoes, hanging tightly to the side of the high furniture with one hand and searching with the other. Finally, in the far back corner of the armoire, my fingers landed on a sharp wooden corner. I pumped my fist and then pulled the box toward me. There was a too loud scrape of wood against wood. I froze.

In the other room, Angela babbled on about her herbs.

I waited a few seconds, heard Angela say some mint tea would soothe Mark's and Diana's stomachs and snatched hold of the box. I lowered myself quietly to the floor, first one foot and then the other. I gave one last glance out the door and opened the lid. Instead of keys and my wallet, however, only the phone was there. Even the charging cord was gone. The phone might as well have been a brick for all the good it would do out here.

I felt as empty as the box itself. Mark must have suspected my plan or followed my tracks to the river and then rehidden what I needed most, my wallet and keys.

I leaned my head back and took deep breaths.

Screw you, universe, I thought.

Angela's voice drifted in from the other room. "Careful. The tea is superhot."

Something thumped outside the window. Quickly, I put the box back in its place, wiped my eyes and made the bed. I pulled the sheet corners tight, fluffed the pillows and stared at the horned skull mounted above the bed. I knew now it belonged to a musk ox that Diana had shot but I still didn't think I would want to wake up every day to the evidence of an animal I'd killed.

When I came out of the bedroom, Mark and Diana were each sitting on the couch with cups of tea in their hands.

Angela turned from the stove with two bowls.

"Here you go, my lovelies. Wonderful soft-boiled eggs."

It snowed the next afternoon, a light dusting that covered the ground like powdered sugar. Mark and Diana were up and dressed but still weak. Dark clouds hung low on the mountaintops. Even the Witness Tree was hidden behind a veil of gray. I brought in armloads of wood splits and fed the chickens and took scraps to the goats. Disappointment dragged like an anchor. What use was trying so hard when everything ended in failure?

I chopped wood, gathered potatoes from the makeshift root cellar and sprinkled lime in the outhouse. I was raw and exhausted, and after dinner I grabbed an armload of wood and went up to the container to start a fire to warm the place before I went to bed. The little stove could hardly keep up with the cold that seeped into the container. I didn't know how much longer I could sleep here without getting frostbite and if I would have to move into the cabin when winter grabbed the farm in an icy grip. Would Mark expect me to share his bed then? As I let myself in, my stomach was gripped by a cramp so hard that the log splits in my arms clattered to the floor. I groaned as my insides twisted. For a moment, I wondered if the universe was teaching me a lesson for insulting it and now I'd caught whatever Mark and Diana had.

I stumbled over to the chair, sat and tried to breathe away the hurt. Another squeezing cramp came.

This time I recognized the pain.

It was either an announcement of a strong period arriving or, as I remembered from the abortion, the ache of a uterus expelling a fetus. An unexpected wave of sadness ran through me at the idea that perhaps this seed of a child had felt my despair and decided not to stick around. That I'd killed it with my thoughts.

I breathed slowly. The pain and sorrow passed about the same time. I didn't have room for sentimentality.

I started the fire, waited for it to catch and spotted something sticking out from beneath my pillow. I lifted the pillow.

There it was. The charging cord.

I didn't even take a moment to think. I stuffed the snake of wire in the bottom of my duffel before anyone might happen by.

Later, when I came back to bed for the night, my underwear was splotched wet with blood.

42.

—— N O W ——

Maybe I should have figured it out earlier. It wasn't like there hadn't been clues. It was more like there were so many clues, I couldn't tell which ones mattered and which didn't. I never saw the full picture until later, when everything happened.

The morning after I'd discovered the charging cord, I managed to slip into the bedroom during breakfast and retrieve the phone. Mark looked better but Diana was still weak and pale. I said I'd take care of the chickens and the goats and went to the coop, where I unplugged the hens' warming lightbulb and plugged in the phone. I apologized to the ladies for the hour of cold they were about to endure, and gathered the five eggs that had been laid (even with the light, the hens' output of eggs was dropping). I was pretty sure it was Rudy, the little camp robber, who'd left the cord for me (there was no reason Mark or Angela or Diana would have done it) and that the things that I'd thought were from Mark and Diana—the feather, the compass, the earrings, even the hidden key case—might actually have been from him.

I think Rudy saw there wasn't much room for him amid our jealousies and squabbles, and even the smallest sign of affection was like a drug to him. I thought of his quiet ways and how he'd surprised me when I was searching Mark's room. I thought there was a good chance he'd seen Mark hide my things.

I was just heading back to the cabin with the eggs when the front door flew open and Rudy scampered outside with Shadow on his heels. A half second later, Angela burst out behind him.

"Come back here, you little shit," she yelled.

Rudy gave one look over his shoulder, broke into a run and was gone.

Shadow hesitated a moment and then sprinted after him, barking all the way.

"He stole my tweezers," Angela said as I approached her. "I set them down and he just grabbed them. He needs a good head slap, something to teach him he can't just go around stealing stuff."

I thought of the trapper who'd beaten him. Violence was not what Rudy needed. "I'm sure he'll bring them back."

"I'm going to go find him and give him what he deserves."

"Let me do it." An idea formed. "He'll just run if he sees you. I'll get your tweezers back."

"OK. Fine," Angela said reluctantly. "I don't know why I'm the only one who sees how horrible he is."

I handed her the eggs and went off. I felt her watch me go and told myself there was no reason for anyone to go into the coop and discover the phone. I had to press down the urge to hurry until I was out of her sight.

I trotted toward the little hut at the edge of Flamingo Marsh. The air was cold and heavy with moisture. It smelled like snow might be coming. Halfway there, I came across a set of fox tracks. I didn't know if it was my fox but its path seemed straight and decisive, its intention resolute. Did a fox always know its purpose? Did a fox ever question its choices?

I hurried on until I saw the tiny A-frame and started to call out, *Rudy, it's me.* Something stopped me, however.

It might have been the way the trees bent over the hut like long-armed monsters, or the overturned bucket near the entrance. That was the only way I could explain the sense of dread that ran up my spine. My dad used to call it someone walking on your grave.

No sound came from the hut. I went forward and then hesitated. I'm not sure what I thought I would find. A trap? A battered and bear-wounded Rudy? It hadn't been long since he'd run away but that didn't mean he hadn't come face-to-face with a grizzly. Gingerly, I pulled back the plastic tarp that served as a door. All I saw, however, were the damp dirt floor; the sad little fireplace; the spruce-bough cot with a navy blanket, which I recognized as having come from the cabin; and Rudy's treasure shelf. Everything was tidy and I recognized the orderliness of someone whose world had always been unpredictable and messy. I wondered if Rudy would grow up to be a house cleaner like me.

Relieved, I righted the bucket, which must have been knocked over by an animal or a strong gust of wind. Then I looked once over my shoulder and ducked inside. What if Rudy had stolen more than just the charging cord?

Squatting on my heels, I retrieved the cigar box from its shelf—it seemed the most likely place to find my things—and lifted the lid. Inside were the silver lighter I'd seen at the beach (the letter T was engraved on it) and a four-by-six photo of a nicely dressed older couple in front of a large stone house (his grandparents?), along with a headshot of a man in a military dress uniform (the ex-sniper?). I also found a key (but not to the Subaru) and a wrinkled and faded Social Security card with the name Annalise May Marshall, whoever she was. Such a puzzling collection of things.

There also was a plain white envelope, which I thumbed through quickly. It contained a bracelet of small black beads; a scribbled message that read, *Need to talk. 10 a.m. The Skull*; a lottery ticket; a two-dollar bill; and Alvin's driver's license, which was strange. Wouldn't he have taken it with him when he left?

Suddenly, a rustle came from outside, followed by what sounded like a footstep on frozen ground.

I stilled.

Whoever or whatever had made the sound was big. Not Rudy or a small animal. More like a bear or an adult human. I closed the cigar box and returned it quietly to the shelf. If Mark had followed me, I didn't want to have to explain why I was digging through Rudy's things. I strained my ears but heard nothing more. My calf muscles protested my stillness. I counted to fifty, moved and slowly peeled back the tarp over the door. Nothing. I waited a few more moments, told myself there was enough danger without me imagining more and crawled outside.

It was only then that I noticed the faint muddy path a few yards from the hut. I went closer and found a half-moon imprint that looked like it might have belonged to an adult-sized boot heel, along with the faint outline of canine paws. Whether the tracks were old or new, I couldn't tell.

"Mark?" I called softly.

Only the wind answered.

A freezing rain started as I headed back to the cabin. The radio announcer on Alvin's little set had said last week that the old-timers were predicting a winter of powerful storms and fluctuating temperatures that could bring blizzards followed by flooding rain and mudslides. Even the muskrats were setting their burrows higher on the riverbanks, the old men said. I thought about the iced-over river and hoped the rain wouldn't melt it before I could cross. As I neared our ruined greenhouse, I came to a halt. Angela was climbing the hill toward the spring. She wore a rain slicker and a colorful beanie. Was she looking for Rudy or was something else afoot?

After she disappeared from view, I hurried around the back of the cabin to the henhouse. I let myself into the coop, intending to unplug the phone and replug the warming light. I couldn't have Angela roaming around and noticing the darkness of the coop and going to investigate. The chickens burbled and fluffed their feathers. I reached for the phone.

My heart leaped.

A single bar on the cell-service icon glowed white. If I had a signal, that meant I could call for help and be rescued. I wouldn't have to cross the ice or trek through the forest to the car. Xander and I could get away from here without risk to our lives. Mark might end up in jail. Or not. I didn't care.

I started to punch in 911, then thought that not only would it take too long to tell a dispatcher about the danger I faced and to describe how to find the farm, but also that she might recognize my name from the news and think that a mother burier deserved whatever she was getting. There hadn't been a television station or news site that hadn't carried my story.

Instead, I located Inspector Hardy's number, hit CALL and pressed the phone to my ear. She would understand.

"Come on, come on," I urged as the silence stretched.

The phone beeped ominously. I pulled it away and looked at the screen. The little service bar was gone. That's the thing about hope.

When it's yanked away, it leaves a far bigger wound than despair ever could.

I stared at the phone's face and lifted it into the air, turning desperately in a circle. No stripe reappeared. Maybe if I got to higher ground. . . . I stuffed the phone into my pocket and hurried toward the cabin. I would make an appearance so nobody would think I was lost again and start looking for me. Then I would head for the Witness Tree hill.

Mark was at the table, rubbing waterproofing cream into his leather gloves. He looked up when I came in.

"No Rudy?" he asked.

I shook my head.

Mark's boots next to the door were dry. I guessed he hadn't followed me after all.

"I don't know why Angela got so worked up about her stupid tweezers," Diana said from the couch, where she was resting. "Like, who has to pluck their eyebrows out here?"

"I think she just loves drama," Mark said.

"Wanna play Candy Land, Mama?" Xander asked from the floor. His hair had grown long and he wore jeans and one of Rudy's old flannel shirts. He looked like a mini lumberjack.

"Maybe later, sweetie. I thought I'd go check the snare line and keep an eye out for Rudy," I said, trying to keep my voice level. "Who knows? Maybe I caught something."

Diana looked out the window. "The only thing you're going to catch is pneumonia," she said.

"What's a monia?" Xander asked. "Can you eat it in a pie?"

"No, baby," I said. "It's when you get sick because you get too cold. That's why you have to wear a coat and a hat."

"Oh," he said.

"Besides," Diana said, "I'm thinking that line is played out. You're going to need to reset at least part of it."

The phone was heavy in my coat pocket and a thought suddenly struck. What if it decided to ping to life right here, right now? I grabbed my beanie from the hook by the door. "That's a good point, Diana. I'll go and reset it."

Mark was bent over his gloves. "What's the hurry? It's miserable out there."

I tried to make my voice light but it sounded brittle, even to me. "The sooner I reset the line, the sooner we'll get a hare. For pie." I tugged the hat on.

"Yay," Xander said.

"At least wait for Angela and take the slicker," Mark said. "She's up checking the spring line for leaks."

I glanced over at the sink. The usual steady flow of water dribbled in a thready trickle. One more trouble added to our woes. Mark was right, though. There was no good reason to rush into the rain. That was, unless you'd figured out a way to save yourself and your son.

I looked out the window. Instead of rain, fat white flakes now floated from the sky.

"Hey, look. The rain turned to snow," I said.

Mark glanced outside. The light through the window cast a shadow across his face. Half in light, half in dark. Like one of those comedy-tragedy masks that theater people hang on their hallway walls.

"So it has," he said.

"I think I'll go," I said. "I've got the wool jacket. I'll look for Rudy too. Maybe he went to the river." I grabbed my gloves from the hook above the woodstove, where we hung them to dry.

I forced a smile and opened the door.

"You might want to take the game sack and the knife, or are you just going to strangle the hare with your bare hands?" Diana said.

"Oh yeah, thanks," I said. My face flushed hot.

"And the bear spray," Diana said.

"Right." I grabbed the game sack and dropped in the knife and bear spray.

Mark set aside the half-finished glove.

"Wish me luck," I said too cheerfully.

I could feel his eyes on me as I went out the door.

43.

—— N O W ——

I walked along the edge of the fallow garden, the game sack in my hand. I strode purposefully toward the snare line in case Mark came outside to watch. I gave myself one star for the crappy acting job back at the cabin.

I walked a few yards into the trees, glanced over my shoulder and turned sharply toward the zigzag trail.

If I got a signal on the phone, I would make the call, then hurry back and move a couple of snares so no one would be suspicious. I hoped Rudy would have returned by then, and I wondered how long it would take for help to arrive. I reminded myself to tell Inspector Hardy about the damaged bridge. Maybe the cops could send a helicopter.

The wet snow slapped cold against my cheeks. My boots left tracks in the layer of white but what else could I do? I had to move fast. I was practically jogging now. By the time I reached the top of the hill, I was out of breath. For a moment, the edges of my vision darkened and I had to stop and bend over. My uterus contracted again, although this time the pain dissolved quickly. There'd been blood this morning but just a single spot. I straightened up.

In front of me was the thick-trunked Witness Tree, with its orange sign and hanging Saint Christopher medal. Beyond that were the fire ring and the sitting stone. I noticed a shallow, bathtub-shaped puddle at the edge of the tree branches; it hadn't registered the last time I had been here. I didn't think too much about it, though. I had to save myself and Xander. I pulled off my gloves, lifted the phone into the air and began to walk. Ten feet past the Witness Tree, the phone came to life. One ping, then two, then a whole chorus of them. I looked at the phone as the text messages popped up. I don't think I'd ever been happier to see that I'd earned twenty gasoline points from the supermarket or that I was eligible for a free flu shot.

The phone showed two bars, then one. Quickly, I tapped open the contact list, located Hardy's name and hit CALL.

The phone rang. I swear the sound echoed through the trees. Six times, seven times. Eight. I imagined Hardy pulling the phone from her pocket, seeing who was calling and silencing her phone.

"Please, please," I begged.

Another ring. Then a click.

"Hello, you've reached Inspector Hardy of the San Francisco Police Department," the voice said.

I cursed, closed my eyes and waited for the familiar spiel: the instructions to call 911 if this was an emergency; the notice to provide a case number if this was an ongoing matter and to call the district attorney if charges had already been filed; the request to leave your name and phone number slowly and clearly; and the final admonition that it might take her forty-eight hours to return a call. Finally, the beep sounded and the words rushed out of me as if I were a dam cracking open.

I told Hardy everything. I was babbling like a crazy person. I couldn't help myself. I was just about to remind her of the address where the cop had gone before and to tell her that the bridge was out, when a long tone sounded. I had been cut off.

"Damn it," I said.

A voice came from behind me. "Liv?"

I turned. The phone was still against my ear.

Mark stood at the edge of the clearing. He wore jeans and a blue wool shirt. He must have hurried after me. His boots weren't even tied.

"What the hell are you doing?" he demanded.

His face, pale, filled with anger.

"Um, nothing. Looking for Rudy." I shoved the phone behind my back like a toddler who'd gotten caught with her hand in the cookie jar.

"Who are you calling?" He took a step toward me. The pistol was stuffed in the waistband of his jeans.

"Nobody."

"Who?" he demanded.

I lifted my chin. I was tired of pretending, tired of being scared of what he might do. "I called the police. I told them you were alive and holding me prisoner. They're coming to find me."

He swore and his hands clenched into fists. He came toward me, his boots splashing through the bathtub-shaped puddle, and I thought, *He wants to hurt me.* I told myself to run, although I knew there was nowhere for me to go. I think he knew it too.

"Give me the phone." He held out a hand.

"No," I said.

"You're going to call back the police and tell them you made a mistake."

"I won't," I told him.

He was a few feet from the Witness Tree when he stopped. "What the . . . ?" he said.

The Saint Christopher medal dangled from the branch in front of him. He took a step closer. "Why is this here?"

I shook my head, glad of the distraction.

"This is Alvin's," he said. "He never took it off. It was his good-luck thing, his protector."

The snow was coming thicker now. Beyond the reach of the tree's branches, the ground had turned white.

"Maybe it was to mark his time here at the farm," I said.

Mark shook his head. "He wouldn't have left it here. This was his dark place." Mark pointed toward the fire ring. "He came here only when the demons showed up. He said it was a spirit hole or something and called it the Skull. It gave me the creeps."

I thought of the note in Rudy's hut about meeting at the Skull. Mark must have mistaken the look on my face for confusion.

"You know, the Skull, like Golgotha, the place where Jesus suffered and died."

"I know."

My gaze went to the puddle. Suddenly, it no longer looked like a bathtub. I thought of Alvin's driver's license having been left behind.

Mark followed my sight line to the watery depression in the dirt. His whole body stiffened.

A raven croaked nearby and I heard the soft whoosh of its wings as it took to the air.

Slowly, Mark knelt and put a hand to the edge of the puddle.

That was when I felt the arm come around my neck.

44.

──── N O W ────

I struggled, dropping the phone and clawing at the strangling hold, but gave up when the arm tightened around my throat, causing black spots to dance in front of my eyes.

"And so, here you are," said the voice near my ear. It was deep, slightly accented.

Mark looked up. "Timur?" His eyes widened.

"Oh, so you remember," said the man, this Timur. "I was afraid you'd forgotten me, the man who gave you a job to do. The one you cheated."

The smell of cigarettes and sweat came off him.

Mark stood slowly. "Listen, I didn't cheat you. The bikes got stolen. It wasn't my fault."

"That is what they all say," said the man, Timur. "Even your friend Tyler. He blamed the theft on his addiction and said he would pay us back and go to rehab. Of course, that was before his unfortunate accident on the highway."

"I'm telling the truth. Somebody stole the bikes," Mark said.

"It doesn't matter. You know what I think?"

Mark shook his head.

"I think blame is the coward's way. A real man accepts what he's done, right?"

Mark didn't answer. Something cold and hard pressed against my temple.

"Now toss your weapon."

"She had nothing to do with it," Mark began.

"Toss the weapon," Timur said, "or I will shoot her and then I will shoot you and maybe then I will shoot the rest of your family."

My knees threatened to give way.

"All right, all right." Mark pulled the pistol from his waistband and set it on the ground.

"Step away from it."

Mark obeyed. A hand shoved me on my back. "Stand next to your thieving husband."

I went and stood beside Mark.

The snow fell straight and thick. Little earthquakes of fear rumbled through me and I recognized the assassin. He wore a puffy down jacket, a watch cap and expensive-looking hiking boots, but there was the unmistakable caterpillar mustache and the asphalt-colored eyes. He was the stranger who'd spoken to Xander that day in the backyard.

"I can pay you back, man. I just need a little time," Mark said.

"Time is what you don't have, asshole."

The gun in the assassin's hand seemed huge. It was all I could look at.

"If you kill me, you'll never get your money," Mark argued.

"Ah, but if I don't, how will people know they cannot steal from us and expect to live happily ever after? You see my problem?"

"I'll sell the farm."

"That would be an ant on the elephant of what you owe."

"I'll do anything you ask."

"Stand still so I can shoot you, then."

Desperation filled Mark's voice. "How did you find me?" He was stalling.

I looked over at the hunting knife and bear spray in the game sack, where I'd left them. Too far away.

"How could we *not* find you after your wife's credit card was used at the store?" Timur said. "Did you think I was a peasant with no idea of technology?"

"No, never," Mark said quickly.

"Even so, this place was hard to find," the assassin said. "Everyone in your town pretended to have never seen your wife, and when I asked about you, they said it was none of my business where you lived. Such loyal friends."

I thought Mark must have counted on that. He'd used my card, weighing the danger of doing so against letting his family starve.

The assassin made a tsking sound. "I'm afraid I had to threaten the old woman at the grocery store to find that you lived off this river. And yet it is a long fucking river, right? I looked every-where. I had to camp in the woods, and you know how I hate camp-ing." He let out a mean chuckle. "I almost gave up, except . . ." He tapped a finger on a black plastic device hanging from his belt. "A very nice man, an animal doctor who lived not too far from here, recognized the photo I showed him and said he gave you some medicine for your goats. I asked for directions and he said all he knew was that you lived north of a flat-topped mountain. And then today, when I was almost giving up, I picked up a signal from a phone."

I thought of the phone lying in the henhouse, sending out its telltale message. What had I done?

"After that, it was easy. I crossed the ice on the river and waited. Then I saw you run up this hill."

A gust of wind made the snow slant sideways.

"Let her go." Mark's voice cracked. "It was all my fault."

"A beautiful sentiment and yet way too late," the gunman said. "Sorry."

Mark leaped for his pistol.

The gunshot was like a thunderclap.

For a half second, I didn't know who had fired. Then I saw Mark on the snowy ground, a bloom of red spreading across his chest like a rose opening up.

"Oh my God," I cried.

"He should not have done that," said the assassin. "I was going to kill you first so you wouldn't have to see him die. He was a very selfish guy."

Mark's hands clenched at his chest. A groan came from his lips.

"I am sorry for what I am about to do, but your husband left me no choice." He raised the gun. My heart stalled.

"You can't," I cried.

He cocked his head. "Oh?"

"My son needs me," I said quickly. "He's only seven and he has heart problems and I have to be there to take care of him. You met him. Remember? He has blond hair and you came up to him that day in our yard and asked him if he'd seen your dog."

"I remember," the assassin said, "although I don't actually have a dog."

I went on. "His name is Xander and he loves country music. Travis Tritt and Garth Brooks are his favorites."

"I also like Garth," the assassin said.

"And he was born without three chromosomes, so he's developmentally delayed. Sometimes he trips on his feet and falls down but he always gets back up and he's the happiest kid."

"My brother was like that too. In the village where I grew up in Chechnya, he was considered good luck."

"Yes, yes," I said. I knew I had to keep talking. "He's a very special boy but he also needs his mother. I have no family. There is no one to take him in, to make sure he eats right and gets enough sleep and stays warm, and to love him like I do. He would be alone. I'm sure your brother was never alone."

The gun barrel lowered a fraction of an inch.

I kept on. "My son is an innocent. A good boy."

The assassin considered me. "Do you know what your son told me?" he asked finally.

I tried to keep the tremor out of my voice. "No, what?"

"He pointed to my mustache and asked when I would turn into a butterfly and I said, 'Maybe one day,' and he said, 'You'll be a very good butterfly.'"

"He is the kindest boy I know."

"So was my brother."

Snow muffled every sound so that the world was as silent as a church. Something passed through the killer's eyes, then disappeared. I held my breath.

He sucked at his teeth, like a man who'd finished a fine steak. "You remind me of my mother. She killed a wild dog with her bare hands after it went for my brother."

I waited.

Slowly, he lowered the gun. "I will let your boy have his mother."

"Oh, thank you," I breathed.

"It is a gift to him," he said, "from a good and noble butterfly. Tell him that."

"I will," I said, although I had no intention of doing so.

The assassin looked around the clearing. "Such a lonely place," he said. Then: "Take good care of your boy. Do not let him grow up to be an asshole like his father."

I watched him vanish into the woods. My legs noodled.

A faint groan came from Mark and I dropped to my knees beside him. I pressed my hand to the bloody hole in his chest, even though I knew he was too far gone to help. A crimson line trickled from the corner of his mouth. I lifted his head onto my lap and felt for his pulse. It was thready and weak. I touched his face. His eyes fluttered open. Snowflakes kissed his lips.

"I tried," he whispered.

I wasn't sure what he meant. Still, I answered, "Yes, you did."

"Xander?" His voice was barely there.

I leaned over him. "Xander's safe."

"Don't let him forget . . ." A gurgle came from deep in his throat and choked off his words.

"I won't let him forget you," I said. "I'll make sure he remembers all the very best parts of you."

Because there were good parts of Mark: his passion for life, his creativity, the way he loved his son.

I brushed the hair back from Mark's face. His blood was slick on my hands. His eyes fluttered closed. A final, ragged breath.

Mark was gone.

45.

—— N O W ——

Mark's body felt empty and yet heavy, rooted. Like it wanted to go back into the earth, where it belonged. I moved out from under him and lowered his head to the ground. This time, I knew he was truly gone and I felt something crack inside me. It wasn't a breaking. It was more like the way an earthquake will move a river and realign mountains. A shift.

I lifted my face to the sky. The snow tapped cold on my cheeks and lips. I was free now but at what cost? And how would I tell Xander that his father was really dead this time?

The crack of wood just outside the clearing stopped my thoughts. I scrambled over and grabbed Mark's gun. Had the assassin changed his mind? I jumped to my feet, holding the weapon in two shaking hands and pointing it toward the sound, remembering only then that I had no idea how to fire a gun. Wasn't there a safety button you had to push or something?

Instead of the assassin, however, it was Angela who burst out of the forest. I sagged with relief.

"I heard a gunshot," she said. Her face was mottled red from the cold and from exertion. Her gaze went to Mark's body. "Oh my God," she cried, "is he dead?"

All I could do was nod.

The snow was falling hard now, an icy white curtain that blurred the brush and the trees.

Angela ran toward Mark's body and knelt next to him. She put a hand to his cheek. "My love," she cried, "what did she do to you?"

"What?" I lowered the gun. "I didn't do anything."

Angela peered up from where she crouched. "Then why is his blood all over you? Why are you holding the pistol?"

"It wasn't me." I set the weapon on the ground. It felt dangerous to even hold it. "It was the partner, Timur. He found us. Mark used my credit card at the store. They tracked us."

Angela stood slowly. Her cat eyes went hard. "And the guy just left you? That's not how they work."

"I told him about Xander and he said he wouldn't shoot me. He had a brother." Even as I said the words, I felt how unbelievable they sounded. I glanced toward the forest where Timur had disappeared. "We should leave in case he comes back." I took a few steps toward the zigzag trail. "It isn't safe here."

The words came out of her mouth like a hiss. "I don't believe you." She stepped over Mark's body. "You killed him, didn't you?"

"What? No. Why would I kill Mark?"

She walked toward me. "Because you were jealous. Because you're old and I'm not. Because your capacity for love is so limited. Because you believe in lies. You thought you could drive Mark away from me. You wanted him all for yourself, and when he wouldn't give me up, you got angry. He loved me, you know."

I shook my head. "It wasn't like that."

"I mean, it's not like it's the first time you murdered somebody because you were angry. I know what happened, remember?"

The breath swooped out of me.

"I didn't kill my mother. Or Mark. What's wrong with you?"

She ignored me. "I told Mark right from the beginning that you weren't ready for this life but he said to give you a chance. He said I had to love you too in order to show you how abundance worked." She mimicked Mark's voice: "'You need to accept her, Angela. You need to make her feel welcome.' Well, I did, and look what happened. You tricked me. You pretended to be my sister, while the whole time, you were trying to turn Mark against me. Just like Alvin tried to do when I came to the farm with Mark. Just like Diana did by blaming me for her accident. All of you are jealous of the way I've been able to evolve. Of the higher consciousness I've achieved. You couldn't stand that I was better than you, so you lured Mark up here. One last try to get him to make me leave. I saw your tracks. You were going to show him, weren't you?"

I took a step back. "I didn't—"

Her voice rose. "Nobody does that to me and gets away with it. My dad used to say, 'Annalise May, you're too vengeful for your own good.'"

Annalise May. The name I'd seen on the Social Security card in Rudy's hut.

Like I said before, sometimes there are so many clues, you don't know which are important. Now, however, I did. The evidence lined up and fell into place: the strange note about the Skull; Alvin's driver's license; the way he had apparently left so suddenly, without a word to his aunt or a goodbye to Mark; his good-luck medal hanging in the tree.

My gaze went to the sunken patch of earth. My scalp tingled. I backed away.

Angela followed my glance. "What else could I do? He snooped through my things. He found my ID and looked me up on the Internet. He found out how me and my brother were wanted for killing my uncle. Alvin should have minded his own business and just left for Thailand, but no. He writes Mark a note telling him to come up here so he could show Mark the story he'd printed out and my ID and convince him I needed to be turned in. Luckily, I found the note before Mark did."

"You told me your uncle went on a trip."

"A trip to hell, maybe." A smile touched her lips and then disappeared. "That guy got what he deserved for treating me and my brother like dirt. One good whack with a shovel and then a nice hole in the ground out in the brush. Like my daddy said, 'Nobody messes with Annalise May.'"

I thought of her tale of abuse and abandonment. I'd fallen for it so easily.

Snow gathered on Angela's shoulders. "Alvin was so surprised when I showed up for the meeting instead of Mark. You should have seen him. I told him that Mark wasn't coming, that I'd sent him down valley to the vet to get medicine for one of the goats. I said the goat had mastitis, which it didn't, but how would he know? Alvin said that I was a psychopath and that I couldn't stop him from telling Mark. That's when I shot him."

I glanced at the medal, which now swung in the wind.

"I know," she said. "I probably shouldn't have left it, but I liked the irony. Besides, Mark never came up here."

I thought of Alvin rotting in the dirt beneath our feet and felt a rush of clammy nausea.

"It was easy after that," Angela said. "I packed up Alvin's things and drove his car into the woods on an old mining trail and hiked back, and when Mark got home that evening, I told him Alvin had just packed up and left for Thailand, accusing us of taking advantage of his generosity. I came back up a few days later and buried the son of a bitch." Her eyes narrowed. "And now you tried to do the same thing. How did you find out?"

I backed up and attempted to keep my voice calm. I'd seen her kind of craziness before in my mother.

"Listen, I didn't kill Mark and I never meant to hurt you. All I ever wanted was to leave."

"If you wanted to leave, why did you get pregnant, huh? Didn't you say having a child together was a sign of commitment and love?"

Too late, I realized wounding words could also hurt those who wielded them.

"And don't try to pretend you're not knocked up." Angela took another step toward me. "You never asked what we did for our periods out here and I know you didn't have any tampons or pads left because I looked. How stupid do you think I am?"

"It wasn't like that. Mark forced himself on me. I didn't want it."

"You're such a liar." She lunged forward suddenly and grabbed Mark's gun, then pointed it at me, her eyes blazing.

I lifted my hands like a shield. "What are you doing?"

"What you deserve for killing Mark and for trying to turn him against me and for taking what I wanted most. I should have been the one having his baby, not you."

My heart pounded in my ears. Desperation filled me. I nodded toward the phone lying facedown on the snowy ground. "I called the cops. They're coming. If you kill me too, they'll find out."

Angela took another step toward me. Her fingers tightened on the pistol grip. "I'll say it was self-defense. Or maybe I'll just bury you where you'll never be found and tell the cops you killed Mark and then took off. I'll tell them that you left Xander behind and that I will take care of him. Wouldn't that be the nicest revenge?"

"Shit," I cried. "He's back!" I didn't know what else to do.

Angela whirled.

I ran.

I sprinted down the zigzag trail. The thin layer of snow made the ground as slippery as glass.

Angela shouted. A gunshot sounded. The trail switchbacked down the hillside.

I could see Angela through the trees above me. She was running too. I hit the first hairpin turn, windmilling my arms to keep upright. Another shot cracked. A piece of bark flew off a tree six feet in front of me. I didn't know if Angela was a good shot but I didn't want to wait to find out. I lengthened my stride and skidded around another turn. My knee twinged with pain.

I knew I was stronger than Angela. I'd been training to escape, after all. She, however, was younger and probably faster, and I wasn't sure I could outrun her to the cabin, especially with my knee.

My boots pounded on the trail. Another switchback. Another windmill of my arms.

I could hear Angela behind me, closing in.

I leaped off the trail then, cutting down the steep hillside, grabbing at the branches of small trees to keep from falling. Twigs whipped my face. My feet slid on the snow-crusted duff.

A crash of brush came from behind me. Angela had followed.

She was close enough that I could hear the ragged bursts of her breath.

I wove right and then left through the trees in order to be a harder target. Finally, my boots skidded onto flatter ground. I had two choices. I could turn right and bushwhack through the thick forest, where I'd have a better chance of hiding and of being less of a target, or I could turn left onto the trail to the cabin. That option would be faster but more open.

I turned left.

Another shot whizzed over my head. I wondered how many bullets the gun held.

I pumped my arms and ran faster than I'd ever thought I could. Ahead of me was a lightning-struck tree I recognized. The cabin was still a quarter mile away. My breath huffed white into the cold air. My head buzzed with adrenaline.

Just past the tree, the trail forked and I turned left again. Twigs snapped beneath Angela's boots. I thought perhaps I'd gained a few yards on her; however, I couldn't be sure.

The path arced around a dark boulder, then straightened. It took me a half second to recognize what I saw just ahead of me then: a small stack of three stones beside the trail.

Angela shouted something.

I didn't look back.

I pumped my arms harder.

Three steps, two steps, one. I leaped.

46.

Most people believe memory is like a video recording. It captures a moment and holds it unchanged. However, I think memory is more like that software that allows you to put one person's head on another person's body in a photograph or splice someone into a video. It can be manipulated. It can be distorted. It can even be locked in a hidden recess of the mind.

The sight of Angela at the bottom of the spike pit, her mouth agape and a stake through her throat, was the key for me. The violence of her death made me stagger backward and lean against a tree, and that was when the memory hit. I was back in the cold in the barn. Only this time my mother stood alive in front of me.

She was dressed in jeans and one of my sweatshirts. Her lips were painted bright red as if she were going to church or town, and yet she carried our sledgehammer in one hand. She was saying something about hearing me come home.

"You're waiting for him, aren't you?" she said.

I remembered how confused I was because of the beers I'd drunk, and asking her, "Waiting for who?"

"Waiting for your father to come running," she said. "I heard about you. I heard about how you've slept with every boy in that school of yours."

Her brittle hair was pulled back into a ponytail.

"No, only Matt," I said, suddenly realizing through the beer sludge in my brain that I'd just admitted a secret I'd be punished for.

In the memory, my mother said, "I saw you," and took a step toward me. I think I took a step back. "I saw you prancing around in your underwear like that. Flaunting yourself," she said.

I told her I had never pranced around in my underwear.

She swung the sledgehammer onto her shoulder and said, "Coming out of the shower like that. You knew your father would be watching. You think I don't know what you and your father are doing? You're screwing him, aren't you?"

I remembered how the meaning behind her words tried to take shape but wouldn't form.

"You knew your father is a weak man, so it was easy to seduce him, wasn't it?" She trembled with anger. "I've seen you sneaking off with him."

"What's wrong with you?" I cried. "Are you psycho or something?"

"I know what I saw."

"That's sick," I told her, "and so are you. Oh my God, how could you think that?"

She called me a whore and, with two hands, raised the sledgehammer and swung it at me.

My mother was a strong woman. Ranch women usually are. I

remembered scrambling backward and the smack of the tool's heavy head smashing into the barn's concrete floor.

"Corrine saw you at the clinic," my mother spit. "You and your father trying to hide the evidence." She hefted the sledgehammer and swung at my head again.

I backed up. "Mom, stop," I yelled.

In my memory, I could feel my back against the barn wall. The only way to escape was to climb into the high stack of hay. That wouldn't stop her from following me, however. I half remembered grabbing the hayfork but I could clearly see her lifting the sledge-hammer again and me jabbing the hayfork at her and saying, "Stop it. Get back."

I'll never know if my mother saw the hayfork. What I do know now is that my mother charged and that the force of her running pushed the handle of the hayfork against the barn wall so the tines plunged deeply into her abdomen. Deeper than I could have thrust them on my own.

In my memory, I saw her drop the sledgehammer, stare at the sharp tines embedded in her flesh, stumble backward and fall.

I had screamed until my father found me.

He'd led me into the house and said he would take care of every-thing.

The only thing he'd missed, apparently, was my hair clip, which my mother must have used to hold her ponytail in place, and I realized, leaning against that tree in the snowstorm, that my father's silence had been intended to save me, not to sentence me. That he'd loved me enough to sacrifice his own life for mine. That he'd died protect-ing me. I thought of how he'd gone after the rattlesnake so viciously, not because he was angry with my mom but because he was keeping me safe, guarding me from harm. Sorrow flooded me but so did a kind of peace, a recognition of what had been lost but also what I'd been to him.

My throat closed and I wiped my eyes. I turned and headed for the cabin.

47.

—— A F T E R ——

I moved in a half crouch through the forest litter. The early-morning sky was the color of a mountain lake. I set my feet silently, one in front of the other. The arrow was nocked. My movements were slow. The buck was probably ten yards away.

I stopped, lifted the bow and sighted. The deer nosed the ground. He was long legged, lightly muscled. Probably two years old. He would give us decent meat.

I steadied my breath, focused my aim and pulled. The arrow released with a clean *thwunk*. The young buck stutter-stepped, stumbled and ran. I stood. He got only about forty yards before he dropped.

It turned out I was a decent shot—some latent talent that had come out.

I'd been here seven months.

After Angela fell into the pit, I'd gone back to the cabin, bloodstained and out of breath. Rudy was back from wherever he'd been and I told him and Xander that I'd found a wounded animal and needed to help it. Then I asked Diana to come outside. I told her what had happened. Her face was unreadable.

"I thought I heard shots. Show me," she said, and told Rudy to watch Xander and to stay inside. She grabbed the rifle. I led her to the pit where Angela lay, the pistol still in her hand.

Diana stared at her for a few moments. "Where's Mark?" she asked.

Mark was already covered in a thin shroud of white by the time we arrived at his body. Diana crouched, brushed the snow from his face and bowed her head.

She stood and I felt her hand take hold of mine.

It was the only time she ever touched me.

"He was good to me and Rudy, and that's enough in my book," she said.

I told her about Angela killing Alvin and about Angela murdering her uncle when she was a teenager and about me calling the detective. She shook her head at that. Then I told her we needed to leave before the police got here. If they found out who I was, I said, I'd probably be the prime suspect in Mark's murder, and after what had happened to her boyfriend, the cops might not believe her either. Diana frowned and I told her what Angela had said about the ex-sniper.

"He didn't kill himself. He's still alive as far as I know," she said. "I had to leave him because of how needy he was. I couldn't handle it anymore."

I told Diana I didn't trust the legal system and I couldn't risk being locked up again, even for a little while. She said that she understood and that we should fill the hole where Angela lay. Explaining to a cop why Angela was at the bottom of a spiked pit would cause its own problems. So that was what we did.

I went back to the cabin and got a shovel, and we dragged logs into the pit, me doing most of the heavy lifting because Diana was still weak from her illness. We scraped dirt and rocks over the logs until the pit was filled. She said that the weather box was predicting five feet of snow and that the storm would finish our work and also hide Alvin's grave from the police. She told me to mark the spot where Mark's body lay with a tripod of tall sticks; she would tell the troopers when they arrived that she'd heard a gunshot and found Mark dead. His death would be confirmed.

She was capable and matter-of-fact, and I was glad for it because I couldn't seem to focus my thoughts. I climbed back to the hilltop, removed the Saint Christopher medal from the branch and went over to Mark.

I knelt beside him and gently slipped the Saint Christopher medal into his shirt pocket. I thought of the dimple in his cheek that appeared when he smiled and of the way that he'd loved Xander. I touched the back of his hand. Snowflakes fell and drifted around us and I thought of the wounds he'd carried. I found some downed tree limbs and made the tripod. I headed toward the cabin. I didn't look back.

Back at the farm, I washed, changed clothes and finished packing Xander's and my things. I made dinner but neither Diana nor I ate much. Early the next morning, Diana retrieved the car keys and my wallet from behind the musk ox skull on the bedroom wall, where Mark had apparently rehidden them. Then she helped me ferry Xander and our things across the frozen river to the Subaru. Her breath came hard but she said she was fine. She was used to suffering on the hunt. Rudy and Shadow trailed behind us.

The snow had stopped during the night but had begun to fall again. Diana said I had about two hours before the storm intensified and I should leave quickly. I loaded our things and settled Xander in the back seat. Rudy climbed in after him and sat staring straight ahead. I got a lump in my throat. Underneath the hurt was a good kid.

"Sorry, Rudy. I'm afraid you can't go," I said. "Xander and I are leaving to find a new place to live."

"That's OK. I want to come too," he said. He didn't look at his mother.

I squatted next to the car door and said that I wished I could take him but that he belonged here with his mom. He said he'd rather be with his brother.

I heard Diana behind me. "If that's what he wants," she said.

I looked up at her. Her face seemed to hold no emotion.

"Take him," she said. "He's Mark's son. I'm not good for him. Never have been. My parents were right."

She looked away and then pulled her quiver from her shoulder and fished out a small wad of cash. "Here's two hundred dollars. From my tips. Take it. You have my friend's address, don't you?"

She'd given me the name of a woman in Anchorage who she said might be able to take us in for a few days.

"I do," I said.

"I'll send more money when I can. Let me know where you land." She looked at Rudy. "Be good, kid."

She turned and disappeared into the trees.

Shadow scrambled into the car and jumped into the cargo area. I shut the door and started to drive. Halfway up the track, I saw a quick flash of red in the car's headlights as it vanished into a snowy alder patch. My fox.

A few hours later, in a gas station restroom, I lost the baby.

Diana's friend let us stay for a week until I recovered, and then said she was sorry but we needed to move on. I had eighty dollars left and no prospects.

The next day, I drove to a Fred Meyer store and panhandled forty-two dollars in the parking lot. Xander said I was trick-or-treating for money and asked if he could do it too. I told him it wasn't a good idea. Rudy shoplifted two candy bars. I made him put them back.

I filled the gas tank, which took a big chunk of our cash. Then I bought a loaf of bread, a jar of peanut butter, some kibble for the dog and two pairs of underwear for Rudy, who'd brought nothing with him. I added a burner phone. Mark's phone had died in the snow where I'd dropped it. Diana had said she would get rid of it later.

I called the only person I could think of: old Mr. Martin, who'd always said if I needed anything just to ask. He had a daughter but she had accused him of helping cause her mother's death by refusing to treat her with coffee enemas and herbs, and she no longer spoke to him. He said I was as close to a daughter as he would ever have. I didn't tell him everything. I just said that I was in Alaska and in a bit of trouble and wondered if I could borrow a hundred dollars. I would pay him back.

"Don't go anywhere," he said.

By the end of the day, I had a five-hundred-dollar money order in my hand, and a few days later, Xander, Rudy, Shadow and I were on an old dirt road, driving toward a cabin owned by a friend of Mr. Martin—an Army nurse named Callie Williams, whom he had known in Vietnam. She had metastatic breast cancer and no one to take care of her. She was too stubborn to get treatment or to move closer to town, he said. She said she'd lived a good life. Her nearest neighbor was ten miles away.

I took care of her for four months. She spent most of her days sitting on the front porch with her dog, Buster, and looking out over her land with its three pothole lakes. When she died, I dug her a grave on top of a rise overlooking the biggest of the lakes, just like she wanted. Xander asked if she had gone to heaven, and this time I said yes, and that his daddy was now there too. He said, "When will he come back?"

Before Callie died, she said she had signed over her property to Mr. Martin, who wanted me and the boys to live there. The land was paid for and he said if I was going to stay in Alaska, there was no better place than this beautiful patch of land. He said he might even visit us someday.

Later, I used her phone to call Diana at the guiding company. I needed to know if I was a wanted woman.

She said that the day I left, the storm had dropped six feet of snow, preventing the troopers from arriving until four days after Mark's death and my call to Inspector Hardy. They came on snow machines and hiked across the river ice, and Diana told them there'd been a shooting and led them up the Witness Tree hill to Mark's body. It turned out later that markings on the bullet that killed Mark were traced to a Colt Python .357 that had also been implicated in a drug hit in Stockton, California. Neither the two officers nor the detective who'd showed up the following day noticed Angela's or Alvin's graves beneath the deep snow.

They asked where I was and Diana said that she didn't know but that I'd been under a lot of stress and had taken Xander and left the day of the call. She said I'd always been free to leave and showed them the note I'd written to cover my tracks.

I'm tired of the dark and of living in this dump was the last line. The cops must have looked around the cabin and understood. Plenty of people can't make it through an Alaskan winter.

I told Diana where we were. She arrived six weeks later.

"I thought it would be better for Rudy without me but I missed him too much." Her eyes filled and she looked away. "I'm going to try to be a better mom from now on."

She said she'd filled in the other two spike pits after the snow melted and sold the farm for twenty thousand dollars to a guy who asked no questions. She'd found the property deed hidden in a Folgers coffee can beneath a loose floorboard in the bedroom.

When I told Diana I'd been pregnant and lost the baby, she said, "I don't believe in coincidences."

I didn't believe in them either now.

As for Kai Huang, according to Diana, he turned out to be an out-of-work software engineer who lived in Arizona and whose real name was Kenneth Hoffman. His story had apparently flooded the Internet in March, after a dentist in Cleveland had been arrested for bigamy and tried to use the book as a defense.

Now I knelt next to the dead buck and pulled my knife from my belt and a tarp from my pack. I began to process the animal the way Diana had taught me. The buck's black eye stared into the sky.

There was a good spring near Callie's house and I'd planted a garden. Diana had put in an order for a dozen chicks and she would pick them up on her way home from her latest guiding trip. Rhode Island Reds and a couple of leghorns. They would be good layers.

Callie had a copy of *Little House on the Prairie*. Rudy was slowly learning to read and I was working on letters with Xander. He loved the ABC song.

I skinned and quartered the deer, then hoisted two quarters onto my shoulders and started off. I'd return for the rest of it later. The scent of blood and sweat was on me.

As I humped the meat back to the cabin, I thought how much I'd changed. How that falling baby had altered the trajectory of my life so that I was no longer a wife, a house cleaner, a woman who lived with a secret even she didn't know. Instead, I was a widow, a hunter, a survivor. I could never go back to what I'd been.

Was I sorry I'd caught the little girl? Not entirely. Saving one life had subtracted a little from having taken my mother's. Did I wish it hadn't happened? I don't know how to answer that. If I hadn't caught the girl, I might not have discovered that my father had loved me after all or that I was stronger than I thought or that there were so many kinds of love, you couldn't fit them into a single mold. On the other hand, I might have kept on with my quiet life and Xander might still have a father.

The one thing I had learned, however, was that you couldn't think too much about the past or the future. Instead, you had to live in the moment. Like the fox and the rabbit and the bear. Like the animals we were.

I shifted the meat on my shoulders and remembered that baby, Molly, and how, if I thought about it, I could still feel the weight of her falling into my arms.

I hoped that wherever Molly was, she was happy. I hoped she would have a good life.

ACKNOWLEDGMENTS

In winter, I spend a lot of time in a small cabin in the woods. Knowing how to build a fire and keep it burning is critical, especially on nights when the temperature dips to zero. A fire builder needs a spark, good kindling, the right wood and enough air to keep the blaze burning. The builder also needs to have done the hard work ahead of time: cutting, splitting and stacking. I think writing a novel is not too different.

The idea for this novel arrived, coincidentally, as I was stacking wood in preparation for winter. That spark of an idea, however, required the care and support of a lot of wonderful people to keep it from being snuffed out before this book could land in your, the reader's, hands.

First, I have to thank my extraordinary agent, Heather Jackson, who is smart and fearless and gave me exactly the fuel I needed to make this book a reality. I wouldn't be where I am in my writing career without her.

I also am grateful to Claire Zion and Cindy Hwang at Berkley, who saw the potential in my pages and gave me the advice I needed to energize this story. They are strong and wise women and I admire them so much.

Just as fire needs air, a writer needs a place to feel safe and supported, and I have that with an incredible community of writers. Meg Waite Clayton, Kathleen Founds, Karen Joy Fowler, Elizabeth McKenzie, Liza Monroy, Melissa Sanders-Self, Susan Sherman and Jill Wolfson are all talented writers whose generous comments helped make this book better from the very first sentence. I feel exceedingly lucky to be part of this group.

In addition, I'm indebted to editor Heather Lazare, who took the manuscript to a whole new level, and to writers Jessica Breheny, John Chandler, Richard Huffman, Richard Lange and Dan White, who have taught me a lot about the art of storytelling. Our gatherings are always an inspiration.

For the early work—the preparation—I have to thank two remarkable women who shared their thoughts and stories about being in a polyamorous relationship with the same man. Their openness and generosity helped lay a strong foundation for my writing, although their experiences were obviously different from those of the characters in this novel. In addition, I can't forget Mark and Kathy Saugstad, who opened the world of Alaska to me, including introducing me to some of the great folks who live there. I'll always remember the raft trip down the Gulkana River and the taste of just-caught king salmon. Encountering a pair of grizzlies across a mountain stream and fishing for halibut in the Gulf of Alaska were pretty unforgettable too.

Just as a fire needs someone to fan its flame into a blaze, I needed the great team at Berkley to launch the book into the world. For that, I thank associate editor Angela Kim, art director Emily

Osborne, cover designer David Litman, assistant director of production editorial Dan Walsh, senior marketing manager Hannah Engler, senior publicist Tara O'Connor, assistant director of publicity Loren Jaggers and the copy editor who finally made me appreciate commas.

For all the love, support and occasional cheerleading (as needed), I am so grateful for my family: Chris and Regina Donohoe, Mary Orr, Cody Townsend and Elyse Saugstad (two of the most adventurous people I know), and, of course, Indiana Townsend.

Most of all, I am grateful to my incredible husband, Jamie, who never complains about the hours I spend at my desk or the research trips I ask him to take with me (an eight-thousand-mile van trip to Alaska and back is above and beyond), and for being my rock. I love you more than anything.

And finally, thanks to you, dear reader, for taking a chance and picking up this book. You're the fire that keeps me writing.